D1707004

I Like You Like that

By Kayla Grosse

Published by Kayla Grosse

Printed in the United States of America

First US Edition: August 2022

ISBN: 979-8841432630 (paperback)

Edited by April Ruhland

Cover art by Nia Oliveira @niaoliveirart

Layout by Nicole Reeves

This book is dedicated to every person
who has ever felt not good enough,
pretty enough, or special enough.
I see you.
You are more than enough.

One

Birdie

"You killed it, Birdie! God, that was fantastic."

I take a water bottle from my tour manager, Eric, practically draining the entire thing in one gulp. "Thanks, E. The energy was wild out there tonight."

"I can't believe a guy threw his underwear at you," he laughs while walking away to talk to our PR person, Gia.

I stave off rolling my eyes. I'm used to men throwing their underwear at me and women throwing their bras, too. It isn't anything new. My voice is sultry and smooth, like if Mama Cass and Janis Joplin had a baby. Or at least that's what my record label told me when I was signed five years ago.

Something about the way I move my hips while I sing and play piano just inspires people to throw themselves at me. I find it funny, and slightly annoying, that Eric still has trouble believing a plus-size woman such as myself could inspire that kind of behavior from people. But I'm confident, sexy, and know my worth. That comes through in my performance and music.

Don't get me wrong, I have insecurities just as other people do. But my weight isn't one of them. When you're in the music industry long enough, you get used to detaching from the endless critiques of how you look and how you sound. You learn that people love you for you, or for your music, and screw the rest who don't. I don't have time to wallow about how Page Six calls me fat or says I shouldn't wear a bikini on my one vacation a year. I don't care if my record executives want me to change my hair or go on a diet. I pay their bills with my voice, not my looks.

As Mom told me in the beginning of my career when it still bothered me, *"You're making more money for their pockets than the numbers on the scale will ever read. Tell them to shove their little insecure baby-man feelings where the sun doesn't shine! They work for you."*

I smile at the thought of her. She lives in Arizona with her boyfriend on a small ranch that I bought for her last year. She loves the energy there and the hot weather. I visit every once in a while when our tour stops over, or I have some down time... which isn't as often as I'd like.

Five years ago, my entire life changed when I won the hit singing competition, America's Next Singing Star. I had the most votes from the American people out of anyone that had ever won in their past four seasons. I was stunned when I found out, but the opportunity led me to a record deal, which led me to three Grammys, three sold-out world tours, brand deals and even some TV appearances. The biggest being SNL just a few days ago. That was a wild ride, and one that I'll never forget.

When Mom said she named me Birdie Wilder because it sounded like the name of someone destined to be famous someday, I never really believed she would be right.

"Great show, B!" a male voice exclaims. I jump as if the boogeyman just yelled BOO! I'd been so lost in thought I didn't see him approach.

"Woah there, didn't mean to scare you. I thought you saw me."

I turn toward my guitarist Kevin's voice. His gaze is full of concern, but I smile at him to ease his mind. "Sorry, I'm just tired."

He cracks a grin, wiping his long, sweaty, black locks off his forehead. "It's been a long week. I'm looking forward to our down day tomorrow. Do you have any plans?"

"Me, a bath, and a big giant bed with cheesy New York pizza."

He high-fives me. "Right on. My boyfriend is visiting if you wanna have a drink or something with us, but no pressure. I can't pass up a night in New York City no matter how tired I am."

"Thanks, Kev. If I can get out of bed, I'll let you know." We've been on tour for over a month straight now, and tonight is our second show at Madison Square Garden. Not to mention life has been a little complicated as of late... between my anxiety, the constant shows, and traveling the country, I'm beat.

Kevin stares at me, his blue eyes penetrating. I can tell he's worried, but I don't want him to be. "You want me to walk you back to your dressing room?" he asks.

I smile warmly at him, "That's sweet of you, but the security in this place is airtight. I'll be fine."

"Okay... but if you ever need me, just say the word. You know I've got your back, Birdie."

"Thanks. You know I appreciate that. And nice job tonight. Your solo in "Desire Reigns" was on point."

His eyes shine with pride. "I'm glad you liked it. Wanted to try something different."

"It worked. Keep doing it."

"Thanks, B!" he smiles wide, his pearly whites on full display. "Well, I've got some interviews then I'm going to go back to the hotel so I can be bright-eyed and bushy-tailed for my man's arrival in the morning."

"Night, Kevin." I salute him before walking off to find Eric again. I think I have a quick interview or two and some fans to meet before I can head back to the hotel and order room service. I'm craving a juicy burger and fries. After all the running around on stage and the stress, I am ready for some greasy food.

When I find Eric, he's standing near Gia next to a small wet bar. Eric's hands are flying everywhere, and he doesn't look pleased. My stomach sinks.

I hope I didn't get another letter... or heaven forbid, notes from the label. They've been on my ass about my hair. I decided to go back to my roots and dye my hair natural blonde instead of my usual black. Apparently, they're still furious, but the crowd didn't care if I had blonde hair or black hair. They came to see me and my band. To hear my music.

"What's wrong?" I question as I approach.

Eric turns, a fake smile plastered on his face. "Nothing's wrong."

I cross my arms over my chest and tap my foot. "Spill, Eric. What is it?"

Gia steps in. She's a small, zippy, powerhouse of a woman. Her delicate hand grasps my forearm and squeezes. "It can wait. Eric is just an overprotective brother bear."

I sigh. She's right about that. Though Eric is often clueless on things like female emotions and, well, just emotions in general, he's a solid guy and runs my tour like he was born to do it. He's also extremely protective of me and the band. Especially when it comes to the press and our private lives. One time he had to take anger management classes after he punched a paparazzo outside of an L.A. show. The guy deserved it full stop, and Eric says he still doesn't regret it.

I take a deep breath, grounding myself. "Whatever it is, I can handle it. Tell me."

Gia and Eric give each other a look—but eventually Gia's death stare wins out. At that moment I'm almost certain these two have been screwing, but they'd never admit it. They're too professional for that. Not that I care. If they get their jobs done, and they do, I don't give two shits about what they do in their free time.

Eric takes a step forward. "Let's go to your dressing room. I'd rather we not get the whole band and all your fans backstage involved."

Agreeing, I lead the two of them to my dressing room. I casually wave at fans from some radio contest I have to take pictures with, letting them know I'll be back soon.

Once we're safely behind closed doors, I give them both an expectant look.

"You should sit down," Gia says.

I shake my head. "I'm fine with standing. Out with it, Gia!"

With one more glance at Eric, she steps forward, her eyes serious. "A popular gossip rag got hold of one of your stalker's letters, it's all over the media outlets."

I clench my jaw. "How?"

"Well, it wasn't anyone here, and it wasn't the label, so I got one of my contacts there on it and it looks like the stalker sent them a copy," she says, her voice laced with anger.

My head spins. "Why would they do that?"

"Stalkers usually want notoriety. This is his or her way of telling the world that they exist."

Now I need to sit. I plop myself down on a nearby loveseat, rubbing my hands over my face. Most of the sweat from the show has dried, and now I just feel gritty and tired. *So tired.*

After a moment, I surrender to the facts. "Well, there's nothing we can do about it. So why are you both so upset?"

Gia's eyebrow ticks up. "You're allowed to be upset by this, Birdie. Having a stalker is serious and scary, and now he's made some weird public announcement to the world that he's got it in for you." Eric shoves Gia a little at that—I guess she was supposed to keep that part a secret.

My mouth goes dry. "Was the letter new?"

Eric's brown eyes look to the ceiling like he's praying, before he rubs his hand over his red bearded jaw. "I didn't want to worry you."

"Well, your plan is flawed. I would have found out from Wren or my mom. I'm sure my phone is blowing up."

"I was going to tell you after you met your fans."

I take a sip of water, willing my nerves to calm down. My stalker started sending letters to me at the beginning of the tour. The first one came in L.A. directly to my home, which was freaking scary, but shit like that has happened before.

The first letter was tame for a stalker, basically just overly admiring. But then a second letter came, then a third, fourth, and fifth. In every city and at every hotel, there is a letter waiting for me at the front desk.

Unfortunately, the letters didn't stay tame. Each one got more perverted and gross, to the point where I told Eric to not let me see them. Now I don't let anyone give me letters unless they're looked at beforehand. We've even upped the security everywhere we go, including on the tour bus. I've been trying not to let it bother me, but now that the press knows, the world knows.

"What did the letter say?" I ask tentatively. I'm going to find out later anyway, and my anxiety won't let me wait.

"They threatened you." Eric says.

I feel like my insides are going to drop out of my butt. "How so?"

"They said they want to hurt you, that it's only a matter of time."

Shivers run up my spine. So far, the letters have been your typical stalker-type language, mostly confessing their love and desire for me. They've yet to threaten me with physical violence. I guess that's changed. Tears prick my eyes, but I don't let them fall.

"Are you okay?" Gia asks quietly. She rests her hand on my shoulder, but I jump at her touch. It gives my fear away instantly.

"Just peachy." The room fills with a heavy silence, and I feel Eric and Gia giving each other that stare again. "What else aren't you telling me?"

Eric sits down next to me, his long legs leaning against mine. "The label called; they want to cancel the rest of the tour until this thing calms down."

"Fuck no!" I yell, my anger boiling up immediately. I stand, throwing my hands around as I pace, trying to get rid of some of my nervous energy. "There's no way in hell I'm going to cancel my tour. Do you know how many celebrities and singers have stalkers? They don't cancel their tours. I have fans that paid a lot of money to see me, people that rely on me to pay their bills. I'm not canceling."

"The label is concerned for your safety. For the safety of everyone. If anything goes wrong-"

"It's a freaking stalker who's seeking attention. If we give in, they get what they want. And what am I supposed to do, just go home and hope they don't attack me in my house instead? There has to be another option."

"Gia and I had a feeling you would say that. So, we came up with an idea we want to run by you first."

I stop pacing, turning to face the worried and anxiety riddled gazes of my two friends. "I'm listening."

"We think you should get a bodyguard."

A snort breaks through my mouth before nervous laughter bubbles up out of me. "You can't be serious."

"Let's Kevin Costner this shit," Eric smirks, proud of his *Bodyguard* reference.

"I'm not Whitney Houston or the President. We can just get more venue security. I don't need a bodyguard."

Eric glances at Gia, and I can see it all over his face.

"Jesus. You already told the label this plan, didn't you?"

"Maybe," Gia squeaks. Literally squeaks.

"Why?"

"Because," Eric sighs. "They were going to cancel the tour, and this is the best we could come up with."

"You're saying I have to get a bodyguard?"

Eric nods. "It's either that or we cancel the tour, Birdie. Those are the options."

I rub my hands over my face. "I want him to be invisible. As if he's not even there. You know I like my privacy."

"He'll be like Casper the Friendly Ghost." Gia confirms. "I already have a few options lined up. Someone should be in New Jersey in the next couple days. I promise I'll pick the best of the best. Maybe someone cute too," she winks.

"I can't believe this is happening." *A freaking bodyguard.*

Two

Liam

I GET UP OFF the bench, setting down the 350 lb. weight. Wiping the sweat from my brow, Ben pats me on the back in happiness.

"Good work. I'm impressed."

I roll my shoulder, it feels good. Which makes me break out into a grin. It's been a long ride getting back in shape after my accident.

I look over at Ben. "Me too. Glad I'm almost back to where I was before."

"You're a fucking beast, man. I'm proud of you."

I take a swig of my water, grateful that I have a trainer and a best friend in Ben. We'd both left Michigan eight years ago after high school for college in New York City—and have been inseparable since the moment we met at summer football camp in fifth grade. Now we're roommates in Brooklyn and he owns a gym where he trains every single kind of person, celebrities even.

He's also been my biggest supporter over the last couple years while I got back on my feet, even got me into private security. Which is much better than being a New York City cop. Paid a hell of a lot better too.

"I think I'm going to hit the showers. Don't want to overdo it like last week." I take another gulp of my water.

Ben smacks me on the back again. "Good idea. I was going to suggest the same thing, but..."

I chuff. *He didn't want me to snap at him.* "Appreciate it."

A chime goes off in Ben's pocket and I immediately know it's Wren's special ringtone. Though she and Ben called it quits after graduation, they still had an on- and off-again fling when she came to town, or he visited his parents. The poor bastard is still in love with his high school sweetheart, though he'd never admit it.

I've been trying to get him to go out with a couple of the women hitting on him constantly, but he always has some excuse. When I suggest he just do long distance with Wren, he brushes it off, though I know he wishes she could move here. The only complication is that she owns a flower shop there and loves living near her family. The last thing Ben wants is to move back home, at least not now while the gym is thriving the way it is.

Ben thinks I miss the smile that flashes across his face when he hears her phone notification, but I don't. The guy is head over heels. He opens the message, and a look of seriousness passes over his face. My gut clenches. "What is it, man? Wren okay?"

Ben makes a noise but doesn't bring his eyes up from his phone, instead he starts reading something. His jaw tightens and a pissed look flashes across his square features.

I'm starting to panic now. Ben never has that look on his face when he talks to Wren. "What's going on? Tell me what's wrong."

"Fucking hell," he mutters under his breath.

I get the urge to take his phone and read whatever it is that's got his panties in a twist, but I don't. "Tell me."

Ben's blue eyes dart up to mine, his face red with anger. He looks about ready to punch something. "It's... well, I don't know if you want to know what it is."

My stomach rolls. That can only mean one thing if he doesn't want to say what all this fuss is about: Birdie.

My mouth goes dry just thinking about her. Though I have no particular feelings about Birdie anymore, I'm not a total asshole. I don't want anything bad to happen to her. "Is she hurt?"

He shakes his head, and I feel a stupid sense of relief wash through me. "Not yet."

Well, fuck. "What does that even mean? Spit it out, dude."

Ben hands me his phone, and it's some article from one of those dumb celebrity magazines. "Read it," he grunts like a caveman while pushing his brown hair from his forehead.

I wipe some lingering sweat off my brow and start to scroll through the article. I'm not going to lie; I do my best to keep all things Birdie Wilder off my radar. But when your best friend's "girl" is best friends with her, and your best friend still talks to her, sometimes, it's hard to keep her completely away from my life.

My eyes go wide as I read the headline:

Birdie Wilder's Stalker Sends Threat

I see why Ben is upset now. He's afraid for Birdie. Stalkers are no joke. I dealt with a few cases while I was a cop, and now in private security, and it's scary how obsessed people can become with someone—especially when it comes to beautiful women and celebrities. Both of which Birdie has going for her, no matter how much I want to pretend otherwise.

When I get to the stalker's note, my jaw clenches. I have to stop myself from throwing Ben's phone at the wall. Whoever this stalker is, they're not playing around.

I read the words on the page. The note is super cliché, like one of those kidnapper movies where the letters have been cut out from newspapers and magazines.

You're mine, Birdie Wilder. When I get my hands on you, you're dead. I can't wait to touch your cold—

I thrust the phone into Ben's chest. I can't read any more of that shit. It feels wrong to even give that fucking creep, whoever they are, the time of day by reading that. I clench my fists and get the urge to punch something. A lot of somethings.

Ben looks the same way, though he has a right to be pissed. I don't. Birdie isn't my friend, and she hasn't been for a long time.

"What the hell," I breathe out, running my hand over the back of my neck. "That's some messed up fucking shit right there."

Ben stares at me for a moment, his eyes calculating. "I thought you didn't give two shits about Birdie girl."

Birdie girl. "I don't," I cringe. But he knows I'm lying.

"Typical," he says under his breath. "You're an ass sometimes, you know that?"

Dragging my hand through my hair, I decide I can't shower right now, I need to work out. I grab some easy dumbbells nearby and get to lifting. Ben studies me, practically burning a hole in my back.

"That was out of line," Ben apologizes, coming to stand next to me. He's staring at the mirror as he talks, looking at me through the reflection.

"Just because I don't care about her in the way I once did, doesn't mean I want some psycho stalker after her. Nobody deserves that shit. Nobody," I say.

Ben lets out a tense breath. "I get it man. Like I said, I was out of line. I'm just upset. You know how Wren and Birdie are. She's like a sister to me."

"I understand." I take short inhales, working through the lactic acid buildup in my biceps. I enjoy the way it burns; it makes me feel like I can take on the world.

Pain, working out— it's my happy place. I don't like that Birdie Wilder is suddenly tainting it, even if it isn't her fault. Now I'm pissed for a whole other reason.

I may have said I care for her well-being, but I never said I care for her. I'm not a fucking saint like Ben. He's right that I can be an ass. And I definitely don't idolize her like the whole town back home. I'm glad Birdie got what she wanted, but she sure as hell makes it hard to forget her face and that damn voice when it's all over the fucking place.

Ben looks into the mirror as a skinny blonde woman comes up behind us. She smiles at Ben like he hung the moon. I'm pretty sure if he let her, she'd climb him like a fireman's pole in front of the whole damn gym.

"Cindy," he says, a fake smile now decorating his face. "I haven't forgotten about you. Just finishing up my session here with Liam," he winks at her via the mirror.

She blushes. "No problem, just making sure."

"I'll meet you by the mats."

She nods, biting her plush pink lips between her teeth. Maybe Ben can give her my number. I need someone to take the edge off. It's been a month since I've had someone in my bed, I think it's about time I get some action before I implode on myself. Like I said before, I'm not a saint— never have been, never will be.

Ben notices my look because he gives me the thumbs up. He's not going to sleep with Cindy, so game on for me. "I'll tell her you're interested."

I nod, putting down the dumbbells before my shoulder starts to hurt. Running sounds like a good plan. It's been a few days since my last cardio session, and I still need to burn off some steam.

"Have a good session. I'll see you at home." I pat Ben on the shoulder before I head toward the treadmills, not looking back. I know he worries about me, but he really shouldn't. I've never been better, and I'm not going to let thoughts of Birdie Wilder ruin my good mood. She has lots of people around her that will help her through this stalker issue. There is nothing I can do for her, and really, nothing that I want to do for her. That ship sailed the summer before junior year, never to return. I'd come to terms with that at sixteen.

I let out a grunt as I step on the treadmill. My gaze moves upward to the TVs above, only to see Birdie's face, her green and gold-flecked hazel eyes staring back at me as some clip from SNL with "Birdie Wilder Has a Stalker" scrolls beneath it. I swallow thickly, memories of the girl I used to know flowing into my mind without permission.

She looks different now, the dyed black hair she used to have is now her natural blonde. Sometimes I'd see the roots peek out in the years we'd hung out, but I've never seen the full effect of her natural hair. It tumbles down her back in golden waves, soft and beautiful.

When she smiles, a perfect dimple graces her left cheek. Her face is round, but her cheekbones are high, adding a delicate grace to her tall frame. She's matured in the last ten years, of course she has, but I can still see the sixteen-year-old girl who loved stupid boy bands and PB&J sandwiches with chips inside behind it all.

I resist the urge to walk away and shower. Instead, I focus on the mirror before me and turn the treadmill up as fast as I can manage. Then I run. I run as fast as I can from Birdie Wilder.

Three

Birdie

Ten Years Ago

TODAY IS THE DAY. Today, I'm going to tell Liam Miller I like him. Like, really, really, like him.

He is everything I've ever dreamed a boy could be. And trust me, I dreamed about boys a lot. Since the moment the Green Power Ranger graced me with his presence on my TV at five years old, I knew I liked boys, especially boys in uniform who have a mean roundhouse kick.

Now, Liam Miller doesn't have long hair or fight bad guys, but he is perfect. He is tall, taller than most sixteen-year-old boys, which is perfect because I'm tall too. At five foot nine and three-quarters I stand at least a head higher than most of the guys in my sophomore class. If I hear one more joke about "How's the weather up there?" I am going to scream.

But Liam, Liam is a bean pole and plays for our high school football team as a kicker. He never asks me how the weather is or if I play basketball or some stupid crap like that. No, he's just my friend. We met while working together last year at our local ice cream shop, The Daily Scoop, and started hanging out in the same social circles. I'll admit, I never thought a boy like Liam Miller could be into me. With his dark hair and even darker eyes, he is the boy that every girl, and guy, at Parker Valley High wants to date and hang out with. I'm lucky he chose me to be his best girl friend.

When we met the summer before Freshman year, we didn't know each other since we'd gone to different middle schools. And I must admit when he batted his chocolate eyes at me, I immediately blushed.

I'm a tall chubby girl who laughs loudly and dyes her natural blonde hair black. He's a beautiful boy with friends that visit him during every single shift. Liam Miller is clearly popular. And though I do have friends, I'm not as adored as he is. That's why I never thought he'd be my friend, let alone give me the time of day. But to my surprise, we became fast friends when we realized we both have a strong love for music and sneaking out of the house.

My "dad" is not in the picture, never has been, and Mom doesn't care where I am as long as I don't do hard drugs and get caught. Yes, I said what I said. Mom is a hippie through and through. She loves me and cares for me, but she also is never on my back like most kids' parents are at my age. Liam's are similar. Except his dad works nights as a cop and his mom is a nurse. Most nights his home is free of parents, and if he's back before five in the morning, he's solid.

It has been two years now since we started hanging out, and every day we do, I think I fall a little more in love with him. I'm sure if he becomes aware of how much I imagine my name as Birdie Miller instead of Birdie Wilder, he might run for the hills. But I blame my teenage hormones and his beautiful smile. Not to mention how nice he is to me...

I've grown up thinking guys would never want to be near a chunky girl, but he's shown me otherwise. He isn't embarrassed to be seen with me. He even talked to me at school and introduced me to his parents. Which led me to believe he liked me for who I was, right?

Outwardly sighing, I make my way into my small bedroom, flopping down on my gray bedspread. On my ceiling are posters of bands like Oasis, Third Eye Blind and, eliciting Liam's teasing, Hanson. Their long hair was once a weakness of mine, what can I say?

I take a bite of the PB&J sandwich with Lay's potato chips within, and chew thoughtfully. School has just ended for the year, and this weekend I have plans to chill and listen to music with Liam before we start work at The Daily Scoop again on Monday. And if all goes according to plan, Liam and I will be doing more than just scooping ice cream and listening to tunes in our rooms together this summer.

A smile spreads across my face. Maybe I could get my first kiss... or even make it to second base! I squeeze my jean clad thighs together at the thought of Liam's dark head between my legs. I blush, trying to keep those dreams out of my head... at least for now.

I take another bite of my sandwich, the silence of our two-bedroom condo enveloping me. I arrived home a couple hours ago from school to find a note from Mom that she'd be gone until tomorrow. She left me a vegan frozen pizza for dinner and made overnight oats for my breakfast. I cringe. Who likes vegan pizza? I shake my head at my crazy mother.

Though the infamous Lorri Wilder leaves me home alone a lot, I never feel neglected. It's weird, and most kids my age pity me, but I'm fine. I have a great life, and I'm lucky enough to have a mom who at least leaves me notes and feeds me. She also supports my dream of becoming a famous singer and listens to all the horrible songs I've created over the years. The worst was my emo phase at thirteen. Those songs were dark!

"I didn't name you Birdie Wilder for nothing," she always says, *"I gave you a name that every person will never forget. And with the voice you have, you're off to the moon and beyond, Birdie baby!"*

I felt excited by the dreams she'd laid out for me before I could even sing a note. And though sometimes I'm lonely when she leaves to teach yoga in other cities and follow her favorite Beatles Cover Band around the states, I fill the quiet with my piano and my voice. And in the last two years, I've also filled it with Liam.

His feathered hair, rectangular face, and dark eyes fill my mind. I know Liam struggles with his parents being gone more than I do, though he'd never admit it. So, I gladly take up that space for him. Just like Mom, he listens to all my songs and is always honest with me when the lyrics don't work, or the melody is off. We just work together, and I hope he feels the same way...

My phone rings and I pick it up immediately thinking it's Liam sending me a new song or asking me what time we can hang out. I'm surprised when a female voice rings out from the other end, but I smile, nonetheless.

"Oh my gosh, Birdie! Guess what just happened!" My friend Wren's voice is laced with so much enthusiasm, I can't help but smile. We'd met through Liam after we started hanging out, and she'd been dating his best friend Ben for the last two years. We quickly became good friends and had movie nights at least once a week or went to a coffee shop to study sometimes. She is a short redhead with a big Irish family and a smile always on her face. She's extremely smart too.

"You and Ben had sex?" I ask.

She giggles maniacally, "You just cut straight to it, don't you, Birdie?"

"Was it good?" I press on, my stomach tight. Wren had been talking about losing her v-card to Ben, they'd already done everything else, but she hadn't felt quite ready yet... until now apparently.

"Oh my gosh," she laughs again. I can practically hear her blushing through the phone. "Can I come over? I don't want to talk about this on the phone."

"Um—" my answer is interrupted by a knock on the door.

"I hope that "um" was a yes because I'm outside!"

I shake my head, "You're nuts."

"Come get me before I sweat to death out here! You know my hair can't stand Michigan humidity. I already look like a frizz ball."

"I'm coming," I laugh, hanging up the phone.

I put down my sandwich and get out of bed then head to the front door. Wren is still pounding on it like I forgot about her within the last five seconds, but before I can even fully open it, the fiery ball of my friend is grabbing my arms and shaking me.

"I'M NOT A VIRGIN ANYMORE!"

I can't help but laugh, even though I'm being jostled around like a human puppet. "O. M. G.," I humor her. We jump around in a circle, dumb smiles plastered on our faces. As soon as she lets me go, she heads for my small kitchen.

"I'm parched, got any lemonade?" She asks, opening the fridge and taking out the pitcher of sunny liquid before waiting for my answer.

She pulls out two glasses from the cupboard like she owns the place and pours us each a glass. She holds up hers, waiting for me to do the same.

"Cheers to me and my cherry being gone forever at the precious age of sixteen-almost-seventeen!"

"Congrats! I'm proud of you." We giggle before we clink glasses and take a sip. The lemonade is tangy and sweet, and the taste of it calms my stomach a little.

I'm starting to get nervous about telling Liam I like him, and all the excited energy of Wren's announcement has got me in a twist. I shove my nerves down and drag Wren to the living room, sitting on Mom's favorite green velvet couch.

"*Sooo*... tell me everything."

Wren's eyes get dreamy, and she sighs dramatically. "It was...awkward."

I snicker. "Well of course it was awkward! What did you expect it to be like?"

"I don't know! Like the movies, I guess. All hot and passionate! Like *The Notebook*."

"Wren, really?"

"Okay fine. Ben's not Ryan Gosling but he is dreamy. And we've been doing other stuff for months now. And I've told you about his wicked tongue."

I shake my head. "Yes, you have. Several times."

"Well, I just assumed his dick would be just as magical."

"He's a teenage boy."

"Okay, but I think for a dick it's pretty big. I just thought..."

"It would be like that porn we watched?" My cheeks flush at the memory. We'd found Mom's stash while she was out of town last month and binged a few classics like *Jungle Beaver* and *A Few Hard Men*. I'll never be the same again.

"Well, maybe a little..."

I try not to roll my eyes. "Okay, well tell me the details. I need to know."

Her green eyes stare into mine, serious. "First, you have to promise you won't tell. If Ben found out I'd told you, he'd break up with me, STAT."

"You know I'm a vault. I'll never spill."

She takes a steadying breath. "After school got out, we were making out near my car in the back parking lot. He had his hand up my skirt and I don't know... it just felt right. So, we drove back to my place since my mom and dad were still at work, and we had sex."

"And you came here right afterward? It must have been REALLY bad then, huh?" I tease.

Wren shoves me. "He had to go to work. It's his first day at the movie theater. He couldn't be late."

That makes sense. "But back to the sex... what was it like? What did it feel like? Do you feel different?"

"It was... fast. Like over *so* fast. I didn't have the big O like when he goes down on me or uses his fingers. We didn't have time. He put a condom on, went inside, and after like... a minute... it was over."

I internally sigh. I may have never had sex before, but I knew enough from reading books and listening to my sex-positive mom yap that teenage boys weren't known for lasting long. Especially their first time. I actually felt a little bad for Ben.

Wren reads my mind. "I can tell by your face you feel bad for him. Don't worry, I told him it was great. I think he thought it would last longer too."

The room fills with silence for a moment before I ask, "Did it hurt?"

"As you know, Ben is not small. So, let's just say I might have shed a tear or two."

My stomach twists. "Are you okay?"

Wren smiles. "Totally fine. I'm over it now. Like I said, it didn't last too long. But I do want to try again. I guess I thought I would feel different, but I just feel like I had sex for the first time with the guy I love, and it wasn't what I expected. I'm happy though."

"Love, huh?"

Wren blushes. "Yeah, of course I love him. I've known for a while now, but we said it in the parking lot and then... you know the rest."

"I'm sure it will get better once you experiment a bit."

"That's what he said too. And don't get me wrong, it was still nice, and I'm ecstatic about it. I'm def sore right now," she blushes.

I lean forward and hug her again. "I'm so, so, happy for you Wren."

"Thanks, Birdie. Now we have to find someone for you to have sex with... maybe a certain boy you always talk about?"

Now it's my turn to blush deep red. "I don't know who you're talking about."

Wren rolls her eyes dramatically. "Oh please. You and Liam are always together. If I didn't know you both so well, I'd think you two were an old married couple. You certainly bicker and bat your eyelashes at each other like my parents do."

I'm blushing so hard my ears turn hot. "Do you really think he could like someone like me?"

Wren rolls her eyes. "I know he does... and you realize you finally admitted that you like him to me, right?"

I groan. Though my obsession with Liam is apparently obvious, I have never told any of my friends I like him. At least not with words. "Fine, I like him."

Wren grins hard. "I knew it!"

My heart stops. "Wait, you said 'I know he does'... are you sure he likes me?"

She smirks. "Well, it's obvious the boy enjoys spending time with you. And Ben may have said something."

"What did Ben say?" I ask quickly.

"Just that Liam is head over heels for you." She says as if it's common knowledge.

My hands turn clammy, and I swear I would faint if I had low blood sugar or something. Not to mention I'm sitting down.

"He said that?" My voice is quiet and sounds pathetic. But I'm in complete shock.

Wren's smile goes wider. "Apparently so. I wouldn't lie to you. So, my question is, what are you going to do about it Birdie bird?"

I can feel red splotches caused by my building anxiety begin to appear on my chest and neck—something that happens way too often.

I swallow hard. Mom would say Wren coming over and divulging this information about Liam on tonight of all nights, the night I plan on telling him my true feelings, is a sign from the Universe. And maybe it is.

An alert nearby from my desktop computer goes off, making us both jump. Wren and I turn our heads toward each other, knowing what that noise is. It's an Instant Message alert. That can only mean one thing. It's Liam. I must have forgotten to put an away message up.

"I think that's a sign you should talk to him, tell him how you feel," Wren chimes, taking the words from my mind. I clench my jaw, the anticipation of what might happen if Liam says he likes me too, or if he says he doesn't, weighing heavily on me. At the thought of the latter, my stomach sours.

Wren places her warm hands on my shoulders. "You're going to be fine. Your friends, no way he's going to hurt you no matter if he *likes you* likes you, or not."

I nod vigorously. "You're right."

"I know I am," Wren stands, grabbing her purse.

"Where are you going?"

"I gotta go home. Mom wants a family dinner or some BS. But I'll see you later this weekend."

"Alright."

"You'll be fine, girl. Text me what happens. Maybe I'll sneak out and come over late if Liam isn't already kissing your face off."

I laugh and blush. "A girl can dream."

"My darling, Birdie..." she winks. "Dreams do come true. Catch you later." Wren leaves as fast as she came, not bothering to let me walk her out, and my computer pings again.

I make my way over, sitting in the office chair and moving the cursor. As the screen comes to life, I click the window open with Liam's screen name on it.

"You can do this Birdie," I pep talk myself. "You're a badass woman who knows what she wants!" Mom taught me that mantra when I was only eleven. It's weird, but I love her for giving me the ability to believe in myself from such a young age. Even if it involves swear words.

"Words are just words," she always says. *"You're the one who gives them meaning!"* I shake my head to rid the thoughts of my mother and focus back on Liam's message.

LIAM_THE_KICKER: You there, Birdie?

BIRDIEBABY: Hey! Sorry, Wren stopped over for a second. She just left.

LIAM_THE_KICKER: Sweet. What are you doing now?

BIRDIEBABY: Talking to you.

LIAM_THE_KICKER: Ha-ha. You're funny.

BIRDIEBABY: I don't know. Mom's gone so I'll probably work on some new music. You?

LIAM_THE_KICKER: There's some end of the year party I might check out. You wanna come?

My heart flutters at the invitation, and normally I would say yes in a heartbeat, but I don't want to agree before I ask him my important question. That would be way too awkward.

BIRDIEBABY: Maybe...

LIAM_THE_KICKER: Just maybe? You already sick of me Birdie girl? If you are, it's going to be a long summer at work.

My stomach clenches at his endearment. He used several, but Birdie girl is my favorite. It's stupid, but I love it. I read over his words and again I'm nervous. I may have to quit my job if this conversation goes south.

BIRDIEBABY: I could never be sick of you, Kicker boy.

LIAM_THE_KICKER: Please never call me that again.

BIRDIEBABY: I need a nickname for you. You have way too many for me.

LIAM_THE_KICKER: I like when you call me Liam. Just Liam.

BIRDIEBABY: Okay, Just Liam.

LIAM_THE_KICKER: HA-HA

I take a deep breath, this is it. I just need to rip off the band aid. I have to trust what Ben told Wren... that he likes me. That he's head over heels for me apparently.

BIRDIEBABY: ...can I ask you a question?

LIAM_THE_KICKER: OF COURSE, B. YOU KNOW YOU CAN ASK ME ANYTHING.

BIRDIEBABY: OKAY WELL... I'VE BEEN THINKING ABOUT THIS THING FOR A WHILE NOW, AND I JUST, I NEED YOU TO PROMISE ME THAT NO MATTER WHAT, YOU'LL STILL BE MY FRIEND.

LIAM_THE_KICKER: OKAY... NOW THIS SOUNDS SERIOUS. DO YOU HAVE CANCER OR SOMETHING?

BIRDIEBABY: NO, OF COURSE NOT. I'M HEALTHY AND TOTALLY FINE. IT'S JUST...

LIAM_THE_KICKER: WHATEVER IT IS, BIRDIE GIRL. YOU CAN TRUST ME.

BIRDIEBABY: JUST PROMISE. PLEASE.

LIAM_THE_KICKER: OKAY, I PROMISE. I PINKY PROMISE AND ALL THAT SHIT TOO.

I smile to myself at his words. There's nothing for me to be worried about. It's going to be totally fine. It has to be. Liam is going to like me; he's just going to.

LIAM_THE_KICKER: BIRDIE? PLEASE TELL ME. I'M FREAKING OUT OVER HERE.

BIRDIEBABY: LIAM, I... GOSH THIS IS HARDER THAN I THOUGHT.

LIAM_THE_KICKER: I'M HERE, YOU CAN TELL ME.

BIRDIEBABY: LIAM, I... I LIKE YOU.

LIAM_THE_KICKER: HA-HA. I KNOW YOU LIKE ME, WHY ARE YOU AFRAID TO TELL ME THAT?

BIRDIEBABY: No Liam, I *like you* like you...

For what feels like an hour, but in reality it's only a few minutes, Liam doesn't answer. My stomach is in my throat, and my entire body is cold, and I feel sick. *Crap!* I shouldn't have said anything, I'm so stupid.

At some point I can see that Liam is typing, and it feels like forever before he finally finishes. Immediately my eyes begin to water as I read his words.

LIAM_THE_KICKER: Birdie, I'm sorry. I... thanks for telling me.

BIRDIEBABY: Thanks for telling you?

I want to laugh at the horrible feeling going through my body. I should have known a perfect guy like Liam Miller would never fall for me.

LIAM_THE_KICKER: Shit. I don't know what to say Birdie. I like you... I do. But not like that. I'll never like you like that. You're my friend.

I'll never like you like that. The words race through my mind. *I'll never like you like that.* Tears begin to fall from my eyes.

BIRDIEBABY: Right... sorry I brought it up.

LIAM_THE_KICKER: Birdie, please don't take it the wrong way.

BIRDIEBABY: No, I get it Liam. Forget I said anything. You promised you'd still be my friend.

LIAM_THE_KICKER: I'll always be your friend, Birdie. I just, I'm kind of seeing someone and you're a good friend.

BIRDIEBABY: No problem, Liam. Look I got to run, my mom came home early, and she wants me to cook her dinner.

LIAM_THE_KICKER: Birdie! Please don't leave.

BIRDIEBABY: I'll see you later. Have fun at the party.

Before he can answer, I log off. I let out a sob, feeling bad for having lied to him, but feeling worse for thinking I ever had a chance with freaking Liam Miller. I was so stupid to think I ever had a chance, and now I just ruined everything. I asked him to promise he'd still be my friend, but I wish I would have made that promise myself. How can I be friends with him now? Especially after what he said...

I'll never like you like that.

I let out another horrible sob.

I'll never like you like that.

I'll never like you like that.

I'll never like you like that.

Four

Birdie

Present Day

"I CAN'T BELIEVE YOU'RE in New York City and you haven't contacted Ben," Wren says through the phone, disappointment evident in her voice.

"Did you tell him I'm here?" I ask, the phone wedged between my shoulder and ear. I'm trying to touch up my signature plum nail polish while we talk. Between the news last night and my shows, I'm attempting to soak up my one free day while I can. I'm unsure of when I'll have another one. The tour is nonstop from here on out, and I'll also have a bodyguard with me. I shudder at the thought. I'm a private person, and the thought of sharing my entire life with someone is... cringe. It's also probably why I've never had a long-term boyfriend. Commitment-phobes please stand up!

"Of course, I told him! He's so concerned about you after he read about the stalker. Just like I am. I hate that you're alone. Are you sure you don't want me to fly out and stay with you for a bit?"

I hold back my groan at Ben knowing I'm in town, and the stalker business. Even if the whole world knew about it now... if she told Ben, that probably means that *he* knows. With everything that's happening in my life, the last thing I want to think about is my ex-best friend/high school crush. Wren brings him up here and there, usually in reference to Ben, but not often. Which I'm thankful for.

I close the cap on my nail polish. "No, I've got plenty of security and people around. Plus, I know you can't leave your shop right now."

"You're right... that's why I'm sending Ben."

I freeze. "He's coming here?"

"Don't act so disappointed," she chides. "Ben loves you. He's one of your best friends."

"I'm not disappointed, I just—I'm tired, is all. I had plans to eat pizza in bed and take a long bubble bath."

"Ben would be happy to eat pizza in bed with you, just keep your hands to yourself," she giggles.

The corners of my lips turn up. Ben and Wren go together like cheese and pizza. Not only do their names rhyme, which is kind of sickening in a cute way, the two of them just get each other. The fact they aren't dating, or so they say, is just crazy to me. But everyone has their own path, so who am I to judge?

Whatever makes Wren happy, makes me happy, and same goes for Ben. After Liam and I stopped being friends, I was very thankful for Wren's continued friendship. She never stopped hanging out with me, even when everything went to shit. And since Wren continues to be my friend, so did Ben. They're a package deal. And I do like Ben, he's a good guy through and through.

I bite my lip. "Did you tell him where I'm staying?"

"He knows you're near Times Square, but I didn't tell him where. He's expecting your call."

"Okay, I'll text him. But I can't promise I'll be good company."

"Just be you, B. That's all you ever need to be around us."

I lean back against the plush red couch in my presidential suite, praying to whatever gods are out there to give me strength. "Thanks, Wren. I'll text you later."

"Send me a picture to show evidence of the meetup. Otherwise, I won't believe you."

I snort. "Okay."

"Bye, B. Cheer up."

"Bye."

I take a moment to collect myself before opening up a blank text to Ben. Even though I'm bone tired and jumpy, I do have to admit I'm a little happy I'll get to see a familiar face. The last time I saw Ben... gosh, it had to have been a year ago at Wren's sister's wedding. Sure, we text, but that is never the same.

ME: Ben, I hear Wren's been meddling in my business. ;)

BEN: Well, well, well! It's my famous rock star friend! I thought I'd lost you to the world of glamour and fame.

ME: HA-HA. Want to come indulge in some fancy room service pizza with me?

BEN: Now you're talking in my language. But screw room service pizza, I'll bring you the real NYC stuff.

ME: Deal. When can you be here?

BEN: 4 work?

ME: Perfect. I'm going to have my tour manager Eric contact you, ok? With everything going on we need to be careful.

BEN: Totally get that! I'll wait for his call.

I say goodbye to Ben and then let Eric know I'll have company. I'm grateful Ben isn't coming for a few hours; it gives me time to take a bath and maybe even get in a nap. Now that sounds like heaven.

"HOLY SHIT!" Ben laughs gleefully as he gives me a giant one-armed bear hug, his other arm balancing a huge pizza box. I'm pretty sure his hugs are the definition of a bear hug. They are all encompassing and warm. He's definitely an A++ hugger.

"Ben Wright, you are a sight for sore eyes."

"Birdie girl! I see your mug all over the place, but it's nice to see you in the flesh. You look good. Tired, but good."

I shake my head. "Your honesty is what I like about you, Ben."

He looks sheepish. "Shit. You know what I mean."

Laughing, I show him in, then lock the door behind us. He puts the pizza and another plastic bag down on the counter nearby, glancing around the suite. His blue eyes shine, and he looks kind of imposing against the backdrop of the fancy room.

Ben is no longer the boy he once was. He's just about 5'10", not much taller than me, but what he lacks in height he makes up for in muscle. The guy is fit, like CrossFit, fit. His left arm is also covered in tattoos, as well as his right leg. He's wearing some basketball shorts and a tight fitted white T-shirt.

"This place is... insane. I can't believe this is your life now."

I stop my perusal of him, grinning. He's right, the hotel room is insanely nice, and probably overboard, but my label spared no expense, especially with the stalker.

"It's strange, isn't it?"

He runs his hand through his short sandy colored hair. "I'm happy for you though, living the way you live seems... thrilling."

"Thrilling is a good word," I say awkwardly. "Thanks for bringing pizza, it smells great."

Ben accepts the change of subject, then walks over to the bag he brought. He reaches his hand in and pulls out a six pack of some craft beer, along with a bag of gummy bears. My favorite.

"For the lady," he bows, handing me the bag.

"Aww, a man who knows the way to my heart. Thank you."

"Beer?"

"Please. I'll grab some plates and napkins."

I make my way to the kitchen area, taking what I need before returning to Ben, who's made himself comfortable on the couch. He's propped his now shoeless feet on the coffee table, and has a beer cracked open waiting for me.

"Here you are, milady."

I take the beer, setting the plates down. "Thank you, kind Sir."

"Cheers!" he says, bumping his can against mine.

We take a sip, and I groan. "This is good."

"Local IPA. Perfect with a New York slice."

I rub my hands together. "Let's get into it before it gets cold."

He opens the box and I'm hit with the delicious smell of sausage and cheese. Again, my favorite. "You remembered."

"To be fair, I may have asked Wren what you like on your pizza."

"Aww," I coo, patting him on the head. "So thoughtful."

He chuckles, putting a slice on a plate for me. My first bite is heaven. God, it's so good. Exactly what I wanted. The company isn't bad either. There is an ease to Ben that I've always enjoyed, and now I'm regretting not telling him I was in town earlier. I should have gotten him free concert tickets, but I was afraid he'd bring the one person I've avoided for the last ten years.

"Nothing like a New York slice," Ben says. "We didn't have anything like this in Michigan."

"This puts Pizza Hut to dust," I agree. "Though, have you ever had Chicago Deep Dish in Chicago?"

"Not in Chicago. It's good, but I prefer a lighter crust."

"Come talk to me after you have it in Chicago. It's heavenly. This is good, too. Totally different pizzas."

"You speak facts."

Grinning, I take another bite, following it up with a drink of beer to wash it down. "So, tell me Ben, what's going on with you? Anything new?"

He swallows. "Not too much. Gym is going great. I'm thinking about opening a second location in Midtown or somewhere... But the rent is insane, and I'm not sure I could afford it."

"Have you considered franchising?"

"I don't think I'm there yet, but maybe someday."

"Open a location in Michigan. Wren would love that."

His face lights up at the mention of her name, but it quickly dims. "It's complicated." He takes another huge bite of pizza, chewing vigorously. Okay, he doesn't want to talk about it. I can relate to that feeling.

"Well, if you ever need an investor, let me know."

His dark and well-manicured brow raises. "Serious?"

"Of course. You're my friend."

Ben nudges me with his shoulder, "Thanks, Birdie. That means a lot. I'll think about that and let you know."

We continue to eat pizza and catch up on mundane things. Family and movies we've watched, which for me isn't many. He tells me about some of his crazy clients and what it's like living in New York City. He carefully avoids talking about Wren too much, even though I can tell he wants to talk about her at every turn. They are hopeless. I know they live in two different places, but they'd be able to figure it out if they really wanted to. Wren thinks Ben just needs time to sort his life out, but I think Ben is waiting for Wren to just tell him what she wants. Like I said, hopeless.

We're on our last beer, and I feel buzzed. I also feel more relaxed than I have in a long time, and Ben makes me feel nostalgic and safe. Like I'm back at home with Mom. I have to stop tears from pricking my eyes.

Ben notices the shift in my energy. He's always been one of my more sensitive guy friends. "You doing okay there, Birdie girl?"

There's a lump in my throat so I take a sip of beer to push it down. "Yeah, I'm good," I lie. "It's been a tough go for a bit."

"I didn't know if you wanted to talk about it..."

I shrug. "There's not really much to talk about. It sucks, and it's scary as hell, but it's not like the creep has actually done anything. It's just mindless words and threats. Sadly, this kind of thing is normal for people like me."

Ben places one of his hands on my shoulder. It's warm and comforting, and now I feel like crying again. God, is my period coming or something? Ugh.

"I can't imagine what it must be like to feel helpless like that. If you had more time here, I'd give you some self-defense lessons."

I grin. "I'd love that. Next time I'm here I'll hit you up."

He smiles back. "Good! I think you'll enjoy it. It's one of my more popular classes here. A lot of women living in big cities feel safer with it."

"Makes sense. I know a little bit, but I should probably know more given the circumstances. I hope it doesn't come to that though, and I'm not sure if Wren told you but the label is making me get a bodyguard. My team is interviewing some men as we speak," I play with the tab on my beer, annoyed at the thought again.

"A bodyguard?" His face scrunches up and I wonder what he's thinking. "Have you had one before?"

I shake my head. "Never needed one. The label says if I don't get one the tour is off, and no way am I doing that."

"You know... I have a friend who does private security. He's great. Super professional. I'd trust the man with my life, full stop."

"Really?"

"100%! If your team hired him, I'd know for sure my Birdie girl is taken care of. I wouldn't have to worry, and then Wren would stop freaking out, too."

"He's that good?"

"Like I said, I'd trust him with my life. He's a good friend and strong too."

"It sounds like you have a man crush on him," I laugh.

He snorts. "I might, just a little."

"Okay, if you think he's the one, you have Eric's number. Text him his info."

Ben pumps the air like he's won the lottery. "I will."

I laugh, then let out a long yawn. I glance at my phone and see it's already after nine. I still have a bunch of fan mail to get to and I promised Mom I would call before I went to bed. We have to be up early to move to New Jersey in the morning—but I hate kicking Ben out. I'm having a nice time with him. It felt like my life was normal for a few sweet hours.

"Say no more. I'll get out of your hair."

I yawn again, then blush. "Sorry. I've been really enjoying myself; I swear."

"I get it. Big rock star needs her beauty rest."

He helps me put away the leftovers and then I walk him to the door.

"Tonight was fun. Don't be a stranger, Birdie girl."

"I'll try not to. When the tour is over, maybe we can get some pizza in the actual pizza shop. I'll fly out Wren," I wink.

"I would love that. She would too. And I'll send that guy's info to Eric."

"Thanks for always looking out, Ben. Talk soon."

With one last bear hug, he leaves. I wait for him to disappear from view before closing the door and locking it. Tonight turned out to be relaxing and just what I needed. Maybe I'd even get a nice bodyguard out of it. If Ben likes him, I'm sure I will too. At least, I can hope. Things are looking up.

Five

Birdie

I OPEN THE DOOR to find Eric's flaming red hair and brown eyes in my vision.

"Morning, B. Hope you slept well. Did your friend Ben spend the night?" He lets himself into my suite, looking around for any sign of him.

"Good morning to you too, Mr. Nosey. But no, he's a friend. That's all."

"Well, that friend of yours did us a solid. We weren't having any luck finding a bodyguard we liked, but he gave us a good referral."

"Did you hire him?"

"I sent Gia to meet him just now. But I chatted with him on the phone late last night and looked over his resume. Seems like he'd be a good fit. He's an ex-cop."

"I'm guessing most bodyguards are ex-cops or military." I pick up my mug of black coffee off the counter and take a sip.

"That's probably true, but he seems cool. Got along with him for the ten minutes we talked. And, lucky for him, he didn't give me a headache."

I laugh. Eric has a hard time liking people right off the bat. He's always suspicious of their motives and if they just want to know him to get close to the musicians he works with, myself included. Him liking the referral from Ben is a good sign.

"Anyway, I really came here to check on you. See how you're doing. Need help packing?"

"You have better things to do than help me pack."

"Shea may have threatened me. She said if I didn't come help you, she'd make sure my mac n' cheese stash would be missing on the tour bus. You know I need my fix."

I bite my lip to keep a laugh at bay. My assistant, Shea, is only 22, but you would think she was a crotchety old lady. She runs my ship like the navy, and I'm grateful for it. I'm not good at schedules and organizing. Without her, my life would be horribly chaotic.

"I'll keep her wrath away, and make sure your mac n' cheese is left alone. I'm already packed. We were only here for 3 nights. I didn't even take much out of my suitcase."

"Okay, then we have some time to kill. Want to walk down and get a real latte from that fancy place on the corner? They have chocolate chip scones."

I lift an eyebrow. "Do they have blueberry?" Eric gives me a 'duh' look and I grab my purse.

We make short work of the walk from the hotel to the coffee shop, it's not even a block away. Since it's hella early in the morning, the streets are still quiet, as quiet as they can be for NYC, which is nice. It means I won't have to worry about signing autographs or taking pictures while I'm wearing a thin faded maroon hoodie and my favorite black skinny jeans.

I'm a simple girl when it comes to fashion. Usually I wear knee-length tight skirts or jeans with cute tops on stage. I'm a sucker for a good pair of dangly earrings though.

We enter the small shop, a lone teenager working behind the counter. Since we don't have security with us, Eric stands closer than he normally does, as if he'd take a bullet for me. The guy probably would, too. I shudder at the thought.

"What can I get for you?" the teenager deadpans.

I bite my lip to stop from smiling. I remember the days of working at The Daily Scoop and hating when I had to work alone. Work was only fun when Liam was with me. My stomach clenches at the thought of him.

After seeing Ben last night, I'd be a liar if I said I haven't thought of Liam more than once. A lot more than once. I hate that I still do. It has been ten years since we were friends, you'd think he'd be a distant memory. But Liam Miller is hard to forget.

A person's first unrequited love always stays with you. The number of songs I wrote about him on my first album is stupid and embarrassing. I often hate myself for it. My first ever #1 hit, "Desire Reigns," is about him. I still think of him while I sing it sometimes. But most of the time I can lose myself in the crowd and my band.

Eric sees I'm lost in my own world, as I often am, and orders my favorite. "She'll take a double dirty chai, half sweet, with soy milk. Make it iced. I'll have an iced mocha with whip, and a chocolate chip scone. She'll take one of your blueberry scones." He hands over his company card and I nod my thanks.

"You're going to get a stomachache eating all that sugar in the morning," I tease.

He pats his abs. "I have a stomach of steel."

"Don't cry to me when you get an ulcer," I snicker.

"So funny in the morning."

Once we have our drinks and scones, I see we have some time till the bus loads. "Want to eat these in Times Square?" I ask him. Immediately I see the hesitancy in his eyes, but I gesture around us with my free hand. "We don't even know if this creep is in New York. He could be in Argentina for all we know. Plus, it's not even eight in the morning."

"I don't think stalkers care what time it is, Birdie."

"I'm going to Times Square, so you can join me or go back to the hotel." I don't wait for his answer, strutting toward the neon lights up ahead. Eric soon falls in step next to me, his body rigid with annoyance.

"Like I would let you go alone. But for the record, I'm opposed to this adventure."

I roll my eyes. "Noted."

Once we're in Times Square, we find a bench. There are some early morning tourists out already, and the city is starting to wake up. People in suits bustle around, talking on their phones and dodging homeless people. I pull out my scone and take a bite. The crystals of sugar melt on my tongue and I can't help but moan. Food is so good. I love it and it makes me happy.

After years of yo-yo dieting in high school and college, I finally said fuck it. Now I don't count calories or care what I eat, I just care that I feel good in my body. And I do. My body carries me through show after show, and my voice is my livelihood. I take care of it as best I can.

Which is why I suffer through drinking soy milk instead of real milk. *"Bad for the vocal cords,"* my fancy voice coach always says. *"Makes you phlegmy!"* Which sadly is true.

I breathe in the muggy city air, then look up at the blue sky. It's going to be a hot day. "I'm going to miss freedom."

Eric pats my shoulder. "You're still going to have freedom. You're just going to have a shadow. Pretend you're Peter Pan or something."

"Why Eric, I didn't realize you were a Disney Adult."

"Disney is cool," he chuffs.

"It is," I agree. "Just teasing you."

He throws his trash in a nearby bin, then looks at his watch. "We should get back. The bus leaves soon and I need to make sure everything is good to go."

I put the rest of my scone in its bag and brush the crumbs off my jeans and hoodie. We stand and start off in the direction of the hotel. We get about two feet away from the bench when a guy approaches, blocking our path. He's wearing jeans and a simple black shirt. He looks average, harmless, but I can't read the expression on his face. Immediately the hairs on the back of my neck go up.

Relax, it's just a fan. Or at least that's what I tell myself. Eric steps close to me, puffing his chest out as big as he can, which I admit is kind of scary. I wouldn't screw with him.

"Excuse me," he says to the guy. But he doesn't move.

"Do you want an autograph?" I ask, my voice timid. Which I hate.

He pulls out some folded paper from his pocket, and Eric blocks it from reaching me.

"This is for Birdie Wilder," the guy says, still not looking at us. His eyes are trained to the ground, like he doesn't want us to be able to recognize him.

"Who are you?" Eric demands.

The guy doesn't answer, instead he thrusts the paper at me again.

Eric snatches it before I can make a move. "Who are you?"

The guy shakes his head then turns and bolts. Eric makes to go after him, but I stop him by grabbing his shirt. "Leave it. It's not safe."

Eric looks pissed as hell, but he doesn't go after him. Instead, he stashes the paper in his back pocket and pushes me forward. "We shouldn't have come alone. Let's get back before I regret my decision not to get the tour canceled."

"Eric—"

"Don't, Birdie."

I stiffen. I hate mad Eric, especially when he's mad at me. Which is rare. Shit, I screwed up. I shouldn't have been this reckless given the circumstances, but I really thought we'd be fine. Thank God it was just some guy with a note.

Or could it have been my stalker? *No, no.* I don't think it was. He was too timid. But that would mean the real creep is hiring people to help him do his dirty work. This is much worse than I thought. Suddenly a part of me is glad I have a bodyguard coming. The last thing I want is for Eric to get hurt trying to protect me. Dying or serious maiming isn't part of his job.

As he pushes me toward the hotel, he beelines for the tour bus. "Get on the bus, Birdie. I'll make sure your stuff comes down from the room."

"I can do it."

Eric rubs a hand over his face. "Please just get on the bus. I'll take care of the rest." He guides me to the door; our bus driver Joe is there loading gear and Kevin is off to the side saying goodbye to his boyfriend.

As Eric turns to leave, I stop him with my hand on his arm. "Give me the note."

He goes still, turning back toward me. "We'll read it later. Just, let me go get your things. I need to make some calls."

"Are you going to tell the label?"

"I have too, Birdie. But I'm going to make sure that your bodyguard is at the hotel in Jersey as soon as possible. Tonight, if he can. This stalker is watching you too closely. That was scary as hell and you're too important."

My throat becomes thick with emotion. "Okay. I'll stay on the bus."

He nods roughly. "Kevin!" he yells as he walks off. "Keep Birdie company, will you? I'm going to round up her stuff and the rest of the band."

"You got it, man!" I hear him answer.

I hold back tears. Let the babysitting begin.

Six

Liam

THIS IS INSANE. I have no idea why the hell I agreed to this. Something must have happened between yesterday and this morning, and I need my damn brain checked.

I walk around my bedroom, pulling clothes out of my drawers and stuffing them into my suitcase. I'm thankful that I had the foresight to do my laundry the other day, or I'd have to find some time to do it on the road.

"Damn dude, didn't your mom teach you how to fold clothes?"

I sneer at Ben, stuffing more clothes into the open case. He holds up his hands in surrender, "I got you a good job, dude. Lighten up."

"You and Wren guilted me into taking it."

"Dude, stop being so ornery. This is a great gig. You get to travel the country, stay in great hotels, eat good food and watch free concerts by one of the world's most popular rock stars."

"Yeah, but did you forget who the rock star is?"

"Birdie was your friend once."

"Once is the key word, Ben."

"I still don't get what happened. One-minute you guys were together all the time, the next minute it was like she never existed. If she hadn't stayed friends with Wren, I wouldn't be friends with her now either."

"You know I don't talk about it."

"Exactly. You never talk about anything Birdie, and you don't want to hear anything Birdie, but now you're going to be in her space all the time. I hope you can get over whatever happened with her all those years ago."

"I'm going to do my job, Ben. The job that you and Wren blackmailed me into taking."

His jaw ticks. "We didn't blackmail you. We just want someone who we trust to take care of Birdie. I was with her last night, Liam. She's downplaying this whole thing, but I can tell she's scared out of her mind. I'd go if I could, but I'm not trained like you are. You can keep her safe. Just put your old feelings and whatever the fuck happened behind you."

"That's easy for you to say."

Ben sighs and runs his hands through his short hair. "Yeah, but since you won't tell me what happened, that's the best I've got for you."

"It was nothing, okay. I'm not even sure what happened."

"That makes no sense."

I groan. Ben wouldn't understand. But he's right about one thing, it was a long time ago. I'm going to have to put my history with Birdie behind me and do my job. I take any and all jobs seriously, and even if Birdie doesn't want me there, I'm going to keep her safe.

"Did you and Wren even think about Birdie's feelings in this? She's going to be pissed when she sees me," I ask.

"Maybe she won't even recognize you," Ben grins.

"I may not be sixteen anymore, but I don't look *that* different."

"You're ripped, dude. All man!"

I shake my head and pray to whatever's out there for strength. "I hope you and Wren are prepared for her wrath. You can't blame me if she never talks to either of you again when she finds out who her new bodyguard is."

"She'd never do that."

"Sure she wouldn't," I say sarcastically.

Ben sits on my bed, taking clothes from my suitcase and fucking folding them before putting them back in. He's like a mother hen.

"If you really don't want this job, don't do it. I'll find Birdie someone else."

I stop packing and look at Ben's concerned face. He really wants me to take this job. When he came to me last night with the idea after seeing Birdie, I laughed in his face. But then he FaceTimed Wren and the guilt tripping began. Before I knew it, I had spoken to not only

Eric, Birdie's tour manager, but met up with her PR person at the buttcrack of dawn this morning. They threw down so much money that my eyes bulged out of my head. My gut reaction was to say no, but I had been out of work for two years prior to working in security, that fat check would dig me out of medical debt.

The deal was sealed when Wren called me again this morning, crying and begging me to take the job and protect her 'bestie.' I couldn't say no to her. And I couldn't say no to Ben either. He'd done so much for me over the years, saying no felt like slapping him in the face. So, I shoved down my feelings and memories of the last time I spoke to Birdie, and I signed the fucking dotted line. For the next two months I'm Birdie Wilder's bodyguard. No more running away.

"I think this is good," Ben mutters, still folding my clothes.

"Why do you say that?"

"This is going to force you and Birdie to put whatever happened behind you. You've changed, Birdie's changed. You're not the same people you were then."

He has a point. We aren't. I don't know much about Birdie, only what I overhear from Ben when he talks to Wren. I sure as hell have changed in the years since we stopped talking. I'm not the music loving, nerdy, football player anymore. I have baggage... a lot of it. I also like to run from commitment and enjoy lifting weights and sleeping with random women.

Hopefully when Birdie sees me, she doesn't try to box me into the Liam she remembers. It wouldn't end well. Not that anything with Birdie Wilder ever ends well for me.

"I gotta jet," I tell Ben, taking a pair of my boxers from him mid-fold.

"Where are you going?"

"I have a brunch date with Cindy."

Shock flits over his face. "Don't you leave this afternoon?"

"Yes. But I need to knock one out before I get on this tour. I'm going to be busy, and I need a recharge."

"I'm sure there's plenty of willing women on tour."

"Birdie is going to be my priority while I'm there. There won't be any time."

"Is she now..." Ben smirks.

"Not like that. Never like that." *I'll never like you like that...*

I shake my head to clear my mind of the memory from that day. I grab my wallet and my keys. "I'll finish packing later. A car is picking me up and taking me to Jersey at one. A few more hours of freedom," I force a grin.

Ben taps his fingers on his thigh. "Well, enjoy yourself."

"I plan to."

I hold my travel coffee mug as I stand on the curb of my Brooklyn apartment. It's trash day, and the smell in the air isn't pleasant. Summer + Humidity + Trash = Satan's armpit.

After I got home from my tryst with Cindy, I packed up the rest of my stuff and said goodbye to Ben. Joke's on me for thinking that sex with a random girl from the gym would make me feel any better. Sure, it was nice, maybe more than nice, but it didn't do much to quell the anxiety of what is to come.

I keep thinking about what Birdie's reaction will be when she sees me. Will she walk away? Smack me? Refuse to let me stay? So many options. I haven't told her people that we know each other, they never asked anyway. And Ben didn't say shit, so it's most definitely going to be a shock for her. Hell, I have no idea how I'm even going to react. I will do my best to be professional, but the last time Birdie and I spoke face-to-face, it wasn't exactly cordial. I try to forget that day a lot.

A black car pulls up, a huge Suburban that could fit at least seven people. The driver gets out and introduces himself as Gary. We load my stuff in the back of the vehicle and before I know it, we're on the way to my new hell. I do my best to remember why I'm doing this—to ease my friends' minds and make some good cash—not to mention the opportunities this gig could bring me, but I know this is a bad idea.

I run my hand through my hair and bite back a sigh. We're driving to Atlantic City, so I have over two hours in the car to think about this horrible life choice—then before I know it, I'll be standing in front of Birdie. When I look beside me, I see a media pass and packet, which

Gary tells me to read on the way down. Fuck; it's a lot of reading. One of the reasons I stopped being a cop is because of all the red tape and paperwork, but I guess there's a lot of details I need to know to do this job. It's a big tour with a lot of moving parts. I've got to be on my toes if I'm going to keep Birdie safe at all times.

I flip open the packet and it's full of pictures and profiles of everyone on tour, including tour dates and travel plans. Birdie is in it, but I skip her profile. I already know the basics. I go over the names of her bandmates: Kevin on guitar, Sarah on bass, Jane on drums, Marta on Violin, and Jenny, Lorraine and TJ on backup vocals. Then I see her team's profiles, Eric who I spoke to on the phone, Gia who I just met, and her assistant Shea. It's going to take me forever to remember these people's names, but I suppose I have two months to do so.

Normally I wouldn't give two shits about these people, but I also want to do background checks on each of them. Make sure their records are clean and none of them have a motive to scare Birdie. Oftentimes stalkers are people that the victim knows. I wouldn't put it past a jealous bandmate to make Birdie's life a living hell just for fun.

After I read over all the tour stops, I get to the info I care most about: the stalker situation. The pages outline the beginning of the ominous letters in L.A. and everything that's followed since. There are copies of the letters too, but not much else to go on. So far, the creep hasn't shown their face, or approached Birdie in public. There doesn't seem to be any evidence of them following her either, minus the letters.

I take a sip of my coffee, relishing the bitter notes of it. I wonder if Birdie still drinks her coffee black or if she's turned into one of those girls who drinks Starbucks frappes. It doesn't seem like something she would do, but like I told Ben, I don't know her anymore. And why the fuck am I thinking about what Birdie likes and doesn't? *Get a grip, Liam.*

I turn my focus back on the letters. At the gym the other night I didn't want to read the latest one, but now that it's my job, I have to study them like some sacred tome. The words and style could give me insight on what type of person this stalker is. Male/Female, Age, Location, etc....

The first one she got in L.A. is tame. Essentially claiming their love for her. It isn't too weird; it reminds me of a high school love letter or diary entry. But the latest one gets straight to the point of their desires.

Dear Birdie,

At night I lay in bed and dream of you. I wonder what it would feel like to hold you in my arms. Do you wonder, too? Your curves against mine, my tongue on you. I hope I get to taste you soon. If I don't, I don't know what I'll do...

Don't let anyone touch you while you wait for me... bad things happen when I don't get my way, Birdie Wilder. Bad things...

The urge to crumple the paper in my hands is strong. I feel my face heat and immediately open the window. Suddenly this giant car feels like a coffin, and I need to breathe.

"You okay back there, Sir?" Gary asks.

I wave him off. "Fine. Just need some fresh air."

"Want the air on higher?"

"I'm good. Thanks."

Gary stops asking questions, which I'm thankful for. The coffee feels like acid in my gut, and I wish I could go punch out the wild emotions I'm feeling. I shouldn't care this much about the damn letters. This is a job and that's it. It doesn't matter that Birdie used to be someone I really cared for. She's a woman I'm protecting. The buck stops there.

I clench my jaw and my anger flares. I hate the way I feel right now. *It's because of what happened two years ago*, a voice in my head tries to reason. I sigh, that has to be why. I lean my head back on the seat and will myself to nap, hopefully a little sleep will clear my mind before I'm confronted with my new reality.

Seven

Birdie

WE CHECK INTO OUR hotel, some fancy casino in Atlantic City. The lights and sounds of the slot machines and people winning, or losing, money fill my ears. I smile.

I love gambling. I don't have an addiction or anything, but it's fun to occasionally bet a little money. The most I'd ever won is one thousand bucks, but it's the excitement I enjoy. Sometimes I need an escape. And after what happened this morning, I fully plan to get my slot machine on after the show tonight. I should have my new bodyguard with me by then, but he'd have to deal with my plan to have fun.

Once settled in my room, Gia asks if she can visit me. Though she's my PR person, she's also my friend and often acts more like a manager than a publicist. Not that I mind, she has my best interests at heart. She also knows what I like and don't like, which is why she hired the new bodyguard. I could trust her to pair me with someone that wouldn't drive me insane.

Gia knocks and I let her in. As soon as I do, she hugs me with such force my breath leaves me for a second. "Gosh, Birdie! I'm so happy you're alright."

I pat her back, pulling her off me so I can take a breather. "I'm perfectly fine, Gia. Eric is being dramatic."

She shakes her head. "He's not and you know it. This morning could have been really bad. Stop downplaying it."

I roll my shoulders back and decide I need a little pre-show drink. I don't care that it's not even noon yet and my show isn't until eight o'clock tonight. On the drive here, I confided my fears in Kevin and had my sappy moment. Now I'm back to doing what I do best—detaching. I had to if I was going to play a good show and not think about that guy in Times Square. I still haven't read the note, but after some time away, I'm glad I didn't. They're screwing with my head, and I can't let my fans down tonight. Whatever the letter said is not important.

I reach into the mini bar and grab a small bottle of bourbon. I don't bother with a glass, just grab it and take it to the couch. I feel Gia's eyes on me the entire time, and I know she's judging me.

"Let me loosen up, okay?" I finally say to her, taking a drink of the burning liquid. I usually like bourbon, but this stuff is shit. *Blech.*

"I'm worried about you. Do you want me to schedule a call with your therapist?"

I shake my head. "No. I'm fine. It was a little scary, but I'm okay, Eric's okay, and soon we'll have the bodyguard here. It won't happen again. I'll be a good little canary and sing in my cage."

Gia sighs, plopping down on the couch next to me. "Is that how you really feel?"

I take another drink and ignore her direct question. "I'm just tired and annoyed. I have a lot on my shoulders, and I want this tour to go well."

"I know you do." She smiles then, "but the tour is going well. We sold out in Atlanta earlier today, and most of the venues are well on their way. I hate to say it but having a stalker is good for business."

I snort then take a final drink from the bottle. "As you always say, all publicity is good publicity."

"Ugh, I hate myself for saying that."

I pat Gia's knee. "It is what it is. But I'm glad to hear we're doing well with sales. I'm sure the label is happy."

"They are. Not about the stalker, but the bodyguard makes them feel a little more at ease."

"When does he get here?"

"Later today. He'll meet you after sound check."

"You really think we'll get along?"

"I do. He's very straightforward and to the point. Not much beating around the bush."

"What do you mean?

"He texted me a bit ago, asking if he could get background checks done on everyone, including myself and your reps at the label."

"Seriously?"

"Yep. I told him he might see my juvie record for stealing a pair of red lace underwear when I was thirteen, but otherwise I'm clean."

I smirk at her. "You really did that?"

"Maybe," she winks. "But in all seriousness, he's a hard ass. But it's what we need to keep you safe. I'm glad he's covering all the bases. And did I mention he's hot?"

"Is that why you hired him?"

"Well, him being eye candy certainly helps. You'll be around him all the time and I want to make sure he's appealing."

I laugh and shove Gia in the shoulder. "Just don't look at him too much or Eric will get jealous."

She picks invisible lint off her shirt. "I don't know what you're talking about."

"Sure you don't."

"Anyway, he's in the suite next to yours. So, if anything happens, he'll be readily available."

"Hopefully nothing will."

"I hope so." Gia stands and smooths the wrinkles from her red skirt. "Security will come get you in a few hours for soundcheck. Afterwards I'll have you meet Liam and get you both acquainted before you get ready for the show."

My heart beats quickly in my chest, and I swear my stomach threatens to drop out of my butt. "L-Liam?" I stammer.

"Yeah, that's his name. Didn't I tell you that?"

I shake my head.

"Why do you look like you've seen a ghost?"

"No reason."

Realization covers her features. "Ex with the name Liam?" she asks. "That's happened to me before, the total worst. I've sworn off all men with the name Brad."

I swallow. "Something like that."

"Well, he's gonna be a good Liam, I swear. If he's not, we'll fire his ass and get a new guy named Tyler or something," she grins. "See you later, Birdie."

She's gone before I can say goodbye, and I'm left with thoughts of Liam Miller swimming in my head yet again. I head back to the mini bar—I need another drink.

"Yes, yes, yes!!!" I cry, pounding my piano keys. "That sounded amazing, everyone."

"Hell yeah it did!" Kevin agrees, strumming out some ridiculous chords on the guitar.

It feels good to get back on stage with my band after this morning. Even with my world being turned upside down, singing, the strum of cords and banging of drums, it rights everything; grounds me.

"Did you hear that high note Lorraine hit?" Jenny, one of my backup singers asks joyfully.

"Hard to miss," I joke, "But it was phenomenal. Should we run it one more time, or are we good?"

"I'm good," Jane says, swirling a drumstick between her fingers.

"All good," the rest of the band resounds.

"You good, B?" Kevin asks.

"I think so. I was a little worried about adding in that last Cranberries cover, but it sounded better than I thought it would."

"We can run it again," Sarah, my bass player adds. "We don't mind, Birdie."

"Nah, I think we could all use a little extra downtime today. We can practice more tomorrow if we think we need it after the show tonight. Let's break."

At that the band all gathers around me. We all have a tradition of coming together in a circle before and after every sound check and show. I don't know how it started, but it's our thing now. We all put our hands one on top of the other in the center and wait for our cue.

"What's the word?" Kevin asks, a grin on his lips.

"Birdie is the word!" we all say together.

"What's the word?" he says again louder.

"Birdie is the word!" we chime again to match his energy.

"What's the word?!"

"BIRDIE IS THE WORD!"

We all push our hands down then up to the sky, breaking into various bird noises. It's absolutely crazy, but I love it. Everyone laughs and then hugs before we disperse. The band is going back to the hotel but I'm going to my dressing room so I can meet Liam the Bodyguard. I had been so involved in soundcheck I didn't even think to look around to see if he was watching.

Eric appears, his face much happier now than the last time I saw him. "You ready to meet your beefy bodyguard?"

"Not you, too."

"He's attractive, I won't lie. Looks like he could kill me, which I guess is a good thing?"

"You're bonkers."

"Come, come. No time to waste. He's in your dressing room scowling like a grumpy old man. Not sure why. Maybe he has RSF."

"RSF?"

"Resting scowl face."

Laughter bursts through my lips. "Again, you're bonkers."

"It's why you love me."

"Maybe," I shrug before following him backstage.

Once we round the corner and arrive at the dressing rooms, I see Gia and Shea in the hallway giggling like schoolgirls. It makes me wonder if my whole band and crew is going to have the same reaction to this guy. They straighten up when they see me and Eric, both smiling wide.

"Ready?" Shea asks. She looks cute today in a knee-length skirt, black blouse and her purple hair pulled back into a high ponytail. Makes me wonder if she dressed that way for Liam.

My stomach burns at the thought of his name again. I'm going to have to get used to this guy's name. Hopefully he's nothing like my Liam. Not that he was ever, *my* Liam.

I nod, and Gia pats my shoulder, opening the door for me. "Watch your step," she says, but it's too late.

My brain expected the door to open to a flat floor, but instead there's a short step down. I go falling. My stomach drops out as I feel gravity pull me down. As I brace myself for the inevitable faceplant, I make a small squeak, but to my surprise, I don't hit the ground.

A warm hand grabs my arm and pulls me up as if I weigh nothing. Whoever this guy is, he's very strong. I'm not a small gal, so hoisting me up from certain death is not a simple move.

"Please don't die on my first day," a deep voice croons. The hairs on the back of my neck stand up on end, and the sudden urge to throw up washes over me.

With my feet planted solidly back on the floor, and my body upright, I turn my head to my savior. Chocolate brown eyes meet mine, and a small half-grin graces the thin pink lips I would know anywhere. My mouth drops open, but no words come out. I feel as if I'm living in a dream. No, scratch that. A nightmare.

"Are you okay?" Liam asks. He knows damn well I'm not okay.

"Take your hands off of me," I demand, my voice quiet yet stern.

Liam's grin widens, as if to say, "*So, this is how you want to play it?*" He takes his large hand off my bicep and steps back.

"What the hell are you doing in my dressing room?"

He lets out a low laugh, brushing his hands through his tapered dark tresses.

"Well hello to you too, Ms. Wilder. It's been way too long."

Eight

Liam

"WELL HELLO TO YOU too, Ms. Wilder. It's been way too long," I say, putting an emphasis on the word Miss. I'm not sure why I'm acting playful. But it feels good to tease her like this. Natural even. Which isn't good.

Her green- and gold-flecked eyes gaze at me with a mix of emotions, but the part that's got me grinning is her pouty pink lips opening and closing like a fish on a hook. It's kind of adorable. My body is in shock at seeing her in person again, but my adrenaline is allowing me to hide it and put up a fake bravado.

"What are you doing here?" she demands again, her face tight and fists clenched.

I put my hands in my pockets, ignoring the stares of people in the doorway. "I'm your bodyguard."

"Like hell you're my bodyguard."

"Sorry Birdie, I'm afraid the paperwork has already been signed."

The woman named Gia steps into the room; her little arms crossed over her chest. "Do you know Birdie?" Her voice is strained.

"Not really." At my words, Birdie flinches. I fight the urge to apologize, but I have to act like I'm impartial. As if I don't care that I know her, and that we don't have a past. It's the only way I'm going to get through this job.

The red-headed sprite turns to Birdie. "Do you know him?"

Birdie's cute mouth opens and closes again. Then she looks back at me. I don't know why I do it, but I give her a challenging stare. Almost daring her to tell Gia she knows me. To have them kick me to the curb. She places her long fingered hands on her rounded hips. Her high cheeks are pink with anger and embarrassment, and there's a light sheen of sweat on her forehead from soundcheck.

The outfit she's wearing, some worn black skinny jeans and a green V-neck t-shirt with a pair of classic Chucks makes me think back to the nights of listening to music in my bedroom till we could hardly keep our eyes open. Teenage Birdie was cute, but adult Birdie... I must admit she's something else. If I didn't know any better, I'd say I'm kind of turned on. *Fuck*, I'm in trouble.

Birdie's dark blonde eyebrows knit together, and her eyes burn a hole into mine. I can see her thinking a million things all at once, and it's doing things to me that I don't like.

"Birdie?" the Eric guy asks from the doorway.

His voice breaks her death glare, and a flash of jealousy runs through me with the way he looks at her. Damn it to hell. I need to work out, stat. This is not how I expected my first meeting with Birdie to go. I forgot what being in her presence is like. It's hard to explain, but it's like someone lit something inside me.

Birdie swallows, and I can see the way she digs her plum-colored nails into her palms. "Can you guys leave us for a bit. I need to get to know my new *bodyguard*."

The way she says bodyguard has my dick standing at attention. It makes me angry. Angry that a woman who basically told me to go fuck off ten years ago, is turning me on by not even doing anything.

"Are you sure?" Eric asks, his voice stern. He looks me up and down while he questions her, practically challenging me to a duel with his glare. This guy screams overprotective brother bear, and it's annoying me.

"I'm sure. I'll call you guys later," Birdie answers.

Gia looks like she has something to say, but Birdie communicates words with her eyes, so she doesn't. She leads Eric out with Shea who's been lingering in the doorway. Once the crowd is gone and the door is closed, Birdie and I stand in silence.

We glare at each other, sizing each other up. I wonder what she's thinking about me. Does she like what she sees as much as I do?

I try to discard those pesky thoughts, reminding myself that the woman before me is not someone I like. She is not someone I want to be friends with, and she is not someone who I should, nor can, have sex with. For all intents and purposes, she's my employer. That's all this can and should be. Hell, it's all I want it to be.

"I'm going to ask you this one more time," she finally says. Her voice is husky and mellow, a voice I've heard people refer to as a bedroom voice. God, I need ice water. I'm feeling hot.

"Ask me what?" I quip, walking over to a pitcher of water that is for her. I pour myself a glass, draining it in two gulps.

"You're the bodyguard Ben suggested?" she asks instead, her voice tight.

I manage a grin. "And Wren."

Betrayal and disappointment cross her features and it's like she dumped the pitcher of water on my head. I straighten my back, my senses coming returning to me. Birdie doesn't want me here, and I knew she wouldn't. Just like I didn't want to be here. The only reason I'm standing in this room is because of Ben and Wren, my pestering friends. Her friends.

"You can leave. I don't need you here."

Despite my thoughts and feelings, her words anger me. "Like hell you don't."

Her chin juts out stubbornly. "I'll find someone else."

"I signed a two-month contract."

"I'll have it voided."

"It's binding."

"There's got to be a clause."

"Maybe so, but you're stuck with me until you find someone new."

She crosses her arms over her chest, her large breasts threatening to push out of the V-neck. She notices me staring, because she scoffs, putting her arms down. She steps forward, her posture imposing.

"I still don't understand why you would take this job. Give me one good reason why you would want to be stuck with me for two months."

I purposely let my gaze flick up and down her body, establishing some sort of stupid male dominance that I can't quite explain. I push any feelings or niceties down, then put on my practiced and well-earned asshole persona that is more than just a safety net for me. It's needed. Especially with Birdie, and especially for the type of job I need to do for her.

"One-word, pretty bird. Money." The lie tastes like acid on my tongue. Sure, the money is great, but I mostly took this job as a favor to Ben, because of my goddamned loyalty to him and Wren.

Birdie's face heats, causing red splotches to appear on her neck. It looks as if her head may pop right off her body.

"Right. Makes sense. You always were a straight-to-the-point kind of guy. I guess nothing has changed."

"I—"

Before I can get another word out, one of her delicate finger's points at me, then she presses it into my chest... hard. "And don't call me, pretty bird. Got it?"

I hold up my hands, palms facing outward. "Okay, I won't. *Ms. Wilder.*"

Her face turns stony, and she steps back. "One mess up and I'll have the label fly you to the moon."

Despite the tension between us, my body relaxes at the realization she's accepted me as her guard. Even if she doesn't like it, she's going to let me stay.

"I don't mess up," I clip, pulling my shoulders back so I look menacing. It works because the poor thing shrinks back. Good. Keeping a safe distance from me is the best option for the both of us.

Birdie's eyes narrow. "You will. And when you do, I'll be ready to kick you to the curb."

Her voice is a threat, but I take it as a challenge. I hold back a smirk. Birdie Wilder has fire. She's definitely different from the girl who used to sneak out with me to go eat shitty pancakes at Denny's at one in the morning. But she *is* the girl I remember the last day we spoke all those years ago.

"Like I said, I won't mess up."

"We'll see about that."

She turns and walks to the mini bar, her ass on full display in those tight jeans. There's a natural sway to her hips that most men would kill to feel beneath their hands, and other places. After she downs a finger of bourbon, her body relaxes slightly. I can tell she's thinking through the situation at hand.

"I have ground rules," she spits out a moment later.

I bite back a smirk. "Of course you do."

"What does that mean?"

"Let me hear them," I say, ignoring her question.

"You're here to do a job, not to piss me off or wiggle your way back into my life."

Now I can't help but grin. "I'm not here to wiggle."

She rolls her eyes in an adorable way. She makes it so easy to want to tease her.

"You won't talk to me unless I want you to talk to me, and you will stay out of my sight as much as possible. As far as I'm concerned, you don't exist. You're just some fly on the wall."

I roll my tense shoulders back. I expected her to lay out these kinds of rules, but I admit a flash of disappointment works through me. "Don't worry, I'm here to do a job. I'll stay out of your hair."

"Right," she mutters, her voice unsure.

"You're the one making the rules. If you want me in your hair, Ms. Wilder, all you have to do is ask."

She throws up her hands. "Who are you and what did you do to Liam Miller?"

Her words smack me across the face, and all the fun thoughts about her I had before go straight out the window. In their place is anger and a familiar pang of rejection and disappointment.

"Maybe you never knew the real Liam Miller, *Ms. Wilder*. Have you ever thought of that?" My voice is harsh and laced with my anger. So much so that she takes a step away from me.

"I think we're done talking now. You can go stand outside and do whatever it is you do."

I take a deep breath and stand tall. I don't want her to see me falter in any way. I'm used to being dismissed, but it doesn't make it hurt any less. "As you wish, Ms. Wilder."

Without so much as a glance in her direction, I turn and walk out of the room, only to be met with her entourage in the hallway. Eric's ear is pressed against the door like a five-year-old. Fuck me. This is going to be a long two months.

Nine

Birdie

WREN AND BEN ARE going to hear it from me. I'm so pissed I could literally breathe fire. Seeing Liam again feels like being stabbed with a million daggers, Julius Caesar style. Sure, staring at him while dying may be a pleasurable way to go, he'd um... filled out... since I last saw him.

His oval face has a five o'clock shadow, his cheek bones look as if they've been sculpted. His chocolate eyes are even darker than I remember, and his tapered carob colored hair screams for me to run my hands through it. And did I mention he's ripped? Like Thor, but a little lither given his six-foot four height. To top it all off, he's in a black suit with a skinny tie.

I smack my forehead to knock some sense into me. No, I wouldn't let my mind go there. I couldn't. Ugh! Why did I even agree to let him stay in the first place? I should have kicked him out of my dressing room and out of my life, just as I did in high school.

Ms. Wilder. Who does he think he is?! Showing up and just plowing his way into my world like he belongs here. He doesn't. He belongs in a swamp, *or in my bed*—no! Dang brain. I look down at the space between my legs and have the urge to scold it for reacting to freaking LIAM MILLER. *I thought we were past this*; I tell myself mentally. Even if my vagina has a mind of its own, I try to focus back on my anger, because holy shit I'm furious.

Before I have a chance to pull out my phone and dial Wren; Eric, Gia and Shea are in my dressing room. They look curious, a little pissed, and amused. Of course they were listening, who wouldn't?

Shea closes the door and I grab a glass of ice water. I would like to drink more bourbon, but I have a show tonight and I can't be drunk. When I turn around, Gia is tapping her foot, waiting for me to speak, and Eric is about to say something, but I stop him with a wave of my arm.

"Can we not talk about what you just heard?" I put down my glass and rub my temples. "I need to get ready for the show tonight. I don't want to mess up my routine."

There is truth to that statement. I have a routine that I do before every show. Shower, meditate, journal, get ready, warm-up, band together time, and then our show. I have to do it like clockwork, or I get too worked up. My therapist once told me it was good for me to have routines so that I didn't binge eat and have panic attacks, but I probably took them too far. Okay, I did take them too far. Now she says I'm too dependent on my routines, but too bad for her. I'm not changing them. Ever.

Shea steps forward, tucking a lock of her purple hair behind her ear. "We can let him go after tonight, Birdie. We'd have to pay him his fee, but we can do it. It's not a problem."

My stupid stomach flutters at the thought of Liam leaving. Crap. I have a serious problem. *I want him to leave*, I try to convince my body, but it has a lot of other ideas. None of them involve Liam leaving, either. It would be better if he left after tonight.

"I'll let you know."

The three of them look a little shocked when I say that, but mostly still confused. They have no idea what Liam Miller means to me, what he *meant* to me. They have no idea how long it took me to get over our little Instant Message conversation; how I still have trouble with his words, "*I'll never like you like that*," when I get close to potential partners in my life.

I may be confident in my body and how I look, but my longest relationship lasted only six months. It wasn't only that conversation with Liam that prevented me from long-term relationships, but also my celebrity status. There's a reason why Eric is hesitant to allow people into his life or into our circle. Status climbers are real. And all of us in the band and crew have experienced someone getting close to us for the wrong reasons.

I roll my eyes at them. "We have history, clearly. I should have known my friend Ben would do something like this. I'm honestly surprised I didn't put it together, but it's done now. Liam needs the money, he's qualified for the job, and he's here. I don't want to piss off the label any more than I already have."

"They aren't pissed Birdie, they're concerned," Eric says. I know he's trying to squash my growing anxiety; I love him for that.

Gia sighs. "I'm livid Liam never said he knew you. He said he had never even listened to your music before unless his roommate or other circumstance forced him too. He said he doesn't even like music."

I clench my jaw. That's not the Liam I know. But as he just reminded me a few minutes ago, I don't know him. And maybe I never knew him. He sure as hell doesn't know the Birdie I am now. He's never met the confident woman that takes what she wants and follows her dreams at any cost. The Birdie that would never let a man walk all over her. But he'd learn, oh yes, he'd learn.

"He should have said something, and with our history, I'm surprised he didn't. But that doesn't matter anymore. You all like him, you said he's qualified, so let's see how I feel at the end of tonight, yes?"

Eric looks shell shocked. "You're very mature. If an ex did what he's doing, I'd kill him."

"He's not an ex," I clip. "And please don't kill him. The label wants him here, and I want the tour to continue. If he doesn't follow my ground rules, then I'll book him a flight back to New York myself, alright?"

The trio glances at each other, but then they all finally agree.

Shea claps her hands. "At least we don't have to try and find someone else. Do you know how hard it is to get a bodyguard on such short notice? Especially one as trained as him."

"See," I snort, "A silver lining in all this for Shea." We all laugh, and I'm glad they're happy. "Just please, nobody treats him like doo-doo. I may not like Liam very much, but only I get to torture him," I wink.

Eric looks a little sad after I say that. "*Okaaayyy*, but if anything changes, you know we all have your back."

"I know, and I appreciate that. Now all of you get out, I have a show to prepare for!"

I give myself a few minutes after my team leaves to collect myself and debate calling Wren. I want to ask her what the hell she was thinking, but a quick look at the clock makes me decide otherwise. I need to get back to the hotel to do my routine, which means I'll have to face Liam again. I take another drink of cold water before opening the door.

I'm met with Liam's cold stare and intimidating stance. I jump, expecting him to be off to the side, not across from the door like a creep.

"Jesus," I say, placing my hand over my heart. "Why are you standing there like that?"

His face doesn't give away any emotion like it did earlier, instead it just screams, *I'm doing my job*. It should have made me happy, but for some stupid reason it doesn't.

"I'm guarding your door."

I place my hands over my chest, and this time his eyes don't go down to my breasts. I'd noticed that little move before, and I'm not going to lie, even if it annoyed me, it made me feel powerful. Like I had some pull over Liam Miller this time around, unlike I did in high school.

"Don't you usually stand next to it or something?"

"I've got it handled, Ms. Wilder."

God, the way he says Ms. Wilder does something to me. You'd think it would remind me of Mom, but no. The way he says it, with so much command... I swallow the lump in my throat. Even if it makes my lady parts go wild, it's better than *'pretty bird.'* That just felt plain condescending.

"I have to go back to my hotel room," I tell him. "Shea has a car waiting outside for me."

He nods, his eyes never leaving mine. "The hallway is clear. I'll follow behind you. You won't even know I'm here."

I want to laugh at my own dumb ground rules. There's no way I won't know where Liam Miller is whenever he is near me. Even if we haven't seen each other since high school graduation, my body still has

Liam radar. Like some stupid magnetic pull that wants me to follow him around like a lost puppy. I hate it. Maybe I should just fire him, I don't know if I can go through the whole tour feeling like this.

"You can follow me, just don't look at my ass," I finally say.

I notice Liam's jaw twitch. I know I shouldn't have said that. But my words just came out of me like vomit. I guess no matter how much I matured over the years, I still can't handle myself around him. But to my surprise, he doesn't retort. Instead, he just holds out his hand motioning me to walk. Embarrassed now, I do as he suggests. I close my dressing room door behind me and walk forward without another glance at him. I take my time to sway my hips like I do on stage. Even if he doesn't like me, and *never* will, I know that a lot of men find me sexy. And my inner damaged teenage girl triumphs in my little power play with him.

It doesn't take long for us to get to the back doors leading outside the venue. But when we do, Liam puts his hand on my shoulder, and the warmth of it causes me to shiver. His touch is like lava, and I feel it everywhere.

"Wait," he says gruffly. He steps in front of me, then looks around the entry way we're in.

"Why?" I'm annoyed now. I just want to get into the car.

"I need to make sure it's safe. Every new area we're in, I need to do a scan. You never know where this person could be hiding or waiting."

A new shiver runs up my spine, but this time it's not from Liam's warm hand. It's from fear, the reminder of what happened in Times Square ever present in my mind.

"Right," I mutter, shrugging his warm touch off me. "Do your job then." I let any kind of good feelings toward him melt away. He's here for a job, and I don't want anything bad to happen to me or my chosen family.

He nods sharply then scans the area. Eventually we move toward the outside, and he looks around there too. He even looks inside of the car to make sure he knows the driver. When he's satisfied, he holds the door open for me and I climb up into the Suburban easily. Once I'm in, he seats himself as far away from me as he can get, then lets the driver know we're ready to go.

The drive to the hotel is short, but it feels like an eternity. Liam is sitting ramrod straight, clearly uncomfortable with my presence. The only sound in the car is the faint talk radio show the driver has on and Liam's breathing. When the ride comes to an end, I want to bust out of the car and take a big breath of fresh air, but Liam stops me from moving, his thick forearm grazing over my boobs. Ugh, why am I being tortured?!

"Wait here," he says again, not even looking at me, completely ignoring his accidental boob graze.

He gets out of the car and I internally sigh. All this waiting is going to annoy the crap out of me. But I do it anyway, because this is his job, and that's what he's getting paid his precious money for. After a few minutes, he opens the door again, telling me it's safe to come out.

Even though I don't need help, he offers his hand to help me down from the car. I reflexively take it, and yet again regret it as soon as I do. My hands aren't dainty or small, but in his hands, they sure feel that way. The calloused pressure of them has me wanting to squeeze my thighs together at the thought of them all over my body. Shit, now I need a cold shower.

As soon as I'm on the ground, I pull my hand away and start to walk. Liam lets out a grunt but follows behind me, thankfully not scolding me for darting off. Once we're in the elevator, I feel like I'm in one of those action movies or something. The air is tight with tension, and I can sense Liam's anger or whatever the hell he's feeling rolling off him in waves. I know he wants to say something to me, but he doesn't. Good, he's taking his ground rules seriously. I have nothing to say to him, and he shouldn't have anything to say to me. Instead, I take a moment to study his profile, the sharp slope of his nose and the cut of his jaw. He looks tired, but for just a moment I can see the sixteen-year-old boy there.

His eyes flip to mine, and he scowls. He doesn't say it, but if he did, I think he'd be saying, *Enjoying the show?*

I straighten and turn my eyes from him just as the elevator doors open. He stops me from walking again, and this time I feel the tension in his arm. He's pissed I'm not following his orders.

He walks off in front of me, scanning the area before motioning me to move. It doesn't take long till we're outside my suite, and I take out my room key. He places his hand to stop me yet again and produces his own key.

"Me first."

"I'm sure my room is fine," I grumble.

"You have no way of knowing that Ms. Wilder. Now step aside."

Begrudgingly, I do. Before I know it, he's opened the door and is sweeping through all the rooms in the suite. He even checks under the bed and in the shower. Once he's satisfied, he moves to the suite door again.

"All clear," he informs me, and I stop myself from saying, *No shit, Sherlock.*

"I leave for the venue around six," I tell him.

He gives a curt nod before making his way to the door. He stops right before he leaves, turning to give me one more good stern stare. "Make sure you secure the swing bar lock behind me. And text me if you want to leave to go anywhere. Even the ice machine."

I roll my eyes. "Yes, *Dad.*" I swear I see a smirk flash on his lips but it's so fast I could have imagined it.

God, why did I let him stay?

Ten

Liam

IT'S EASY TO FORGET how boring being a bodyguard is. And I need better shoes with how much standing I'll be doing. For the next two months I'll be spending most of my time outside of Birdie's doors and making sure nobody gets near her.

Since she's currently safe in her room, I take the time to grab a quick shower and a bite to eat. But not before sending a text to Ben to let him know I'd seen Birdie and she's mad as hell at him and Wren.

Naturally, he just sent a thumbs up. A fucking thumbs up. Ben is used to dealing with girl stuff, so I guess he thinks Birdie is going to get over it. And maybe she will. I heard her little conversation with her team, and I admit I'm surprised she told them to treat me well. I thought she'd revel in her friends taking cheap shots at me.

I groan, shedding my suit jacket and button-up, hanging them to keep everything free of wrinkles. I look down at my forearm, the one that accidentally grazed Birdie's ample chest. I scratch it to try and rid the feeling of her shirt and the weight of her breasts lingering there. Even though it was just for a moment, now my mind is wandering to thoughts of the elevator ride and the tension between us.

Immediately all my blood rushes to my downstairs brain. I didn't expect seeing Birdie again to cause such a "rise" in me. Now I really wish I could go work out, but I can't leave her alone in the other room. Not after what happened earlier.

When Eric filled me in on the Times Square incident, I was furious. She should never have gone to such a busy place with him. He's a big dude, but he's not trained. Today could have been bad, and by the look on Eric's face, he knew it too.

He mentioned that Birdie didn't seem to think much of it, which made sense given the way she just tried to walk everywhere without me scanning the area first. I'd have to make sure to do more perimeter checks with the band's venue security before and after all shows and sound checks.

For how famous the woman is, she sure doesn't have any self-preservation. Which we need to fix if our time together is going to work out. The anger I feel when she doesn't listen is going to make my head explode if I'm not careful. She shouldn't anger me so much, but ever since we stopped being friends, I couldn't help but feel a certain amount of animosity toward her.

I promised her during our Instant Messenger conversation that we'd always be friends, no matter what she said, but she's the one who couldn't stay friends with me. She's the one who ended whatever friendship was between us, not me.

I didn't deserve her anger, which I think is what ultimately pissed me off the most. And that only grew every year that I had to see her walking around school with my friends—laughing, joking, having a good time. Well, I wasn't having a good time, and I needed a friend like her back then and she wasn't there.

I scrub my hands over my face a couple times. The rational side of me knows that I should just let our sordid past go. That we should move forward as the adults we are now, instead of who we were back then. But she hasn't let it go either. We have some unfinished business, and I just don't have the capacity to dig it up and discuss it. I don't know if I ever will.

So that brings me back to just doing my job and ignoring the way that Birdie Wilder gets me riled up in more ways than one.

"You've really never seen Birdie perform? Like ever?" Shea yells over the noise.

I'm watching Birdie from the wings. The band just started their first song, and the crowd is going wild for them, especially for Birdie.

"No," I confirm, not looking at the kid. My eyes are completely on Birdie, watching her do what she does best.

In the two years we were friends, I never would have imagined her being here now. She was a quiet girl back then. I mean, she was super passionate about music, and could talk to me for a long time about the bands she loved. She even sang me a couple of her songs, but a famous rock star? I never saw it coming. But seeing her now, on stage like this, I can see why she's so good at it, why she's loved by so many fans.

Birdie looks like some sort of voluptuous vixen, her hips swaying in time to the music. She's got on a pleated evergreen skirt that's swirling at her feet as she moves. She's barefoot on a colorful area rug the crew has set up, and I think I see a toe ring glimmering on her pinky toe. She's wearing a black T-shirt, cropped short, and when she reaches her arms up, I can see a small sliver of peach skin peeking out. My small brain starts to wonder what that skin would taste like; feel like.

"I can't believe that! Not even on TV?" Shea yells again.

"Nope, never."

"You're in for a good show. Some of these people paid big bucks to see her tonight. But every cent is well spent, trust me."

My eyes stay locked on Birdie as she croons a low beautiful note. I feel the soul of it vibrate under my feet. The crowd is cheering loudly, and I can't help it, I smile. Her gift is beautiful, and her spirit on stage with her band is contagious. Just when I think it can't get any better, Birdie sits down at her piano and starts pounding away. It's insane to watch, and I can't believe she's hitting those pedals barefoot. She's a beast and a musical force. Even though I've stopped listening to music like I had when I was younger, I still have a great appreciation for it and a knowledge that would never go away. Birdie Wilder and her band know their stuff, and the entire world loves them for it.

Song after song, I find myself unable to look away. The more she sings, and the more the band plays, the more I become enraptured by her sound. Shea mentioned she gets compared to Mama Cass and Janis Joplin a lot, and though I can hear that in her sound, Birdie is something uniquely her own. Like wild sex and deep love has been bottled up somehow.

"ATLANTIC CITY!" Birdie yells to the crowd, sweat dripping down her face, and a wide smile covering her features. I watch as her lips, the dark red lipstick now worn, move to the vowels of each word she speaks. It's sexy as hell, and I can't find any power to hate myself for thinking that right now.

The crowd goes wild, and Birdie eats it up.

"I keep hearing some loud requests for a certain song!" she yells again. The crowd gets crazier, and before long, the words, *Desire Reigns, Desire Reigns, Desire Reigns*, work through the crowd. "Should we give it to them?" Birdie asks her band.

"HELL YEAH!" They answer back. Jane does some crazy shit on the drums to rile them up even more.

Birdie motions for the crowd to calm down with her hands, and to my shock, they listen.

"Alright, we heard you, Atlantic City! We heard you!"

Birdie turns back to her band, and Jane counts them in. The song that they begin to play is one I know I've heard before. No matter how much I've tried to avoid everything about Birdie Wilder, this is her most popular song. It plays at the gym sometimes and on the radio—and even during commercials and some movies.

"This song made her famous!" Shea echoes my thoughts. "It's amazing live!"

Birdie starts the song and the notes flow from her mouth in smooth succession. I focus on the words she sings, and they wash over me like an ice bath.

Hold on baby girl,
Look at what he's put you through,
He's broke your heart,
He'll never like you like that,
So why do you let your desire reign?
He took your heart,
Held it in his palm,
Crushed it tight and let you die a little inside,

You should move on, yet you let your desire reign.
You're the one who wants to be with him.
Deep inside you hope he feels it too,
You waited for his heart to grow,
But he doesn't want your desire, no....
Yet you let your desire reign, desire reign, desire reign.
As you grew, you wanted the desire to wane,
But instead, it followed you
from state to state
It's hard to keep him from your mind,
He hates you, yet you want him,
You love him, yet he forgets you
You should move on, yet you let your desire reign.
You're the one who wants to be with him.
Deep inside you hope he feels it too,
You waited for his heart to grow,
But he doesn't want your desire, no....
Yet you let your desire reign, desire reign, desire reign.
In the end, there is no dream to dream,
In the end there is no hope to hope,
Yet you hold onto memories of summer,
Of should haves and what ifs
You hold on to desire, that strong desire.
You let your desire reign.
You let your desire reign, desire reign, desire reign.
You let your desire reign, desire reign, desire reign.
You let your desire reign, desire reign, desire reign.

The music fades out and for a moment, the crowd is silent. My ears are ringing, and my hands are clenched at my sides; nails digging into my palms so much they hurt. That song is about me. Who the hell else could it be about?

I'll never like you like that. Those fucking words. But those words aren't the only ones ringing in my ears. She loved me back then; and now she thinks I hate her. Well, I guess in a way I do, but I didn't hate her back then. There was no reason to. She's the one that made our relationship weird, not me.

I wonder if Ben and Wren know this song is about me and her. Ben claims he never knew what went down between us early that summer, but maybe he did. Maybe he's just trying to get me to say it. He has to have an idea if he knows that song, which I know he does.

"Birdie says that song is about some unrequited high school love. Think he knows?" Shea asks, breaking my thoughts.

I don't answer her or look to see if she's trying to get information from me, instead I walk off the stage to get ready for the fan meet-and-greet and press interviews after the show. That's where I'm needed now. I can't watch any more of this. It's too much. Too many memories and feelings. Things I shouldn't be feeling while on a job.

I need to get my damn head in the game.

Eleven

Birdie

I CAN FEEL LIAM'S eyes on me during the entire show, yet I manage not to look at him once. Instead, I focus on the amazing energy of the crowd and my talented band. I use his burning gaze to put more passion behind my songs. I didn't even think about the fact that at least one-fourth of the ones we sang tonight came off my first album, *Desire Reigns*, and most of the songs are about him.

After we finish said title track, we come off stage before our encore. I'm a little surprised Liam isn't there anymore but don't think too much of it. He must have slithered off to 'check the perimeter' or whatever.

I take a swig of water and wipe my brow, then the band and I are back on stage for two more songs. It's a wild rush, and over in a blink of an eye. When we're back off stage again, we gather for our end of show huddle, then Eric is sweeping me away to my dressing room.

"Liam will meet us in the green room. He'll be following you throughout the fan meet-and-greets and press interviews."

"Perfect." The sarcasm in my voice is evident, but Eric doesn't respond. Once I'm in my dressing room, I collapse on the couch to take a breather. Shows are so much fun, but also a lot of work.

"You sounded great tonight. There was some extra gusto in "Desire Reigns" I haven't heard in a while. Any reason for that?" Eric's brown eyes gaze into mine and I see he's got my number.

I decide to play dumb. "No idea what you're talking about."

"Sure it doesn't have to do with a certain bodyguard named Liam?"

I stand and make my way to the bar. Since the show is over, I can get drunk if I want to, and I want to. "I had a good audience. And, after what happened this morning, I wanted to put on a good show."

Eric taps his fingers methodically on the bar counter. "If you say so."

"I say so."

He's about to speak again, but there's a knock on the door.

A voice calls from behind the door. "It's Liam."

"Speak of the devil," Eric mutters. "Come in!"

Liam enters, stepping down into the dressing room. His stance is tight, and his face is stern. He looks a little more pissed than usual. Eric's right, he has RSF.

"The press is requesting an interview with Birdie. It's someone from Waves Magazine," he says, all business.

I pour myself a shot of tequila and down it quickly. Gia told me they might send someone, and she suggested I say something to send a message to the stalker. Not sure I have it in me, but I'll give it a try. I stop myself from taking another shot, and instead grab a beer from the fridge.

"Let's get this over with."

I catch Liam's gaze going from the empty shot glass then to the beer. He probably thinks I have a problem. Which I don't, but I let him think what he wants. He can judge me or accept me. I may sing "Desire Reigns" almost every day, but the words aren't relevant anymore. At least that's what I tell myself. I catch his eyes and don't back down from his searing stare.

He holds out his arm to signal me to go. "After you."

I unlock our eyes and make my way past him. I can feel his eyes on my back as we walk to the green room. It makes the hairs on the back of my neck stand on end.

When we enter the room, to my surprise, Liam puts a hand on my lower back and the other out in front to stop people from approaching me. In some cases, this might be hot, but I'm immediately embarrassed. I've always allowed my fans to approach me in the green room, that's what they're there for.

I don't say anything to Liam, instead I just push his arm down. Since he's not expecting it, it gives willingly. He tries to utter his disapproval, but I don't listen, nor care. Two curvy teenage girls approach me, both wearing Birdie Wilder T-shirts and ask if they can have hugs.

"Of course you can!" I put out my arms and the girls come right in. After we briefly hug, I ask them if they have anything they'd like me to sign. We finish with a picture, which Eric takes. I had a feeling if I asked Liam he'd sneer at the poor girls and scare them. He's in a mood tonight. He's acting more like a mad dog than a bodyguard. I ignore him and continue to do the rounds.

I take more pictures and sign more CDs and posters. Liam stands close to me the whole time, ready to pounce if one fan makes a wrong move. It's seriously putting a damper on my good mood. By the time I reach Waves Magazine, I'm grumpier than I have been all week. Gia is there, thank God. I hope she can stop me if I say anything stupid.

"Katelyn, this is Birdie."

"Hi Katelyn. Nice to meet you." I smile and hold out my hand for her to shake.

"You as well, Birdie. I'd just like to get a few quotes if possible?"

I look at Gia and she nods her approval. "Sure."

Katelyn holds out a tape recorder, then starts to shoot off questions. They start off simple. Questions about the tour, some about my new songs, and then she asks if I'm dating anyone. I notice her gaze move to Liam, and I immediately shake my head. "He's my bodyguard. I'm single."

Katelyn blushes after Liam gives her a small grin. It makes me want to puke. Is he seriously flirting with this reporter? I can't believe him right now. He's been acting moody all night, then he sees a pretty reporter and he's all smiles. I can't wait to get my gamble on. After this day, I really need it.

After what is probably only a few seconds, but feels like minutes, Katelyn eventually focuses back on me. "I'm glad you mentioned a bodyguard. I want to ask you about the stalker situation. How are you feeling?"

I set my shoulders back and put on a brave face. "I'm feeling fine."

"That's good to hear. If you could say anything to them, what would you say?"

"That I'm not afraid. That if he or she needs professional help, I'd be more than happy to pay for their needs," I respond, hoping that didn't come off too asshole-ish.

Katelyn opens her mouth to ask another question, but Liam steps forward. "I think that's all for today, Katelyn. Birdie thanks you for your time."

"Wha—" I don't get the full word out of my mouth because Liam is practically dragging me away by the upper arm. I don't want to make more of a scene, so I follow him with a fake smile plastered on my face.

Once we're in the hallway away from prying eyes, Liam pins me to the wall. His body is so close I can smell his sweat and aftershave. I'm tall, but he still has five inches on me, so I feel small. Smaller than I ever do. Again, this would be hot if I wasn't so upset at him and his shitty behavior. And if he was, well... not Liam Miller.

"You can't say stuff like that to reporters," he scolds.

His voice is harsh, but I manage not to let it get to me, at least not on the outside. I put my chin up and puff out my chest, "I just did what Gia asked me to do."

"From now on, you don't say anything about the stalker to the media. You shouldn't provoke them or offer them help like some savior. It's going to get you hurt, or worse."

His face is only a few inches away, and I can feel his hot breath against my already heated cheek. This close, I'm able to *really* look at him for the first time in our adult lives.

I can see the way his skin is tight over his cheekbones, and he has slight bags under his eyes from lack of sleep. I notice how his eyelashes kiss his skin and his eyebrows need a slight trim. From the depths of his chocolate irises, I see the concern for me within them mixed with his visible anger and layers of another emotion. If I had to guess, I'd say it's pain. For what, I don't know.

Liam's hand flexes on my bicep, and for a moment I think he's going to kiss me. Or hit me. No, Liam would never do that.

"Liam," I breathe, my voice comes out huskier than usual. The sound breaks his trance, and he steps back like I've smacked him across the face.

"Sorry," he clears his throat. "I shouldn't have gotten in your space like that. It's unprofessional."

I swallow thickly, "You're right, it is." With the spell of him now broken, I come back to my senses. I remember how embarrassed I am that he pulled me from the green room like a child.

"And, Mr. Miller, I'd appreciate it if the next time you want to tell me something, you just ask. You don't need to drag me out of a room full of people who admire and look up to me. You potentially made a PR nightmare for Gia."

He nods roughly. That stony look back on his face again. "Understood, Ms. Wilder. Would you like me to escort you back to the green room or to your hotel?"

"I'm going back to the green room. I have more press to do and fans to meet."

He makes his "after you" motion again, and I quickly make my exit, happy to not be alone in a room with Liam Miller any longer.

I'm on my fourth shot of liquor, and a few beers have been thrown in here and there.

After I met with my fans, the band stuck around, as well as our openers, to toast to our amazing show. Now we're gathered around discussing some of our wild fans. Tonight's show was fruitful. I got one bra, two thongs, and three pairs of briefs. They'd been thrown out long ago, but it's hilarious to talk about.

I can practically feel Liam's brooding from where he stands in the corner thinking about whatever it is he's thinking about while he watches. Kevin even tried to get him to join us a few times, but he politely declined each time. After our little showdown in the hallway, he hasn't so much as looked in my direction. But the more I think about it, the more I realize it's for the best. We need to stay complete strangers if I don't want him to invade my life again.

"Well," Kevin says, slapping his knees. "I need to hit the hay, or I'll be asleep on-stage tomorrow night."

"Me too," Jane chimes while she stretches her hands over her head. "I'm already going to have a hangover after all these drinks."

That starts a chain reaction, and soon everyone gets ready to go. I text Eric to get our cars sent and make my way to my dressing room to collect my things. Liam follows me, but I don't acknowledge him.

I make my way over again to the little bar. It's after one in the morning, but I'm not tired. I'm also not *quite* drunk enough yet. I take another shot, and once I hit the empty glass on the table, I feel Liam's eyes on me. I can tell he wants to say something about that last shot, but he bites his lip. Smart man.

I grab my bag and head toward the door. Liam is still trailing me like a puppy. The hallway and outside are already clear so I don't have to wait for him to do his lookout. Once we're in the car and on the way back to the hotel, I start to get giddy at the thought of finally hitting the slot machines. I've been waiting all day!

"Why are you smiling?" Liam's gruff voice startles me.

"I forgot you were there," I laugh. Okay, it sounds more like a giggle. Dang. I might be more drunk than I thought.

He shakes his head. "Good. That means I'm following your rules."

I snort. An actual snort. Pretty soon I'm laughing so hard I think I might pee my pants. The whole time Liam watches me, a faint smile on his pretty pink lips.

"Why are you laughing so hard?"

I laugh louder. "This whole situation is laughable."

He rubs his stubbled jaw. "How so?"

"Wouldn't you like to know," I giggle.

"You're something else, Ms. Wilder."

"I've been told."

Liam raises his eyebrow, but the car comes to a stop in front of the hotel. He buttons his suit coat and makes his way out of the car, then gives me the okay to follow after a minute. Once we're in the lobby, the sound of slot machines calls to me and I make a beeline right for them.

"Stop!" Liam commands.

I stop like the good dog I am.

I turn on my heel. "Yes?" *Is the room spinning?* I look up at the ceiling and I think it's spinning. I should have stopped at four shots. I'm probably going to lose a lot of money tonight.

"Where do you think you're going?"

"I'm going to gamble."

He shakes his head. "No. You're not gambling tonight, Ms. Wilder."

"Whoa there, buddy! You're not my keeper."

He comes closer, his voice low to not draw attention. "Trust me, I know I'm not. But I'm your bodyguard, and I'm not equipped or prepared to keep you safe in a full-blown casino at this time of night. It's not safe, and I'm not putting you or myself at risk so you can blow all your money."

I giggle again. "That would be a lot of money to spend in one night."

He bites his tongue, but I can tell he wants to laugh. Or maybe scream.

"I'll take you back to your room."

I whine. "But... gambling."

"It will have to wait for another night. A night when I'm prepared and not falling asleep on my feet. It's been a long day."

I push my lips together, trying to quell my irrational anger. I know he's right, but drunk Birdie is not happy at having her plans foiled.

"You're so boring."

"Call me whatever you want. I'm just doing my job."

"Fine. Take me back oh Boring One." I stick my tongue out at him like I'm five. "I'll get my kicks some other way!"

"As long as it's in your room with the door locked."

"And if it isn't?"

Liam's jaw clenches, but he doesn't take the bait. "Let's go, Ms. Wilder. I think you need some sleep."

Twelve

Liam

THIS WOMAN WILL BE the death of me.

I don't know if I should stay outside of Birdie's suite tonight or not. I'm worried the moment I go to my room she's going to try and sneak out to play slots. She's drunk enough that doing so is one hundred percent possible. Not that I can blame her, the bright lights called my name a few times today too. But once I've made sure she's securely locked in her room, I make an executive decision to stay just outside her door for the next hour, or at least until her room quiets down enough that I think she's passed out.

Part of me wants to stay in her room to make sure she sleeps on her stomach and drinks enough water, but as she reminded me, I'm not her keeper. And I'm not her friend either. They hired me to be her bodyguard, not her babysitter.

I let out a troubled sigh. I should have asked Eric if Birdie struggled with drinking. If tonight is a regular occurrence, I'd need to up my OT hours. Birdie can pack them away like the guys from the gym I went out with some nights along with Ben—I find it alarming. Granted, tonight is just one night, and she and I did just rekindle our... whatever it is that's going on between us. Truth be told, if I could have had one drink, I would have. But I'm on the job, and I try not to drink too much anymore, especially to escape from stress.

Since it's late, and there is nobody around, I slide down the door. My feet ache, so I text Ben to have him order me better shoes and send them to our next stop. He can be my bitch for a second since he got me into this situation. I may be fit, but bodies aren't meant to stand on their feet all day, especially in a stagnant position.

With the quiet of the hall, and my tired body propped up on the door, my mind wanders. Was it only just this morning I had sex with Cindy? She was certainly bendy.

The way she felt... that thing she did with her hips while she was riding me. I can see it in my mind and instantly my dick is half hard. In my mind's eye, I reach forward to pull back the blonde locks of hair, but when I do, instead of Cindy's perky nose, it's Birdie's round face.

My eyes pop open and I groan. I blame our heated conversation in the hallway after the show.

The way her body felt pressed into mine, all soft curves and heat. Her height made us more evenly matched, and if I didn't dislike her so much, and if she wasn't my boss, I would have propositioned her right then and there. *Fuck...* it's almost too easy for me to picture what it would feel like if I sunk balls deep into her warmth.

I smack myself across the face.

My little brain has me thinking with him again. Now I need another cold shower. I look at my watch, it's only been fifteen minutes. I press my ear to the suite door and still hear Birdie milling around. She's not talking, but she's doing something.

I will her to go to sleep, but it doesn't work. I slam my head against the door and for a moment the movement pauses. Then it starts back up again a few seconds later. I guess I'm going to be here for a while.

A loud noise startles me awake. *Shit!* I fell asleep. Way to be professional.

I stand and scan the hallway, but thankfully there's no one there. Once I put my ear against Birdie's door, I think I can hear something. The noise that woke me had to have come from inside her suite. I check my watch and see I've only been out of it for a few minutes, but I can't let that happen again. Worry fills my stomach that something might have gone down inside the suite while I was sleeping. I knock on the door loudly, but no answer.

"Birdie?" I knock again, a little stronger this time. But still nothing.

Without another thought, I make an executive decision that I need to check on her. She's drunk, and something could have happened. I know for a fact there's no stalker in her suite, so if the noise did come from inside, it's because she's done something.

"Birdie, are you okay?" I yell one more time. When there's still no answer, I take out a copy of her room key Eric had made for me and slide it in. The light turns green, and I step inside.

My eyes first go to the empty beer cans and little bourbon bottles on the kitchen counter. Oh no, she drank more. The sound of running water from the bathroom keys me into where she is. I stalk toward the door, my stomach now in knots. I hope she didn't kill herself. Damn it. I suck at my job, and it hasn't even been twenty-four hours.

When I reach the bathroom, the door is wide open, and Birdie is lying awkwardly in the tub. She's still wearing her black crop top, but she's managed to remove her long skirt. The shower curtain is on the floor, and water soaks her. I try to keep my eyes off her lower waist, which is covered in sheer black high-waisted panties. Those are soaked too, and I can see the outline of her pussy, hair in a perfect triangle. If I wasn't so concerned about her well-being, my dick would have been extremely happy at the sight.

Her hazel eyes gaze up at me, and a weight lifts in my stomach. Thank fuck she's alive.

"Hey Liam Miller," she slurs. "What are you doing in my room?" *Hiccup.*

"Geez, Birdie. Are you okay?" I get down on my knees and water begins to soak my nice suit. I turn off the shower, it's ice cold, then move to lift Birdie by her shoulders.

"Never been better." *Hiccup.*

"How much more did you drink?"

She groans, acting more like a dead fish in my arms than a human. "Why are you in my room?" She demands again. Her eyes are hooded and mouth sweetly pursed.

"I'm making sure you don't die. Has anyone ever told you not to drink and bathe? You could have seriously injured yourself."

"Not like you care!" She tries to push me away but I'm stronger than her, so I don't budge.

"Come on, let's get you out of the tub. You're going to get sick."

She snorts. "That's an old wives' tale. Getting wet and cold doesn't make you sick. A virus does!"

I drop my head to my chest. "Only you would give me facts while I'm trying to save you from dying."

"I'm not dying," she mumbles.

"Yeah, because I'm here."

She rolls her eyes at me, and I continue to move her out of the tub. She's swaying on her feet, but thankfully she's standing. I keep an arm on her as I reach for a towel. Wrapping it around her shoulders, I bring her to the kitchen, then make her sit on a stool.

"Liam Miller," she says my full name again, and I swear my cock twitches. Her coal black makeup from her show is smeared around her eyes, and her dark lipstick is completely gone, but God she looks... *No, don't go there, Liam.*

"Birdie Wilder," I say, her name like syrup on my tongue.

She holds the towel close to her body. "I like it when you say my name. I shouldn't like it, but I do," she admits, her voice hoarse.

"I thought you didn't like anything when it came to me." I get her a glass of water and some Tylenol I find in one of the cabinets. She's going to have a killer headache in the morning if she doesn't take any. Probably some body aches too.

"I don't! You're an asshole."

I can't help but grin. "You're right about that."

"What are you doing here, Liam?"

"I told you, I'm helping you."

"No." *Hiccup.* "What are you doing HERE?" she exclaims.

I get the picture now. "I told you. I'm here to do a job."

"And that's all?"

"As I said, I need the money."

"But why do you need the money?"

I roll my shoulders back and crack my neck. "What is this, twenty questions?"

"You just... UGH! You make me so mad, Liam Miller. I look at you and—" she pauses.

I stare at her hooded eyes and messy lips. Fuck, her lips... they look like delicious pillows. I want to lay my own lips on them and... "And what?" I ask, my mouth now dry.

She doesn't say anything, instead she stands and almost falls over. I grab her and keep her steady. "Where are you going?"

"I'm cold. I need to change... but the floor seems to be moving."

I let out a breath. This woman! I pull her into my side, "I've got you." She doesn't seem to notice the hitch in my voice, or the way I hold her closer than I should.

We walk together to the bedroom, and I gently settle her on the edge of the bed. I turn to walk toward her suitcase, but she stops me by grabbing my hand.

"Did you hear your song tonight?"

Her eyes are still glassy from the liquor, and I want to tell her to shut up and go to bed, but there's also some sort of pleading in her eyes that makes me answer.

"So, it is about me?"

Her cheeks flush with embarrassment. "I don't feel that way anymore. Just so you know. It's an old song I wrote when I was a stupid obsessed teenager."

I don't know why, but my stomach flips at her words. "Whatever you say, Birdie."

"You hurt me then, Liam. You know that, right?"

A lump forms in my throat. "I was a teenager too, Birdie. I didn't mean to hurt you."

"I get that you didn't want to date a fat girl, but you didn't have to be so cruel. You were my best friend."

"Woah! When did I ever make anything about your weight?"

She contorts her face, her tone sarcastic as she says, *"I'll never like you like that."*

I rub my hands over the scruff on my jaw. "It was never about your looks, Birdie. I may be an asshole, but I'm not a shallow asshole. I never have been."

"You're saying I'm ugly?" Her eyes water.

Damn it. This conversation is way out in left field. Birdie's drunk, and clearly out of her damn mind. The last thing I want to do right now is rehash old drama that shouldn't even matter anymore.

"I think you need to go to sleep. You're not going to like yourself in the morning if you keep going."

"I'm fine."

"Yeah, and pigs fucking fly," I grunt.

"You're an ass."

"I am, and you're drunk." I take my hand from hers, which I didn't realize I was still holding, and grab some shorts and a shirt from her bag.

"Change and get some rest, Birdie. I'm going to sleep on your couch. Make sure you're okay."

"Yes, Dad," she sneers again. But this time I don't get any kicks out of her teasing, instead I'm just livid. This is not how I expected my first night to go. I'm tired, and I'm going to say something stupid if I stay in her line of vision any longer.

"Just do it, Birdie."

She pushes her towel down, and before I can exit, she strips off her shirt. She's wearing a black lacy bra that's see-through. Her heavy breasts are straining against the wet fabric, and her stomach looks like a nice place for my head to land.

Damn it. I'm giving myself whiplash with my up and down feelings. Seriously, what the hell is wrong with me? I need to be medicated or maybe knocked out.

She smirks at me... the little vixen knows exactly what she's doing. I lift my eyes from her dark nipples, my body heating from the visual stimulation and heated tension. *Remain professional, Liam.*

I put my poker face back on. "Go to bed, Ms. Wilder. We aren't going to play this game."

"I don't know what you mean," she chirps innocently.

"Like hell. Now go to bed. I'll see you in the morning." I close the door on her and hope she'll be okay. I'm sure she will be, it looks like she's pretty functional... and feisty.

I make my way to the living room, my pants still wet from the bathroom floor. I stare at the fancy sofa, then at the door that leads to my bedroom with a nice big King bed. I guess this couch will have to do for the night. Fan-fucking-tastic.

Thirteen

Birdie

I THINK I'M DYING. Or maybe I've already died? My head's pounding, and my body feels like I've been in a fight. The last time I'd felt like this was at my first college party during my years at Michigan State.

Blech. My mouth tastes like shit. Why did I drink so much? Oh right, Liam Miller. I gasp and sit up way too quickly.

My head pounds. "Fuck."

With a groan, I lie back down. Liam. Stupid face. Miller. He saw me practically naked. The things I said... Oh man, just shoot me already. I told him I wrote "Desire Reigns" about him, why did I do that?

It's official, I'm never drinking again.

There's a light rapping on my door and I look up to see Shea standing in the doorway with a black coffee and a brown bag that's got an oil stain coming through it. It's probably an egg and cheese bagel. I don't know if I want to eat it or puke but eating it will probably help the acid now burning a hole in my stomach. I don't think I ate anything for dinner last night, which is also why I got so wasted. Again, I blame Liam.

"I figured you'd need this," Shea says quietly, and I want to kiss her for how thoughtful she is. She sits on the edge of the bed, handing me the coffee and food. "You look like crap by the way. Maybe just go straight to the shower, don't bother looking in a mirror."

I cringe. "That bad?"

"You kind of remind me of Bozo the Clown," she giggles.

"Great. Just great." I take a sip of the black coffee, enjoying the way it burns the taste of shit from my mouth.

"Sooo... you and Liam make up?" She gestures her head in the direction of the living room.

"Why would you say that?"

"He was sleeping on the couch when I came in. Either the guy takes his job way too seriously or something happened last night."

"Most def the former. Nothing happened between us last night. Or at least, nothing of mention. Is he still here?"

She shakes her head no. "What happened then? Why do you look like death warmed over?"

"I got drunk and fell in the shower." *And tried to strip in front of Liam.*

"Goodness, B! Are you okay? Do you need me to get you a doctor appointment?"

"No, I'm good." I force myself to open the bag of food. I pull out the bagel and take a bite. When the carbs hit my stomach, I immediately feel better.

"Are you sure?"

"I broke the fall with my ass. Mostly I'm just embarrassed and sore. And did I mention hungover? I don't even know how I'm talking to you right now."

"I don't either. But I came to remind you that you have a meeting with Rolling Stone."

"Dang it! My interview."

"Yep. Forgot that was today, huh?"

"I sure as hell did. Do I have hair and makeup coming?"

"No, but I can get them if you want me too."

"Yes, please. I need a miracle."

She picks at my tangled hair. "I'll agree with you there."

I take another bite of food and sip of coffee as Shea explains how the interview is going to go down. We're meeting in the hotel bar for lunch, then we'll go for a walk around Atlantic City. The reporter is going to ask me some questions, get to know me, then we'll be done. Surprisingly, I've never been featured in Rolling Stone before, so this is a big deal. I can't believe I forgot.

"Penny for your thoughts?" Shea grins. "You're awfully quiet."

"I just hope they don't ask anything about the stalker. Liam said I shouldn't talk about it at all."

"Then don't. I'll make sure Gia lets them know. Only talk about what you're comfortable sharing."

"Okay, cool."

"Are you going to tell me what happened between you and Liam last night for real? He got all weird when I told him "Desire Reigns" is about an unrequited high school love. He was all goo-goo eyed at the show up until I said that. Then he stormed off like he wanted to punch something. Is that song about him?"

I drink more coffee, but it doesn't keep my stomach from jumping. I'm sure Liam was not goo-goo eyed at my show, she's exaggerating, but now I understand why he was so angry last night before the whole shower thing.

"It's a long story that I'd like to keep to myself for now. My head is pounding, and I need a shower. Can I take a rain check?"

Shea smiles then stands. "Of course. I'll get to work and have hair and makeup here within the hour. Go get cleaned up, and remember, don't look in the mirror."

"Roger that!" I salute. But as soon as I hear Shea leave, I beeline to the bathroom and look in the mirror.

She was right, I shouldn't have looked.

After a long shower, followed by aspirin, a lot more coffee, and then hair and makeup, I'm a brand-new woman. But nothing can erase the embarrassment I feel at how I was with Liam last night. Sadly, I'm not someone who forgets what I say and do during a night out—I remember every word.

Not only did I talk about "Desire Reigns" being "his song," I can't believe I told him he didn't want to date a fat girl. I thought I was over that body hating BS. Apparently not when I'm drunk... and not when my high school obsession is my bodyguard... a very sexy bodyguard.

I rub my eyes, careful to avoid the dark eye makeup. I don't want to turn myself into a messy racoon again like I did last night. *Ugh!* Liam saw that too. I try to push my thoughts away, dreading when I see him again in a few minutes.

He's going to trail me and the reporter during the interview to make sure everything stays kosher. He probably hates me even more after last night. Not that I'd blame him. He was only trying to help me, and I was being a drunken bitch.

There's a staccato knock on my door. Time to face the music. I open it to find Liam's disgruntled face.

Today he's dressed in another suit, no tie this time. Just a white button up with navy slacks and matching jacket. His hair is still wet, and I swear I can see where he ran his fingers through it. His five o'clock shadow is gone too, and I notice a tiny red dot on his jaw from where he must have nicked himself. His brown eyes are weary, but he doesn't look like a guy who just slept on his boss's couch.

"You should look through the peephole to see who it is before you answer, or at the very least ask who it is. I could have been anyone," he clips.

I straighten at the tightness of his voice. Right, he's angry. Rightly so. Well, today is going to be a fun day. "I looked," I lie.

He swallows, his Adam's apple bobbing up and down. "I know you're lying. Just look next time, Ms. Wilder. It's for your own safety."

Ms. Wilder. "Right, I will."

Liam lifts one of his dark eyebrows, surprised that I didn't give him a hard time. But I have to admit he's right. I should have looked.

I raise my eyebrow back at him. "What, do you want me to argue with you?"

"Of course not, Ms. Wilder. Are you ready to leave? The reporter from Rolling Stone is downstairs."

I bite my tongue so I don't say something snarky. "I am. Just let me grab my purse."

Liam waits dutifully in the hallway instead of coming in, so I grab what I need before making my exit. I take my position in front of Liam, and he steps behind me, his footfalls heavy as we walk. Nobody is around and I can feel his eyes burning holes into the back of my head.

Once we enter the elevator, I can't take it anymore. I don't know why I do it, but I apologize.

"Liam…" My voice is unsteady. He turns his head toward me, but his body remains facing forward. "I just want to say I'm sorry for last night."

He stares at me for a moment, and for a split second I think he's going to say something. Instead, he just nods, then goes back to looking forward like a perfect statue.

I want to scream at him, beg him to say that he's accepted it, but it would be stupid of me to. Clearly, he's back in work mode. And even if I'm sorry for what I said last night, I said those things because that's how I feel. He hurt me back then and helping me last night after I fell in the shower did not change the past.

As soon as the bell dings to the lobby, I breathe a huge sigh of relief. I need to leave this damn elevator. As I walk, I take some deep breaths to collect myself. I want this interview to go well, and I can't let my beef with my bodyguard get to me. I'm a grown woman. I accept that I made a fool of myself last night, and now I'm moving on.

Gia is in the hotel bar when we arrive, talking to the reporter. "She's here," I hear Gia say, and the reporter looks up at me. I'm struck immediately by how beautiful she is. She's got dark red hair and black lipstick on. She's dressed in a black crop top that shows off her toned midriff and a pair of short jean shorts. Great. Now I feel self-conscious in my thigh-length mustard yellow sundress.

I blow out an annoyed breath. Liam's presence has really screwed me up. Normally this crap doesn't bug me, but now that he's here, all of sudden I'm questioning myself? I'm a sexy rock star and I know it. My ex-high school crush should not be determining my worth or how I feel about myself right now.

"Birdie Wilder!" the reporter says happily. She holds out her small hand for me to take. "I'm Tawny Black, I'll be interviewing you today."

I shake her hand. Of course, her name is Tawny Black. It sounds like a model's name. "Nice to meet you as well."

"Shall we get started?"

"Of course."

Her eyes trail behind me to Liam, who's now sitting at a table only one away from us. He glances at us then around the room in a routine of sorts.

"I'm sure Gia told you about my bodyguard. He'll be with us the entire time. Like a little shadow," I say. I raise my voice just a bit so that Liam can hear me. It's petty, but I do it anyway.

"She did. And it's no problem, would you like a drink? I think lemonade sounds good."

"A lemonade would be nice," I smile.

"I'll get them," Gia cuts in with a wink.

I turn my focus back to Tawny; her blue eyes are alight with excitement. She must be a fan. That makes me feel a little better. I'm also happy that she isn't making eyes at Liam like Katelyn from Waves Magazine was last night. Not that I should care, but again, I'm showing no signs of rational thought since yesterday afternoon.

"So, Birdie, I'm so glad we're finally getting to do this. The interview is going to be super straightforward; your publicist already gave me the rundown. I promise it will be painless. Just be yourself."

"Great." I relax a little. I'm happy that Gia told this woman what's up. I don't want another day to be ruined by this stupid stalker.

"First, I'd love to talk about your upbringing. Tell me a little bit about yourself."

Immediately I feel Liam's eyes on me. Even though it's been a decade since we've been in the same place together, I still know exactly when he's watching me. I guess he wants to know what I have to say. I take a sip of the cool and sugary lemonade that Gia just brought over, and let my tongue do the talking.

"I'm sure you've heard most of this before, but before I was born, my mom decided that her kid was going to be famous, and that she intuitively knew her baby was going to be a girl. When she was one month pregnant, she decided to name me Birdie Wilder. Thought it sounded like a famous name."

Tawny laughs. "Really?"

"Yep, really."

"It's a great name. And your mom turned out to be right on all fronts."

"That she did. Which she always likes to remind me of."

"And when did you start singing?"

"Gosh, from the time I was maybe... two? My mom loves The Beatles, so I grew up singing a lot of their music, and of course I fell in love with Mama Cass's voice too. I get compared to her a lot, but I don't mind. She was a musical genius and an icon."

Tawny raises a perfect eyebrow up at me. "Do you think that's just because of your sound?"

I tense up. Is this chick for real? The air becomes thick, and I force a smile on my face. "If you want to say it's because I'm fat, be a woman about it and say that."

Gia gasps at my words, but I'm not in the mood to deal with fatphobic bullshit today. Or any day for that matter.

Tawny cheeks turn pink. "Oh man. I'm so sorry! I didn't mean for it to come out that way."

I tap my fingers on the bar methodically. "Mama Cass was a victim to the music industry and to society. She was a brilliant artist, and it's a shame that people still focus on her looks and how she died instead of her talent.

"I fight every day to make sure that I'm remembered for my music and not as 'that tall fat Grammy winner.' I just hope that when I die, I'm not remembered for my body, but for what I gave to the world. I think most of my fans recognize my true value and worth, and I'm grateful for it. I've been blessed with success and notoriety, but make no mistake, I fight to be taken seriously every day. Even by reporters."

Tawny is the same color as a strawberry, and I think she may want to cry. I was probably too harsh, but I had to say that. I can't stand by and let people walk all over me, even if they don't realize they're doing it.

After a few heavy moments, she finally speaks, but I can tell she's choosing her words carefully. "Again, I'm so sorry for how that came out. But thank you for sharing that experience with me. It's not every day an artist gets so candid so quickly with me. I do appreciate it, and I will try to be better with my words."

"Thanks. No hard feelings." I give her a small smile because I can tell she's genuinely embarrassed. I'm not sure her apology is meaningful, but at least she tried. Which is more than I can say for most people. Because it's true, no matter how famous I am or how many Grammys I win, I still get put down for the way I look. If I had a penny for how many issues of *Worst Beach Bodies* I'm on, I'd be richer than Oprah.

"Good. Next question?" she asks hopefully.

I nod. "Next question."

Fourteen

Liam

FOR A MOMENT, I thought Birdie was going to lose it after that reporter's asinine words. Hell, I wanted to throw the woman out of the hotel bar for her assumption. But Birdie took care of herself; she more than took care of herself. She put the woman in her place. It made me feel oddly proud.

Which is better than the feelings I felt this morning.

After my night on Birdie's couch, my shoulder is sore. I'm tired, I'm annoyed, and even more than those three things, I'm confused. I've only been with her for twenty-four hours and it's as if my whole world has been shifted upside down. I'm doing my best to keep myself upright, but it's hard.

When I took a shower this morning, I seriously considered just leaving. I don't like feeling vulnerable, and I sure as shit don't like feeling unstable. I've worked hard in the last two years to get where I am, and I don't want to slip back. And yet, I didn't leave.

A horn on the street honks and I do my best not to jump at the sound. Fuck. *Focus, Liam.*

We're walking around Atlantic City with the reporter, and I have some extra security tailing us in a black Suburban. I didn't like the idea of walking around, but Gia practically begged me to make it happen. She didn't want Birdie to feel like a caged bird or some shit. I don't know how a woman like Birdie could ever feel like that with the world at her feet, even if she does have a stalker. But I did my best to make this happen for her, and here we are.

I can't hear everything they're talking about, but they've pretty much covered every topic under the sun. It's been surprisingly nice to hear her talk about Parker and her mom. I didn't know Lorri Wilder well, but she was always nice to me when she was around. Which wasn't that often. Birdie and I bonded over the fact that our parents were mostly absent. But while Ms. Wilder often left homemade food for Birdie, my parents left me pizza money and Chinese leftovers.

I do love my parents, and I know they love me, but I really went through it as a kid. In more ways than one. To this day Birdie doesn't quite understand how much I struggled. I was honest with her back then, but only to a point.

The reporter's next question breaks me from my memories of the past. "So, tell me about your hit song."

"What do you want to know about it?" Birdie asks, her tone cheeky.

I know she's still annoyed at the way this woman asked about her similarities to Mama Cass. After witnessing that exchange, and hearing Birdie's response, I understand a little more about Birdie's insecurities and why she may have thought our Instant Message conversation all those years ago was about her looks. Which is just not true. Honestly, it never even crossed my mind.

Sure, guys in high school may have referred to her as "the fat girl" but I never cared what a girl looked like. If she had a good personality and wasn't a psycho, that's what mattered. My mom may have worked a lot, but she did raise me to be a gentleman. I guess I never thought Birdie would take my words like that. I only wanted to get my point across at the time. In hindsight, I should have never said them. But I did, and I can't take them back.

The reporter laughs, "Who's it about? When did you write it? It's a heavy song, I'm sure people would love to know who you wrote it about."

I gaze at the back of Birdie's blonde head, wondering what she's going to say. Now that I know it's about me, I'm curious if she'll admit it to the world.

"I had a good friend in high school," she starts. I notice her shoulders roll back, and she makes it a point to ignore my presence. I'm sure she doesn't want this woman to get any ideas.

She continues, "I was obsessed with him. It was that silly teenager kind of love, where he's all you can think about."

The woman nods, "I can relate to that. I think most people can."

"I think so, too. We spent a lot of time together, bonded over music, snuck out of our houses, and met for walks and late-night pancakes at Denny's."

"Sounds romantic."

I swallow hard. Was it romantic? I guess I never thought of it that way. I'd been head over heels for Birdie back then, but not in a romantic way. She was a great friend, a best friend, someone who made me laugh and feel less alone. I enjoyed every moment we spent together, and I never wanted to lose her. Unfortunately, that's exactly what happened.

I spent many nights after that wishing she would have never told me she liked me. No, *loved me*... fuck. It may have been obsessed puppy love, but she said it in her song and now to this reporter. I guess I never knew the extent of how she felt. How could I? After that night online we had a big fight the first day of Junior year, then we never spoke again.

I can see the side of Birdie's mouth tilt up in a smile, like she's reliving our time together right now. It does something to me, warms me from the inside. She hums. "I guess it could be seen as romantic, but he didn't like me like that." Immediately that warm feeling is doused, and I'm cold again.

"He told you that?"

"He did. Then shortly after that we stopped being friends. It was too painful to be around him, knowing I would never be more to him when that was all I wanted."

"Sounds like you still have feelings."

I give my complete attention to Birdie's answer. Hanging on her every word. She just exposed herself more than she ever had when we were sixteen, and it made me upset she didn't just say that to me back then. Maybe we could have found a way to still be friends.

Birdie laughs, she fucking laughs. "No, I don't have those feelings anymore. I did, for a long time, but I'm a grown woman now. I've had other relationships and a lot of time to think about that season of my life. He was a good friend, an obsession, my first love, but he didn't love me back. So, I took that love and put it toward my music. I let my desire, pain, and sadness fuel my art. It worked out for me in the end. So, I guess I should say thank you to him for giving me so many feelings to work with."

I clench my fists. Is that all she's reduced me down to? Fodder for her albums? Sure, we stopped being friends, but I did cherish the time I spent with her when we were kids. I thought she did too. Suddenly I feel like I'm going to be sick. Not that I have a right to be angry with her, we aren't friends. We aren't anything, but I can't help the stupid emotions this woman keeps stirring up in me.

"If men are good for anything, they are good for providing us with stories and fuel to achieve our dreams," the reporter smirks.

Birdie swallows, not agreeing with the reporter, but also not disagreeing with her. "I'm grateful for the time I had with the boy who broke my heart, but now he's just a memory within a song."

Right. Well, I'm glad I know how she feels. Not that I should be surprised. For a moment I thought that maybe Birdie and I could work out our shit, or at least have a cordial relationship over the course of the next couple months. But if that is how she feels, if that's how she wants to continue to deal with me being here, then so be it.

I'll be the bodyguard she wants me to be. Nothing more. Nothing less. It's better for me anyway. I can keep all my secrets and feelings away from her... and away from her damn songs.

I skip Birdie's show and wait in an empty dressing room for it to be over.

Venue security has her covered while she's on stage, so I sneak in a good meal and even a short nap. My shoulder is still killing me, so I take off my shirt but leave my pants on. If I can't get to the gym today, I may as well do a little yoga. As Ben says, "*No excuses.*"

There's an area rug in the dressing room; I cringe to think what's been on this floor, but since I don't have a mat, this will have to do.

I start off with a few sun salutations then stretch my arms over my head. The twinge in my shoulder is there, but I'm glad I can stretch it out before it has time to get worse.

I go through several different poses, including a few hip openers, which are hard to do in these tight pants. After I do downward dog, I end my practice in corpse pose.

My brain wanders while I'm there—I haven't allowed myself to feel this many emotions since the accident. Birdie is pushing my boundaries, and I felt like I may snap if I don't at least try and keep my cool.

I count to ten and attempt to focus on my body, breathing through any pain just as my therapist taught me. In and out, in and out, in and out. My breathing calms, the bass from Birdie's band thrumming in the background. My body buzzes with the vibrations from the floor and I can hear my beating heart in my ears.

Thump. Thump. Thump. Thump.

I enter a meditative space...

I'm back in New York City on patrol. My partner Maria smiles at me, jelly on her cheek from the raspberry filled doughnut she just consumed. I'd make a funny cop joke if she wasn't so damn cute.

"You like what you see, Miller?" She quips, licking some sugar from her lips.

"You have jam on your lip."

She reaches to get it, but misses. I shake my head and lean over to take care of it. She stills as my finger touches her cheek. I get the offending jelly, and before I think about what I'm doing, I lick it from my finger. My face heats with embarrassment, but all she does is smile.

"When you do things like that, Miller... it makes a girl think things."

I swallow the lump in my throat. "And if I do want the girl to think things?"

She laughs. "Then maybe you should ask the girl out on a date?"

Normally I'm a confident man, but Maria, she does something to me that makes me feel like a giddy boy. I'm about to ask her on a date when we get a call over the radio. Someone called in a 10-20, a robbery, on the Upper East Side.

"10-4, en route," I quickly turn the car around. I guess asking her on a date will have to wait.

Knock, knock, knock!

I'm startled from the memory. Fuck. I haven't thought of that day in almost six months. Now I really know my head's not in the game. I think about calling Ben, or maybe my cousin Hammer—I know they'd both hear me out without judgment.

The person behind the door knocks again, so I stand and rub my hands over my face to clear some of the cobwebs. "Come in," I say.

A second later Shea's purple hair is in my line of vision. Her eyes drop down to my chest, taking in the muscles and light sheen of sweat. I'm pretty sure she licks her lips, but I try to ignore it. She's a cute kid, but way too young. I don't usually do under the age of 25, and she can't be more than 21, maybe 22.

"I found you," she says, her voice a little hoarse.

"What's up?" I move to put on my shirt and shoes.

"The show's over. You're needed in the green room for fan meet and greets."

"Roger that."

She smiles but doesn't leave. I finish buttoning my shirt. "Something else?"

"Umm, no. Nothing."

"Right, well. See you, Shea."

"See you," she gives a little wave.

I feel her eyes staring at my ass as I walk away.

Shit. I think I have an admirer.

Fifteen

Birdie

"HAVE YOU AND LIAM spoken yet?" Wren asks through the phone.

It's been three weeks since Liam joined the tour. Three weeks of the cold shoulder, clipped answers, and a lot of tension. Even though it annoys me to no end, he's following *my* ground rules. But after the last show in Atlantic City, he came to the green room with his usual RSF. I didn't want to get into an argument with him, so I just let it go. Three weeks later, here we are.

"He grunts at me and orders me around when he needs to."

"Sounds kind of like normal Liam to be honest," Wren chuckles. "Ben won't tell me anything about it. Says it's between you and Liam."

"It's probably because there's nothing between us. He's here for a job, just like you asked him to do, and he's doing it well."

In fact, we haven't heard a peep from the stalker in the weeks Liam's been here. Maybe the sound bite in Waves Magazine kept him at bay. I know that I wouldn't want to go against Liam in a fight. Dude is huge.

Wren lets out a dramatic sigh. "Have you tried to talk to him?"

"You know the answer to that question. There's nothing to say to him."

"You know that's not true. Have you ever thought to just talk about what happened back then?"

I groan. "It's not going to happen Wren. He's here doing a job, not to reconcile with me, and I'm here to entertain people."

Wren pauses for a moment. "Birdie, you know you're not just entertainment, right? You're a real person, and I think you and Liam could actually be something if you both—"

"I'm going to stop you right there. I'm fine. My life is good, and Liam is doing what Liam has to do. I don't want to talk about it anymore."

"But—"

"Nope," I cut her off again. "No buts."

"Fine. Then tell me where the hell you are in the US."

"Orlando."

"*Ooh*, Disney World?"

"I wish. But we don't have any time. We have our third show tonight then we go to Atlanta in the morning for another couple of shows."

"Dang. No rest for the wicked."

"None," I laugh. "But I'm going to the spa today. Liam got the whole place closed off for me so he can keep the perimeter clear or whatever."

"Sounds romantic."

I snort. "More like expensive."

"You could ask Liam to give you a massage."

"Wren—"

I'm cut off by a rapid knocking. "Hold on."

I make my way to the door. When I look in the peephole, I see Liam standing there.

"Who's there?" Wren asks.

"Who do you think?" I open the door to find Liam's RSF is in full force. He's about to say something, but Wren wants to put her two cents in first.

"Liam are you there?!" she calls from the phone. And to my surprise, Liam's face breaks out in a smile. Not just a half grin or a smirk like the ones he'd sometimes give my team or Kevin, somehow the two have become friends over the last few weeks, but a full blown one. White teeth and all. A pang of jealousy hits my stomach, but I push it away. I have no right to be jealous.

I put Wren on speaker and against my better judgment, invite Liam in.

Liam speaks louder so she can hear. "Is that Wren Jones?"

"What other Wren do you know?"

He laughs. "You're right. You're the one and only."

"Is my girl treating you well?" she asks him.

Liam's brown eyes flash to mine. He's no longer smiling when he says, "All is well. It's a long tour, but things are good. Ever thought about coming to visit?"

My stomach drops at his suggestion.

"*Ooh*, now you're talking." Wren's voice is giddy.

"You should. Bring Ben, too," Liam adds.

"That's not a bad idea! What do you think, Birdie?"

My throat feels thick, and my nerves are wound tight. Ben, Wren, and Liam... all here? Sounds miserable. Like a double date gone wrong. I can't believe Liam even suggested it. Maybe body snatchers have taken him over.

"Umm, yeah. If you guys want. I won't have much time to hang out, but I can give Liam the day off when you come."

His jaw clenches, like he's offended I'd give him a day off. He's so weird. I can never tell what he's thinking, if he really cares about me, or just about doing his job well so he can get his paycheck.

"We won't mind! You know Ben and I can find things to do. We haven't seen you in concert in years."

"Okay, pick a date and let me know so we can arrange it."

Wren squeals. "Sweet! Good idea, Liam."

"I hate to cut this chat short, but I have to get Ms. Wilder to the spa," Liam says, back to business.

Wren snorts, "Please don't tell me you call her Ms. Wilder all the time?" Silence. "Birdie?" she asks. But I'm currently in a stare down with Liam. He's trying to get a rise out of me.

"We'll chat more about it later, Wren." I start to grab my things so we can leave.

"Fine. But don't make Liam call you Ms. Wilder. That's ridiculous."

When I find Liam's eyes he's smirking. *Ugh.* "Bye Wren."

"Bye you silly goose."

I let out a breathy laugh as I hang up the phone. Part of me regrets it because the silence that follows is deafening. Liam is still smirking, and I honestly wish I could smack him. But I don't have time to question it, my massage and facial await.

I don't think I've been this excited for anything in a long time. I seriously need an afternoon of care and attention. The shows every night are intense, and touring is stressful. I think my hair is starting to fall out with all the added anxiety of the stalker and a certain bodyguard.

Even my band has started to question if I'm okay. Which does not fly with me. I need to get myself together. I have to hold up the crew, give a good show. It's my job. It's why I get paid what I do and win the awards I do.

"Let's go then." I clip.

When our eyes meet, Liam's smirk is gone. "After you, *Ms. Wilder.*"

I stop myself from rolling my eyes. Instead, I just bite out a short thanks, and we head out the door to my awaiting paradise. Thank goodness.

The spa is located not far from the hotel, but since it isn't walking distance—not that Liam would have let me walk—we're driving there.

Liam's texting on his phone, which is unusual for him. Normally he's glowering out the window.

"Are you talking to Ben?"

Liam jumps slightly, not expecting me to talk to him. We've made a routine out of riding in silence the last three weeks.

He lifts an eyebrow. "You're talking to me now?"

"Oh please, it's not like you were talking to me before either. I'm just asking if it's Ben you're texting, given you just invited my friends to visit without asking me."

"You realize they were my friends first, right?"

Oh, so we're being petty now. Granted, I've been petty since I spoke to Tawny at Rolling Stone. I knew he could hear every word I said, specifically when she'd asked me about "Desire Reigns." I have a feeling that's what led him to be so annoying the last few weeks. That and my drunken admissions. I still can't believe he saw me partially naked!

My cheeks redden. "Right, well... you could have asked."

"Do you not want them here? I'll tell Wren that."

I scoff. "Of course I want them here."

"Doesn't sound that way."

"I want them here; you just should have asked me first."

"Fine, next time I want to invite my friends for a visit, I'll make sure to get a permission slip signed."

"Now I remember why I don't talk to you. It's like speaking with a petulant child."

"Then please, by all means, go back to silence. I prefer it that way."

My body aches at his comment. We really can't get along, can we?

I should've kept my mouth shut. I'm only upset that he invited them with no regard for how I felt about it. I do want them here, but I'm worried what might happen when they are. Not to mention, what if the stalker decides to strike while Wren is with me? I'd never forgive myself.

I look out the window. It's hot outside, summer in Florida always is. I'm grateful for air conditioning, but right now it isn't doing anything for me. My body is hot, and I can't wait to get out of this car. Thankfully we pull up to the spa before I open the door and literally jump out while it's moving.

Liam does his usual routine and gets out of the car first before holding out his hand to help me down. Just like I have for the last three weeks, I ignore it. I don't know why he keeps on trying. Probably to piss me off.

As soon as we're inside the spa, I'm greeted by Sarah, the owner.

"Welcome to Sun Spa, Ms. Wilder. If you'd follow me this way, we can get you started." The pretty woman smiles and starts to lead me away.

Liam immediately protests. "I need to know where she is at all times."

Sarah stops and smiles at him. As I've learned in the past weeks, every woman has some sort of reaction to Liam. Wren even goes so far as to call it the "Liam Effect."

Sarah bats her eyes at him then flips her short blonde bob over her shoulder. "Don't worry, Mr. Miller. Ms. Wilder will be well taken care of. I'll show you to the room she'll be in. The only time she'll leave is while she's in the sauna."

Liam smiles, his charm turns up to ten. But there's still a seriousness about him. "I understand, Sarah. And thank you so much for taking care of Ms. Wilder. I appreciate your help during this difficult situation."

She giggles wildly. Actually, it's kind of scary. "Of course. Anything for Birdie Wilder. We're such big fans here. We play your music in reception all the time."

I smile at her. "Thanks, that's nice to hear."

Sarah flips her hair again. "Well, shall we get started?"

"Yes please." I'm itching to get away from Liam's burning gaze and Sarah's flirting.

Liam must notice something different about me because he looks at me with concern. As if he's silently asking, *Everything okay?*

Something must be in the water today! All I can manage is a sigh and then I'm following Sarah through a hallway and into a large room. Inside there's a personal hot tub, and a view of the ocean and lots of palm trees. A little patio is outside with a hammock, and I can't wait to sip on some coffee and enjoy the heat and ocean breeze on my skin.

Sarah tells Liam that we're going to get started, so she closes the door. The last thing I see is Liam's chocolate eyes on me, his gaze still questioning. I shove down a shiver and get ready to be relaxed.

Sixteen

Liam

THIS WHOLE SPA TRIP is a bad idea.

Renting out the entire place wasn't cheap either, but that didn't matter to Gia or Eric. I know Birdie is wealthy, but damn. Not that money matters, but sometimes I forget how famous Birdie is, especially when she's ignoring me. But it's what I wanted... *she wanted*... so I can't complain. It does make my job easier, but also makes it monotonous and boring. One thing I'm glad for is that we haven't heard anything from the stalker since Times Square. But that doesn't mean they aren't around. That's why this whole spa excursion makes me nervous.

I stretch my shoulder a bit as I stand outside Birdie's private room. It's feeling much better this week than it did the week prior. I finally have a routine down now that I've been here for a bit. Since Birdie usually keeps to her room, I have more free time than when I first started.

Thankfully, big interviews like Rolling Stone don't happen every day. That means I can wake up early, work out at the hotel gym, shower, follow Birdie around wherever she needs to go, do yoga backstage while she performs, then do green room duties. Oftentimes we travel in the evening after a show, or the morning after if we're lucky.

I'm also thankful I get to travel on the second tour bus with the crew, I don't know if I could handle sleeping in tight quarters with Birdie. Being around her almost every day is bad enough. Not that I hate it, it's just so heavy, the tension is getting to me. This morning it boiled over when she answered the door with Wren on the phone. It had been good to hear Wren's voice, and it made me wish that Birdie and I could be more cordial. We do share friends after all.

At first, I didn't understand why I invited Wren and Ben to the tour. But the look Birdie just gave me a moment ago reminded me. The past week I've noticed her shrinking into herself. I shouldn't care, but I'm not a robot. And the last thing I want is for Birdie to become angrier. At least that's what I tell myself. Being concerned for her is to my benefit, not hers. By inviting Wren and Ben, I hoped it would boost her spirits, but I just stressed her out even more.

That means this spa trip better be worth it. If she doesn't come out a new woman, I don't know how else to get her to let loose. And I sure as hell am not going to give that woman a drink. I still have random daydreams about her breasts and those damn sheer underwear. My phone pings, and I see a message from Shea. I hold back a groan.

Ever since she walked in on me doing Yoga, she's been a constant presence in my life here on tour. I've done everything I can to get her off my scent, but nothing seems to deter her. I don't want to tell her off and risk losing this gig, or angering Birdie, so I keep things cordial.

She's been asking me questions about Yoga and being a cop. The questions are tame, but I know she wishes I'd give her more in-depth responses. Lately, she's been asking if I can give her pointers at the gym, but so far, I've avoided it. I don't want Birdie to see us and get any wrong ideas. Not that it matters to Birdie who I have sex with, but I learned a long time ago not to shit where I eat. Shea is off limits, not that I want her anyway.

After I reply with a short answer, I turn my attention back to the spa. Meditation music plays over the speakers, and it smells like peppermint and incense. My stomach churns. I've been avoiding sitting in quiet meditation with myself since I had a flashback to the accident. Every night I've been fighting hard to keep the nightmares at bay. It works most of the time. But sometimes I wake up covered in sweat with the feel of warm blood on my hands.

I take a deep breath, count to ten, and remind myself I'm fine. That I'm here in the present and I need to be alert. Today is a big day, and I have to be on my guard while I'm in unfamiliar territory. This building is big, and although the place is fairly empty, and all of the doors are locked, I still don't trust it. Anything can happen in this type of situation.

A while later, Sarah comes out of the room and gives me a smile. "She just had her facial. I'm going to get the masseuse to start with her, then I'll rotate back in to remove her mask."

I give a curt nod. "Thanks."

She touches my arm lightly. "Would you like anything to drink?"

I shrug her off gently. "A black coffee would be great. Thanks."

Her face falls a little, but she tries not to be too disappointed at my rejection. "No problem. I'll be right back."

After Sarah leaves, the masseuse walks down the hall shortly after. It's a man, which I don't much like. I try to get a read on him, but he ignores me and knocks on the door. I'm fully aware there are a lot of men who are massage therapists, but the thought of his hands touching Birdie's naked flesh makes me feel... jealous? No. It makes me feel protective. Stress creeps into my shoulders and I clench my arms at my side. *Birdie's fine. There's nothing to worry about. You did everything right here. She's in good hands.* That thought makes me want to vomit.

I listen through the door for a second, but nothing sounds amiss. I know Birdie will call out to me if she has any issues with the man in there. So, I will myself to relax. I'm just on edge. I count to ten again, and just as I finish, Sarah brings me a coffee.

"Here you are."

"Thank you." I take a sip. It's hot, but I swallow it down anyway.

"Can I get you anything else? You know, I could give you a massage while you wait?"

My jaw ticks. Did this chick really ask me that? "Then I wouldn't be doing my job." I turn my gaze from her to the wall.

"Just thought I'd offer." She tries to sound chipper. "You look tense."

I grind my teeth. "I'm good."

After that, Sarah finally takes the hint and leaves. I take a large gulp of coffee and suck in another deep breath. It's times like these I wonder if I have a sign on my forehead that says, *I'm available and don't require commitment.* I admit that screwing a random woman who's into me isn't an unusual occurrence, but sometimes I feel like an objectified piece of meat. I shake my head, curious if that's how Birdie feels sometimes.

Day in and day out I watch her do as she's told. She wakes up, does interviews, works on new songs, or has meetings with her band or the label. Her schedule is insane, and on top of that, she does a show almost every night and never misses a beat. I'm surprised she's not dead on her feet, and we're only one-third of the way through the tour. She's a beast, and despite our dislike of each other, I respect her work ethic and ability to take things in stride.

After about an hour, and another cup of coffee, I hear some noise inside the room and then the door clicks open. The masseuse walks out and gives me a nod, then walks off. Like magic, Sarah appears, this time she manages not to flirt with me.

"I'm going to take Birdie to the sauna, you're welcome to follow us if you need to."

"Great. Thanks."

After a few moments Sarah returns with Birdie behind her. When I see Birdie's face, I must admit she looks refreshed, although still tired. Today she hasn't worn her usual dark makeup, and her skin is slightly red from whatever they did to her in there. She's wearing a fluffy white robe, and little white slippers. I'm so used to seeing concert Birdie, who looks like a sexy vixen, or daytime Birdie, which is usually in some type of pant/T-shirt combo or hoodie, that I'm slightly caught off guard by this relaxed and comfortable version. It's nice, and for a second my dick takes over. I find myself wondering what it would be like to untie the robe from her curves and taste what I saw between her legs in Atlantic City.

Birdie glances behind her and gives me a weird look. It's then I realize I've been staring and not following. And these damn tight pants I'm wearing... thank fuck they're black, or she'd probably have seen the beginnings of my hard-on. I stop my thoughts in their tracks and stick my shoulders back. I take a few strides to quickly catch up.

"Daydreaming?" Birdie asks me, not caring that Sarah can hear us.

"That robe leaves little to the imagination," I say a little too quickly.

Birdie flushes, the round apples of her cheeks turning pink. *Shit.* Why did I say that? *Because you're thinking with your dick you idiot.*

Without saying more, Birdie turns her head forward, leaving me to wonder what she's thinking now. I try to remind my little brain that we don't really like Birdie. And that she doesn't like us. But he doesn't care. He's seen the assets that lie underneath that robe, and he wants to wet his whistle.

Not quickly enough, we end up in the room that houses the sauna. It's hot in here, which immediately kills my sexy thoughts. Wearing a suit near a sauna isn't going to be a pleasant experience, so I decide to wait in the hallway. Just as the door is closing, I hear Sarah tell Birdie that she can disrobe and sit in the sauna in the nude since no one will bother her. I groan.

Great. Now I have to stand out here in the hallway and think about a naked and sweaty Birdie. Sometimes the world is a cruel and unusual place.

This time when Sarah exits, she doesn't even look at me. After my comment to Birdie, she probably assumes we're together. Which is only going to annoy Birdie more. Especially if this woman goes to the tabloids.

I rub my hands over my face and train my eyes to the wall. I can't wait until this excursion is done. I need a shower and some "me" time before the show. If I don't take the edge off, I'm going to keep thinking about my boss, my ex-best friend, my... sex fantasy? God. I'm losing it.

I strip off my suit jacket, the heat of this place starting to get to me; and try to focus. It doesn't take long before I hear what sounds like a sob. At first, I wonder if it's some random noise, but then I hear another, followed by another. I put my ear to the door. It's coming from inside the sauna. Something in my stomach clenches. For me to hear her cries, Birdie is crying loudly. Against my better judgment I open the door.

I can see Birdie through the glass panel on the door of the sauna she's in. Thankfully, or not, depending on the way you look at it, Birdie isn't naked. She's in a sexy red bikini. I have no idea where she got it from. If she wasn't crying, I would've taken way more time to observe the way it hugs her soft skin in all the right places, how it pushes her breasts up just enough to make me want to kiss the soft skin there.

She's crying you idiot.

With an internal sigh, I make my way toward the sauna door with caution. I don't want to scare her. I watch her for a moment and see tears dripping down her cheeks, a little snot coming out of her nose. Her long blonde hair is tied up in a messy bun on top of her head. She's very much sobbing; heart wrenching sobs that sound like grieving. Shit. I hope I didn't make her cry. Now I feel like an even bigger asshole.

When there's a small reprieve from her cries, I gently tap on the glass panel. I call her name just loud enough so she can hear me. My desire to not scare her doesn't work though, because she jumps and bangs her head on the top of the box she's in. *Fuck*. Way to go, jerk-hole.

Without a second thought, I quickly open the door, not caring I have all my clothes on. I'm already sweating, so at this point it doesn't matter. I need to make sure Birdie's okay.

"Liam! What the hell are you doing in here?" She grabs hold of the top of her head, tears still tracking down her cheeks.

"I didn't mean to scare you, I swear. I just heard you crying and got concerned."

Her face, already flushed from the crying and the heat, turns a brighter shade of red. "I'm fine." Her voice goes into business mode. "You didn't hear anything."

I clench my jaw. "Don't play this game with me right now, Birdie."

"No more Ms. Wilder, huh?" Clearly she's trying to change the subject.

"That's not going to work. Tell me what's wrong."

She rubs the wet tears from her cheeks and turns her chin up in stubbornness. "I told you. I'm fine. Nothing's wrong."

"Why are you lying to me?"

"Why are you impeding on my private time?"

"Because I'm concerned."

"So you say—but are you really?" she huffs and crosses her damp arms over her chest. Which makes me look at her heaving breasts once more. This is a bad idea. Why did I come in here? Oh yeah, because sometimes I can be a freaking nice guy.

"Birdie..." My voice is tired. "I'm trying to be nice here. I may be an ass a lot of the time, but I'm not a complete dickhead."

She scoffs. "Questionable."

Sweat drips down my face. "I'm in a sauna, in a very expensive suit. I wouldn't be here for just anyone." I cringe. Birdie makes me say and do things I shouldn't. I'm starting to realize that even though we stopped being friends all those years ago, I could never turn off the way I really feel about her. What exactly I feel, I can't name it. It's not love, but it's something alright.

Birdie stares at me, her eyes dilated from the heat. "Ugh! Why are you so confusing?!" She throws up her hands.

I quirk a brow at her. "Why do you say that?"

"You're nice, then you're not, then you're nice, then you ignore me for weeks, then you make that comment about my robe in front of Sarah. Honestly Liam, you're giving me whiplash."

I wipe more sweat from my brow. I really need to get out of this hot box soon or I'm going to melt. "That makes two of us," I grumble.

"See? Confusing! What do *you* mean by that?" she points at me.

I groan. "Can we talk somewhere that maybe isn't one hundred degrees? Also, nice diversion. Making this whole thing about me. I came in here because you were sobbing."

"I wasn't sobbing."

"Ughhhh! You're so stubborn. You were crying, Birdie. Not just a little cry, like a soul crushing cry. You've been worrying me the last few days; I want to make sure you're okay."

She goes quiet. "What makes you say that?"

"You think I don't notice how quiet you've become? Or how you snap at Eric when he asks you simple questions? Kevin asked me what's going on with you the other day."

Her face crumples. "They shouldn't worry about me. I'll do better."

Birdie stands up to leave, and I stop her by grabbing her clammy hand. "What does that even mean?"

She shakes her head. "Nothing." Yanking her hand from mine, she opens the sauna. I gladly follow, but I'm not done talking to her yet. Sadly for my eyes, she grabs her robe, covering her scantily clad body. Once she's secured the sash, I turn her back toward me.

"I'm not going to drop this, Birdie. Tell me what you meant when you said you'll do better."

She lets out a long breath. "I didn't mean it that way."

"Like hell you didn't. You're not some monkey that does tricks for treats. Your band, your people, they all care about you a lot. I see it every day."

Anger creeps up in her features, but she keeps her voice tempered. "You don't understand, Liam. You'll never understand. Please, just drop it, okay? I just needed a good cry. It's that time of the month."

I stop myself from rolling my eyes. "Bullshit."

"Like you would know my cycles."

"I remember you have bad cramps; I would know if you had your period. You're lying to get me off your back and it's not going to work."

Her ears turn pink. "You remember that?"

"It's hard to forget something like that. I was a teenage boy with a best friend who happened to be a girl and a mom who's a nurse. I used to bring you ice cream and pretzels when you stayed home from school."

"You did," she swallows, saying it like she forgot that memory.

"Birdie, I'm here to take care of you. Let me help if I can."

Birdie's features change and she stiffens. "You're only doing this because it's your job?"

This woman makes me want to scream. "Stop twisting my words, that's not why I came to you."

She throws up her arms. "Then why the hell did you?!"

Sweat drips down my face and into my eyes. My clothes are damp, and I'm fucking hot and uncomfortable. "You know what, I give up. I'm trying to be nice to you, even if you have given me no reason to since I got here. So, if you want me to treat you like a job, then I'll treat you that way. But I'm trying to extend an olive branch. If you don't want it, just say so. But stop being such a bitch!"

By the time I'm done with my rant, my chest is heaving, and I've stepped closer to Birdie than I should have. We're close enough that I can feel the heat from her body and her chest is almost touching mine. I should take a step back. I should leave her here to think about how she's been acting. But instead, I stay where I am. I stare into her beautiful hazel eyes and wait for her to say something, anything.

The air crackles with an energy I haven't felt in a long time, and I push down my own impulse to run. Birdie Wilder makes me so angry yet turned on. I should hate myself for wanting to close the space between us and kiss her pouting pink lips, but I don't.

In fact, the longer we stand this close, the more I start to think it's a great idea. And no, I wouldn't just kiss her lips... I'd suck on her neck, kiss the skin of her soft stomach, strip her bare and eat her like she's my last meal. Fuck the people who work here, they could watch if they wanted.

I lick my dry lips, and look down at her soft blonde hair, then to her lips again. She holds her bottom lip between her teeth, and her body is taut, as if she's waiting for me to make my next move. I tilt my head and lean down, but right before anything can happen, she clears her throat and takes a step back.

Her eyes move down to her bare feet. A drop of sweat falls from her brow and plops onto the hardwood floor. When she looks back up, I expect her to be pissed at what I just did... well, almost did. But instead, she lets out a breathy laugh.

"I don't think anyone has called me a bitch to my face before."

I can't help it, but I smile. "Really?"

"Does that surprise you?"

I shrug. "I'm afraid to say if it does." This time she really laughs, and it's a beautiful sound. The dimple on her left cheek indents, and I want to reach down and touch it.

"Listen Liam..." She brushes a strand of hair behind her ear. "I still don't really know why you chose to come here. I know Wren and Ben wanted you to, but you could have said no. And the way we are together, it's, well it's confusing me. This stalker business mixed with work and my music, it's a lot. That's why I'm having a hard time, I feel a lot of pressure. I needed to cry, okay? I thought nobody could hear me."

"I think the entire state heard you," I joke to lighten the mood.

"Ha-ha!" she retorts. But she smiles still. It makes my heart pang just a little. Then, she holds out her hand. "Let's just move on, alright? Forget the past and just be friends. Shake on it?"

A knot forms in my stomach. *Friends*. I wonder if adult Liam can be *just friends* with Birdie Wilder. Not to mention, I don't think she can forget the past, especially when she sings about it every damn night. Hell, I'm not sure I can either, but this is better than the anger and tension filled days we've been spending together. Part of me thinks if I get some peace with Birdie, it also might lessen my nightmares. So, I make a decision.

I take her hand, my large one engulfs her delicate fingers in my calloused ones. I want to say a million things, but instead, I say the only thing she'll accept.

"Friends."

Seventeen

Birdie

TEENAGE BIRDIE IS HAVING a moment right now. Scratch that. She's been having a moment for two days now. After we left the spa, incident free, Liam and I rode back to the hotel in easy silence. I think we were both still digesting what took place. But it was nice to not be at each other's throats.

I've been feeling slightly better after the spa treatment and my "cry heard around the world," as Liam now calls it. I know he's making light of it to make me feel less embarrassed, but honestly, how could I not be embarrassed? My old crush saw me ugly sob and then he almost kissed me while I was all sweaty and pissed off. Though we left the spa as friends, if you could call it that, I'm still very much confused by his behavior.

Does he want me? That seems impossible. His words, *"I'll never like you like that,"* still haunt my heart and mind. The only sense I can make of it is that he was caught up in an emotional moment with me. That I felt familiar, safe, and available. From what I understand, he dates a lot of girls back in NYC. Maybe he just needs a release? God, I know I could use one, maybe... No! I can't sleep with Liam. He's off limits!

I shake my head and rub my temples. I can't sleep with my bodyguard/ex-best friend/first love. It will complicate everything, and my life is already complicated enough. The tour bus goes over a pothole, and it startles me out of my thoughts.

My eyes find Kevin, he's sitting across from me with a stupid grin on his face. Liam is next to him reading a book. It's weird to have Liam on our bus, but he and Kevin are friends now. That means he invites Liam to play chess while we travel. Yes, chess. They must have finished their game, but I'd been too involved in my racing thoughts to notice.

"What are you grinning at?" I ask him.

"Writing something good, B?" he winks.

I look down at the pages of my journal covered in lyrics. I intended to write new songs today, but my brain has been consumed with thoughts of the man next to Kevin.

When Liam walked onto the bus in dark jeans and a tight white T-shirt, my mouth went dry. From shock, and from a hormone rush. It's not the first time I've seen him without a suit on, but it's the first time I've allowed myself to really look at him since the Rolling Stone interview. Dressed so casually, it makes me feel like I've been thrown back in time to sophomore year.

I shrug at Kevin. "Writer's block, I guess."

At my statement Liam's eyes flick up to watch me, but I stop myself from meeting his gaze. His stare makes the hair rise on the back of my neck.

"Want some help?" Kevin flips his long brown hair over his shoulder.

"Sure. That would be great."

Kevin and I have written a few songs together. I always enjoy working with him both on stage and off. He's fun and somehow makes everything feel lighter. I'd never say it out loud, but he's definitely my favorite band member, and he knows it. I have no doubt I'm his, too. Jane is a close second.

Kevin stands then comes to sit next to me on the small gray couch. He pulls out his acoustic guitar from under the seat, then glances across to Liam. He's gone back to his book, but I don't think he's reading it. I haven't seen him turn a page in a while.

"Do you mind, bro?"

Liam looks up and shakes his head. "Not at all. Have at it."

"Right on," Kevin grins wider. "Let me see what you have so far."

I give him my notebook and settle back against the couch. It's then I remember that the words on the page might say more to Kevin, and to Liam, than I want said out loud. But it's too late now, Kevin has the notebook and he's already reading.

His icy blue eyes meet mine then dart over to Liam, who thankfully is "reading" his book again.

"It's good, B. I think the structure just needs some work, maybe a few words in the chorus need to be switched up."

"Really?"

"Yeah, it's heartfelt. You thinking a ballad?"

I tap my chin. In my brain it's more of an upbeat song, but he's right, it's probably better as a ballad. "I hadn't been, but I think it's a great idea."

He starts strumming out some chords on his guitar, and as the mellow notes wash over me, I feel at peace. I'm thankful that we're driving to Atlanta. I need some time to make music and rest. Even if it's only for a day.

I begin humming to the notes Kev's playing and fiddle around with the melody. Liam turns his gaze to me and our eyes lock.

I'm thrown back to a memory of a summer night with him ten years ago...

Sometimes I forget that Liam Miller and I are actually friends. Not just friends, but best friends.

We're sitting outside in his backyard. Both of his parents are at work and Mom is at some Yoga retreat, so Liam invited me over to listen to music while we watch the meteor shower tonight.

We set up a bunch of snacks and Liam even lit a little bonfire for us. I brought my little keyboard too, which was a pain to get over here without a car. Thankfully Liam isn't that far of a walk from my place.

"Have you been working on your new song?" He throws some popcorn in the air and catches it in his mouth.

"A little. I had an English paper due that took up all my time. But now I'm free!"

"I'm sure you'll ace it, Birdie girl."

My heart flutters. "I hope so. Anyway, I worked on it a little last night. Wanna hear it?"

"Play away, Piano Man," he winks.

I grin at him. Gosh, he's so beautiful. The firelight reflects in his eyes, and it makes the pools of chocolate dance. He's so cute... actually, he's dreamy. I really don't get why he hangs out with me. But he's here now, and I'm not going to question it any further.

I put my hands on the keyboard and begin to play the intro to a song I started writing a few weeks ago. It's got a soulful vibe to it that I've never really tried before. Mom's been playing a lot of Janis Joplin around the house, and it's all that's been on my mind lately.

As I play, Liam starts to hum in his deep voice. It's a little off key, but I love the way it sounds. Once I finish the intro, it picks up a bit, and I start to sing along.

Sweet summer boy
With your eyes so full
You've got the look of a man
And the touch of a bull
You take what you want
You give all you've got
Sweet summer boy
I know how much you care
You love with a force
of a thousand volts
Your eyes show your soul
And your lips tell a tale
Sweet summer boy
You're gonna go far
Sweet summer boy
Don't let your dreams pass you by.
If you do, you'll regret
All the time that you spent
Sitting alone with your heart on the fence.
Sweet summer boy
Your eyes full of joy
Take in life while you can
And go where you please
Sweet summer boy
You're going to go far.
Sweet summer boy
Don't forget me when you go.
Sweet summer boy

I'll remember you and everything you adore
Sweet summer boy
Keep your head high above
Sweet summer boy
You are the sweetest boy I know.
Sweet summer boy...ooh, ooh, ooh
Sweet summer boy...ooh, ooh, ooh
Sweet summer boy...ooh, ooh, ooh

I finish the last few chords, and when I look up, I find Liam staring at me. Did he know I wrote that song about him? Crap. I'd been too obvious about it. Gosh, I could be so stupid. I ruined everything, I—

Abruptly Liam stands up, a wide smile on his face. He starts to clap and then lets out a big whoop. "Birdie! That was amazing. Your voice, it's like... I don't know. It's so good. You really wrote that?"

Warm relief rushes through me. He didn't realize it's about him. Quickly, the relief is replaced by sadness. Part of me did hope he knew it was about him. Then I could finally come clean about how I felt.

"I did write it. You really think it's good?"

"More than good. That was... I don't really know how to describe it."

"Thanks, Liam."

He sits back down and pops a cold marshmallow into his mouth. After a few moments, his eyes flick back to mine. "So, are you going to tell me who the boy you're crushing on is?"

My stomach sinks and my cheeks turn pink. Liam Miller thinks the song about him is about another boy. F my life.

A hand waves in front of my face.

When I come back to reality, I find Kevin looking at me funny. I can't help the embarrassment I feel from drifting off while we were collaborating. My neck is probably covered in red splotches.

"Where'd you go, B?" he asks.

My eyes dart to Liam. He's wearing that concerned stare of his.

I turn my attention back to Kevin. "Sorry. The lyrics... it made me think of a memory."

"A good one?"

I can't help but glance at Liam once more. My heart aches. It's as if I'm looking at my sweet summer boy all over again.

"Yeah," I whisper, "it was a good one."

The rest of the trip to Atlanta is filled with song writing and Kevin and Liam playing way too much chess. It amazes me how long they can play for. It looks super boring to me, but I've never been one for games.

Once we arrive, and everyone has left the bus, I'm left waiting, as usual, for Liam to get everything secure. I tap out a text to Wren about her and Ben's impending visit. They decided to meet us in New Orleans in another two weeks, which gives me some time to figure out where my relationship with Liam stands.

Since we'd just called a truce of sorts, I'm curious what will happen from here on out. I hear footsteps come up the stairs of the bus, so I go to pull my travel keyboard out from under the seat across from me. I'm on my hands and knees when I hear the steps stop behind me. I yank on the case, but it's stuck.

"We'll don't just stand there Liam, help me!" There's a pause before I hear a throat clearing. Okay, not Liam. My arms break out in goosebumps.

Still on the ground, I turn my head to find a man, covered head to toe in black. I can't see his face because he's wearing a ski mask. My heart pounds in my chest.

"JOE!" I call out to our bus driver. He doesn't answer. He must be outside somewhere. How the hell did this guy get on the bus? *Fuck.* Why am I thinking about that right now? "LIAM!" I cry next. But he's probably in the hotel. *Shit. Shit. Shit.* This is it, I'm going to die, or... *No!* I can't think like that.

"Birdie Wilder," the man says, his voice higher than I expected for such a big presence.

Realizing I'm still on the floor, I quickly stand up, slowly backing myself down the walkway of the bus. If I turn and run, I can make my way out of the emergency exit in the back. Call it a moment of insanity, but I don't run.

"Who are you?" My voice comes out shaky.

"That's not important."

I don't know how to respond to that, so I don't. After a few moments, he smiles through his mask and my stomach churns. What if this *is* the moment I die? *Liam...*

"I wanted to see how close I could get to you. It's easier than I thought," he mutters. This time he takes a step forward, which makes me take two steps back.

"Who are you?" I ask again, attempting to stall in hopes that Liam or Joe will walk on the bus any second. "What do you want from me?"

"You'll find out soon enough," he winks. "See you soon... *Little Bird.*" Then, he just walks off the bus, cool as a cucumber.

I continue to stare after him for I don't know how long, my body completely frozen. I'm not even sure if what just happened is real. Eventually my body starts to shake and the world around me becomes hazy. I sink to the ground and put my hands in my hair. I feel like I want to cry, or scream, but nothing comes out. I should get help, call someone. 911?

Footsteps approach again and it feels as if time stops. But it's not the man in a mask, it's Liam. He's gently smiling as he approaches, until he sees me cowering. Then his entire demeanor changes.

"Birdie! What the hell happened?" he demands. He crosses the bus to me in a few long strides, then gets down on the ground. His warm hands grasp me by the shoulders. When his concerned brown eyes lock onto mine, I try to say something, but nothing comes out. Instead, I throw my arms around his neck and fall apart.

What the hell just happened?

Eighteen

Liam

ANGRY IS NOT THE right word for what I'm feeling right now.

Furious? Livid? Nothing is right.

I held Birdie in my arms as she cried for over ten minutes trying to get her to tell me what the fuck happened. When I came on the bus and saw her, she looked like she'd just seen a ghost. I'd never, not when we were kids, and sure as hell not in the last few weeks, seen Birdie Wilder look so weak and afraid.

When her tears finally subsided and she told me what happened, I jumped into action. The police were called, Birdie gave them her statement and then I secured her in her hotel room. It was time to get to work.

Joe is pulling the security footage from the bus, and my leg is bouncing from my own impatience. I want to see how the hell this creep got near Birdie in the first place. I should never have left her. If something happened... I clear my throat. I have to reassure myself or I'll spiral, which I can't do right now.

"Looks like he was hiding in the trees here watching, then waited until I went under the bus to get some of the suitcases to make his entrance," Joe says gruffly. I can tell he's sorry for what happened, but it's not his fault. He's not here to protect Birdie, I am.

I rub my jaw, "He had a lot of balls to do what he did. It's not your fault, Joe. I'm going to get more security hired for our transfers so this doesn't happen again. I should never have left her on the bus."

"The hotel security radioed that we were secure to bring her in. This is the way we've done it the last few stops. There's no reason to blame yourself either, Liam."

My stomach sinks. "*Shit*."

"What is it?"

"What you just said. The stalker... we haven't heard from him in three weeks because he's been observing. He knew Birdie would be alone on the bus. Fuck!" I throw the walkie I've been holding on the ground.

Joe puts one of his big paws on my shoulder, giving it a rough slap. "Don't be so hard on yourself, man. You've been doing your job. This sicko has upped his game. You're simply learning it now. None of us will let this happen again. We're a team here, and we all care about Birdie."

I give him a sharp nod. Though Joe's words are meant to soothe me, they don't. I failed. "Can you give a copy of this to the police? I'm going to head up to Birdie's suite."

"Will do. Take care of her."

My throat becomes thick with a foreign emotion. "I will."

When I approach Birdie's suite, hotel security is outside. I have them move to the end of the hall to keep watch, then knock on the door.

It doesn't take long before Shea answers. She gives me a coy smile then pushes her purple hair over her shoulder. I bite my tongue. I want to cuss her out for smiling at me like that right now. Her boss, *her friend*, just came face-to-face with a dangerous threat. A threat that could have killed her.

I must scowl because her smile drops. Instead of her usual bubbly greeting, she just opens the door and lets me in. *Good choice*. When I enter the room, my eyes search for Birdie.

Kevin is sitting next to her, her blonde head rests on his shoulder. She's gazing at the television. I can tell by her glazed-over look that she's not watching it, it's just on for noise. Eric and Gia are sitting close to each other, talking quietly. Every so often they glance cautiously at Birdie. I'm glad she has her friends around her, though a part of me wishes it was my shoulder under Birdie's head instead of Kevin's, which is a ridiculous thought.

At my approach the three of them look up, but Birdie's eyes remain staring forward. Eric stands and waves me over to the bedroom so we can talk in private. I notice Shea takes his spot on the couch, her eyes watching us leave. Her stare inspires me to go over her background check again, I'm starting to wonder if this girl is here for the right reasons. Even if she shits rainbows, maybe I can find something to convince Birdie she can get a better assistant. One that doesn't flirt with her bodyguard on the daily.

Once we're out of earshot, Eric starts giving me the third degree. "What did you find?

I run my hands through my tousled hair; I could really use a hot shower. I tell Eric what we found on the security footage, and that the police report has been filed, but as of right now, there's not much we can do besides up security and keep a closer eye on how we transport Birdie to and from locations.

"Do you think we should fly her instead?" Eric asks.

"That's an option. But if you can get me extra guys hired in each town, we shouldn't have any issues. I think this creep just wanted to flex a bit. He probably gets off on these types of power plays. Between the public letter, the incident in Times Square and now tonight... he's showing us he's watching. That he sees the weak links. Whoever he is, he must have some sort of police or military background."

"Are you sure?" Eric asks.

"That's what the signs point to right now. But I'm going to investigate it more tomorrow. I just want to make sure Birdie's okay tonight." Eric pats my bicep, a small smile tugging at his lips. I lift an eyebrow at him in question.

"I'm glad to hear you say that. I know you and Birdie have history you won't tell us about, but I've never seen her like this. Ever. It's scaring me. We may be her friends... hell, we're her family, but I think it would be good if she has someone from her past around tonight. Someone familiar and safe."

I don't know if he's right or not. Birdie may hate me right now after what happened, but I'd do anything to make sure she feels safe tonight. "I'll be here for her," is all I can say. I know he wants me to divulge more of our past, but that's her story to tell.

"Good. I'll clear everyone out so you can speak with her."

"Thanks, Eric."

I follow him back out to the living room. Gia must have been in on this plan because Kevin and Shea are already gone. Birdie stands by the door now and Gia is hugging her for dear life. Birdie's hugging her back, but her body is still. I think she's in shock. Once Gia sees Eric and I, she pulls back.

"Call me if you need anything, I'll come right over," she tells Birdie.

"I will," Birdie says, her voice small. Something in my heart pangs at the sound of it. Eric echoes Gia's words, then after a minute they're both gone. Birdie closes the door and locks it, her hands shaking just slightly as she does. When she turns around, she jumps a little at the sight of me.

"Sorry, I thought you knew I was here."

Her hazel eyes flick to the floor. "I didn't see you come in."

"You were watching the news." I say awkwardly.

She lets out a harrumph. "I'm pretty sure I wasn't, but I know what you mean." She forces herself to breathe, then straightens her shoulders. "Did you need something?"

My ego deflates a little at the fact that she dismisses me so quickly. Maybe she's planning to fire me after tonight. I wouldn't blame her. "I want to make sure you're alright."

"I'm fine," she clips as she heads for the mini bar.

It under a minute, she's throwing back a little bottle of bourbon.

"That just screams okay," I mutter.

She rubs her temples then puts the empty bottle down on the counter.

"Liam, what are you doing here?" her voice is tired, but I decide I'm not going to leave until I know she won't drink herself into a stupor and fall in the shower again.

I make my way to the bar then sit down. "Pour me a drink."

She looks intrigued now. "You're serious?

I probably shouldn't. But after tonight, one drink won't hurt. "I'm technically off the clock."

She lifts her hands. "I'm not judging. I think you deserve one after putting up with me."

I sigh. "That's not why I need a drink and you know it." Her face falters a little, but I watch as she quickly detaches. I would know that ability anywhere. I do it all the time.

After a second, she reaches down and pulls out a little bottle of vodka. I smirk slightly. "How did you know that's what I like?"

She shrugs. "Just a guess."

I tap my fingers on the counter. "Tell me why it's your first guess."

Birdie slides the bottle to me. When I reach for it, our fingers touch just slightly. It warms me more than this shot of vodka ever will. She pulls back her hand too quickly, that's when I know she felt it, too.

She clears her throat. "Well, you work out."

I let out a barking laugh that makes her smile. "I have no idea what that has to do with me liking vodka."

"I've heard it has the lowest calories," she shrugs.

"And that's the only reason?"

"And it's Ben's favorite, so I assumed..."

"Now that answer makes more sense." I open the small bottle and quickly drain it. "That's disgusting," I wince. She hands me an open cola, which I gratefully accept. After I take a swig, she slides me another vodka.

I shake my head. "I'll hold off for now."

She gives me a challenging stare. "You scared, Liam?"

More than you know, I want to say. But instead, I push my shoulders back and crack open the second bottle. This one goes down smoother, but it still tastes like shit. Birdie does another shot of bourbon, then opens an IPA for each of us.

"Are you trying to get me drunk?" I ask.

She bites her lower lip. "Not drunk, maybe tipsy. After tonight we both need a little help to relax."

Though I don't like to drink to get rid of stress, tonight is one of those nights I'll make an exception. I grab the beer and take a drink. Then another.

I let the hoppy liquid enter my veins and mix with the cheap vodka. Birdie's right, my body does relax a bit, but not enough for me to be off my game. If anything were to happen, I'd be able to take care of Birdie. That's what matters most.

After a few moments of silence I ask, "What now?"

She taps her fingers on her chin and smiles. It's very cute and reminds me of something teenage Birdie would do. "Listen to music on the patio?"

My stomach twists. The trauma of tonight must have made her feel nostalgic. Her desire to feel safe with the boy I once was makes me nauseous. For a second, I want to deny her, my own fear of being vulnerable getting in the way. But I don't.

I stand, beer in hand. "Lead the way."

"I need to grab my iPod and speaker. I'll meet you out there."

Before I can think twice, she's rushing off with a giddy pep in her step. It's fucking adorable. I'm glad to see it after what happened earlier.

While I wait, I make my way to the patio of her suite. We're high enough that I don't have to worry about any stalkers creeping on her, but the open air still makes me slightly nervous.

I push it down and try to relax. Once I sit, I prop up my feet on the table in front of me. It's after nine, and the sun has gone down. The Atlanta air is humid, and I can hear crickets chirping. I look up at the muddled stars, and I wish we were somewhere north where the sky looks like a painting. That's one thing I miss about living in Michigan. NYC didn't lend itself to stargazing. Maybe when we hit Nebraska we'll actually see the stars.

After a few minutes the sliding door opens and Birdie walks out. When my eyes take her in, I feel my temperature rise. She's changed into short little pink pajama shorts and a tight white t-shirt with a rainbow printed over her breasts. Her hair is up in a messy bun again. I immediately have the desire to grab her by it and press my lips into hers. For a split second I wonder what her hair smells like. Maybe hotel shampoo, or something like peaches or strawberries. When she sits, her breasts bounce slightly, and my eyes go straight to her dark nipples peeking out from the white shirt. Shit, she's not wearing a bra. Is she trying to kill me?

She plugs her iPod into the speakers, not noticing my dick is happy to have her here, dressed like that. Maybe I did drink a little too much. I better nurse my beer or shit might happen that shouldn't happen.

That day in the spa when we'd called a truce, I almost kissed her outside the sauna. When I came to my senses in the shower later, after

I'd released some pent-up frustration, I was glad I didn't let my small brain win out in the moment. I still want to kiss Birdie. Hell, do way more than just kiss, but it's not a good idea. Especially after her stalker just traumatized her.

My eyes go back to watching her as she looks through her iPod selection. Once she's settled on a song, she leans back, still oblivious to my rampant sexual desire. Her gaze flicks up, she looks a little tired, but surprisingly happy. Much better than when I first walked into her suite.

"Are you ready to hear what I picked?" She smirks.

"Will I know it?" I take a small sip of my beer.

"Oh..." she practically purrs. My dick goes hard again. The sound she just made makes me think of what it would feel like to have her lips wrapped around my cock while she makes it.

"You'll know the song," she finishes.

I cross my leg, putting my right ankle on my knee. It didn't do much to hide my hard-on, but it's better than nothing. She presses play on her iPod, then leans back. Her nipples are hard, which makes me think she's aware of what she's doing to me. Or maybe she's just a little cold. My bad judgment hopes it's the former... even though it's hot outside.

Music fills the air and warmth fills me from head to toe at the familiar notes. "American Pie, Pt. 1" by Don McLean plays. I tip my beer to her. A great song choice, and one that holds many memories.

"Remember when we used to play this on your dad's old record player?"

As if I could forget.

"Those were simpler times," is all I manage to say. Sitting here with Birdie, listening to this song is doing things to me.

I shift in my seat again and this time it doesn't go unnoticed by Birdie. She can tell my demeanor has changed. She leans forward and puts her hands on her knees.

"Does being here with me make you upset, Liam?"

I chuckle. "You cut right to the point, don't you?"

She shrugs. "If I said I wanted to talk about what happened ten years ago, would you?"

I swallow, my throat feeling as if it's about to close up. "Why do you want to talk about it, Birdie? Can't we just leave it in the past? We're very different people now."

She drums her plum-colored nails on her beer can. "I know, but I need to ask you a question."

"Birdie—"

"Please, Liam?" She begs, her green- and gold-flecked eyes locked on mine.

I run my hands through my hair. *Fuck it*. I chug the rest of my beer. I'm going to need liquid courage if we're doing this conversation.

Nineteen

Liam

BIRDIE'S VOICE IS STEADY when she says, "That night when we talked online. Why did you say it?"

My stomach knots as I lean back in my chair. Now I'm wishing we were in the air-conditioned suite instead of on this hot balcony. My skin is crawling, and my shirt is getting sticky with sweat. "American Pie" is still playing softly from the speakers and Don McLean's voice sings soulfully around us.

I let out a breathy sound. "Why does it matter now?" Birdie blinks rapidly at me, then to my surprise, tears spring to her eyes. *Damnit.* "Birdie..."

"It matters to me, Liam. Shouldn't that be enough?"

I pick at the tab of my beer can. "It's complicated..." My eyes dart to the sky and I pray for some type of strength. Birdie's warm hand appears on my knee, and she squeezes my jean clad leg. When my eyes meet hers again, I'm surprised they don't show any anger.

"Just tell me. Whatever it is, I can handle it. I'm not the girl I was all those years ago."

I smile at that and place my hand over hers, giving it a squeeze. "I know."

All too soon she removes her hand and leans back. My body hurts at the loss.

"Then please...," she says quietly, "for me. Just tell me why. I've spent way too long wondering, even after all these years. I lied when I told that reporter it didn't matter anymore. Your words, they still haunt me whether I want them to or not."

Regret hits me. "I never meant for you to be hurt. I swear, Birdie. But that day..." I pause to collect myself. "That day I was so scared of losing you. I said what I thought I had to, and I—" I stop and wonder if I should really tell her the truth.

She worries her bottom lip. Before I can stop myself, I reach my hand out and press my thumb to the soft flesh. I gently pull her lip out from her teeth and rub my finger over the indentations. She stops breathing and her gaze flicks to my lips, then back to my eyes. I pull back before I lose my nerve and take my mind back to that last day of sophomore year...

"Holy shit, dude." I tell Ben over the phone. "I can't believe you did it."

"Me either," he says. I swear I can hear him blush over the phone.

"It just kind of happened."

"And you said the L-word, too. That's huge. I mean, I'm sixteen and I can't imagine saying that to anyone like... ever."

Ben laughs. "Not even to Birdie?"

I roll my eyes. "We're friends, you dirtbag."

"I thought you said you were head over heels for her or some crap the other day?" he questions.

"I didn't mean it like that. She's my best friend. I said I'd go head over heels to do anything for her, not that I want to have sex with her."

"She's got great boobs though."

I shake my head. "Dude. Seriously?"

"What? I speak facts. So, you really don't like her like that?"

My mind flashes to Birdie, her pretty black hair and soulful eyes. Her one dimple is cute, too. But I don't think I like her more than a friend. "No, I don't. And even if I did, I kind of kissed Jen Brown the other night after football."

"The senior cheerleader?" His voice is in awe.

"The very one."

"Damn dude. And you're just telling me now?"

I shrug even though he can't see. "I've been busy with the last day of school and everything, not to mention I got into it with my dad last night."

"Is he drinking again?"

I clench my fists. I hate that Ben knows my secret. "He's trying to get better. Mom thinks he should go to rehab. They got in a huge fight over it last night before they left for work. Then I laid into him for how rude he was to her. He left for work, and he was sleeping when I got home from school."

"Does Birdie know about it?"

"No. You're the only one."

"Have you ever thought about telling her?"

"Why would I?"

"Because she's your friend. You practically live together at this point."

"Wow. You're just so funny today, Ben."

There's silence for a moment before he speaks again. "Listen man, I have to come clean about something."

My stomach sinks. "You didn't tell Birdie about my dad, did you?

"No man, nothing like that. I would never."

I breathe a sigh of relief. "Then what?"

"I may have told Wren that you said you were head over heels for Birdie."

Shit. "Why would you do that?"

"She was asking a bunch of questions. Said that Birdie really likes you... like more than friends. I thought the poor girl had a chance with you. I misunderstood. Sorry man. I hope I didn't screw things up for you."

I run my hands through my hair, a nervous tick of mine. "Thanks for telling me." I squeeze my eyes shut. "I have to get going. I'll talk to you later. Have a good first shift at the theater."

"Are we good, bro?"

I take a deep breath. "We're good."

Once I'm off the phone with Ben, I can't help but head toward my computer. My head is reeling from Ben's confession. Birdie likes me.

I rub my temples. I feel a headache coming on. I can't imagine a girl like her liking me. She's better than most girls my age, and I enjoy spending time with her. We talk about a lot of stuff, and she keeps me company while my parents work... or rather, my dad passed out upstairs, oblivious to the fact I didn't come home until four in the morning.

Dad's drinking was an issue before I was born, or so Mom says. He got some help when I was a baby, but now he's fallen back into it. He isn't mean or anything when he gets drunk, but he's useless. I got so used to him working or drinking and mom working long shifts at the hospital, a lot of days it felt like I didn't have parents. So, I filled my time with Birdie or Ben, then of course football and the summer job at The Daily Scoop.

I log on to Instant Messenger and see Birdie's screen is active.

Could I like Birdie more than a friend? Sure, she's beautiful, funny, likes my kind of music, pancakes, and even my stupid jokes. But what would she think if she found out that Dad drinks and forgets that he even has a son sometimes?

Even if I like Birdie, dating a girl like Jen Brown is easier. She doesn't know my life; she won't ask questions or get too committed. She's going to college soon, and there won't be any strings. If I date Birdie and we don't work out, I'd lose one of the only friends I feel one hundred percent myself with.

So... I decide, right here and now. No matter what, I can't like Birdie more than a friend. If I lose her, I... I don't want to think about it.

I message Birdie and hope that she never even mentions that she likes me, but it doesn't take long for her to do exactly that. When I see the message on the computer screen, telling me she likes me, I freeze. All my fears are coming to life right before my eyes.

Without thinking, I type the only words I can muster. The only words I can think of that will get her to understand that we aren't going to be a thing—even if she doesn't realize it's for her own benefit. Not because I don't find her cute or one of the best girls I know. Yes, this is the only way.

I hit send, the words "I'll never like you like that" hang in the air around me like smoke, as if they're choking me. I immediately wish I could take them back—but I can't. I just hope Birdie will still be my friend, because if she doesn't, I don't know what I'll do...

I finish telling Birdie the truth and brace myself for her reaction. She'd listened quietly to my side of the events from that day ten years ago, not saying a word the entire time. Somehow, she's managed to keep her eyes clear of emotion, which makes it hard for me to determine what she's thinking or feeling.

We sit in silence for several more moments, before she makes a small movement to reach for her iPod. She starts to scroll through songs, and I'm left to wonder if I fucked up by telling her the truth.

My voice is thick with emotion when I speak again. "What are you doing? Aren't you going to say something?"

Her eyes dart to mine then she leans forward. She brings her pointer finger up and presses my lips closed. "Shh, just listen."

She presses play on a song, and Birdie's voice echoes through the speakers. I follow her plea and listen carefully. This must be an earlier song, because her voice sounds younger, less seasoned; though still beautiful.

It doesn't take me long to recognize it; I think it's the one she sang while we watched the meteor shower in my backyard. I thought it was about some boy she was crushing on, but now I understand. It's about me.

Sweet summer boy
I know how much you care
You love with a force
of a thousand volts
Your eyes show your soul
And your lips tell a tale
Sweet summer boy

I listen to the words; they really are beautiful. But she had it wrong even back then, I'm not a sweet boy, nor a sweet man. I'm... I don't even really know anymore. Broken is probably a better word. I used to think the accident made me harsh, but really, it was the day the woman before me left my life. And the worst part is, I can't even blame her. She didn't do anything wrong; I was the one who pushed her away. She had every right to tell me to fuck off.

After a minute or so the song finishes. When I finally bring my eyes to meet Birdie's once more, I study her for a few seconds. Her pupils are dilated from the alcohol and her skin looks sticky from the humid air, but she's beautiful all the same.

I breathe in. "Why did you play that for me?"

Birdie scoots her chair closer, surprising me. She puts one hand on my knee and the other one under my chin, tilting my face up to look at her.

"You..." she says, her voice hoarse. "You're so sweet, Liam. And I... God, I'm so sorry for the way I acted back then. I should have seen that you were struggling. I was so blinded by how much I liked you. And—"

This time I reach up and grab her face in my hands. "No Birdie. There is no way you could have known. I was—or I should say, I am—ashamed of my father's illness. He... it hasn't been an easy road for him. And back then, it was so new, and I was only sixteen. I didn't know how to handle it. And you were such a good friend. Looking back, you would have handled the information like a champ. I should have just been honest but—I didn't deserve it. I didn't deserve you."

Birdie lets out a strangled noise and shakes her head back and forth. "You did though, Liam. You did deserve it. You were the sweetest boy, you..." She looks down for a moment and I watch as her cheeks turn a light shade of pink. I'm still holding her face, so I gently urge her to look at me again. When she does, I see a deep pain there that stabs at my heart.

She takes a shallow breath. "Do you even know how much your friendship and attention meant to me? I was the fat girl who boys never gave a second look at! You made me feel visible, even if it was only for a short time. Liam..." she leans her forehead against mine. "You helped me find my voice."

We're so close now I can feel her hot breath on my cheek. I lick my lips, staring into her eyes so she knows I mean what I'm about to say.

"No. I may have helped, but you found your voice all on your own."

She lets out a breathy laugh as her gaze flicks to my lips and then back to my eyes. "Thank you for telling me the truth."

"I should have told you a long time ago."

She smirks. "Yes. You should have."

I laugh a little at that. "So sassy."

Birdie brings her hands to rest over mine. Her gaze penetrates me as if she can see my soul. This moment feels surreal. It's more than the moment at the spa, it feels like it's the start of something completely new. I know I still have a ton of baggage to work through, but whatever's happening with Birdie, it makes me feel a whole lot of things I never thought I could feel again. At this moment I'm teenage Liam again sitting with the girl he's head over heels with. A little shock runs through my system...

"Birdie—" But my words come up short.

"Don't. Whatever you're thinking. Just don't say it."

I run my nose over hers and our lips brush gently. She smells like vanilla hand soap and IPA.

I nudge her nose with mine. "What if I was going to ask if I could kiss you?"

"Then I'd say, ask away."

I brush my nose along her jaw then then press a kiss just behind her ear. When I bring my lips to the curved shell I whisper, "Can I kiss you, *Ms. Wilder*?"

A shiver courses through her and she pulls away just slightly so we're nose to nose again. Then she says the words I never thought I'd hear.

"Yes, Liam. You may kiss me."

Twenty

Birdie

I'M DREAMING. NO, I'M dead. No, it's real. Holy. Shit. Liam Miller is really kissing me.

He tastes better than I could have ever imagined. He's like rich dark chocolate and fire on a cold winter night. I want to be consumed by him every hour of every day for the rest of my life.

Liam's hands tangle in my hair as best they can with it up in a bun and he pulls me closer. When his tongue strokes mine, I groan as he explores deeper. Damn he's passionate. Just like his work, he gives everything he has. I place my hands on his shoulders and lean awkwardly from my chair to try to get even closer. Before I can shift positions, Liam's pulling me up. His kiss only breaks for a second as he pushes me against the sliding glass door.

Our eyes meet, I'm swallowed up in chocolate brown, so deep they're almost black. He grins at me devilishly. I squeeze my thighs together, which he notices. His gaze travels from my bare feet, up my thick thighs, to my short shorts and finally my breasts. He pauses for a moment and stares at my hardened nipples. Right before I'm able to grab him myself, he crushes me to his lips again.

I sigh into his mouth as his strong hands grasp my bottom and he pushes my hips into his groin. He's hard, more than hard, and I have to stop myself from dry humping him. That would be embarrassing. But my body is living its dream right now. Real Liam is much better than the shower wall I pretended was him when I was sixteen.

His strong grip on my ass brings me back to the present time where the real thing is kissing and groping me. At that I kiss him harder, then run my hands up from his muscular chest and into his feathered hair. It's silky and soft between my fingers; I want to feel it on my thighs as he licks me to his heart's content.

Liam tugs at my bottom lip with his own then moves them to suck on my neck. He groans as he tastes my skin while rocking his hips against me. It's as if he reads my thoughts and knows exactly what I want. He brings one of his hands up from my ass and palms my breast. Once he's found his prize, he rubs his thumb over my nipple. He teases it gently against my too tight T-shirt and I stifle a very loud moan.

"God Birdie," he groans between his nips and sucks. "You're perfect."

I want to laugh. Sure, I'm good looking and my soft roundness never disappoints a man, but nobody has ever called me perfect. It's funny though, because when Liam says it, part of me believes it, even with the history between us.

He kisses back up my neck and our lips meet. He takes his hand from my ass and brings it up to grip the back of my neck. When he starts to knead it in a possessive way, my panties melt. His other hand still plays with my nipple as he smiles against my mouth.

"Birdie," he presses his erection into me. "I—"

I kiss him to shut him up and to take the lead. I get that he wants to be in control, but I can tell he's trying to overthink the situation. After his confession, I know he wants to make sure that I want this. And I do—I really do. These last few weeks have been torture. And after tonight I need to feel alive, feel safe, feel... him. And boy oh boy do I feel him.

I grind into him and let myself enjoy how we only have six or so inches of a height difference. It makes us evenly matched, and I feel powerful yet protected. I move my hand to the handle behind us and push him slightly so I can open the sliding door.

"Let's go inside," I say, my voice huskier than usual. I'm so turned on I can't think straight. I want to feel him everywhere, and I most definitely want to see what's behind his jeans. I can tell it's going to be a nice show, and I have my ticket ready.

We make it to the bedroom in no time, the short walk there filled with Liam smacking my ass and telling me to hurry. His energy is contagious, and I find myself smiling. He's already more playful than I expected, and I want to find out everything I don't know about adult Liam, and everything I didn't know about teenage Liam.

Before I can make it to the king-sized bed, he pulls me back by my hips, his hard cock encountering my butt again. He groans, then turns me around so he can push me down on the edge of the soft mattress.

My breasts are heavy and aching to be touched. I can't help but rub my legs together to relieve some of the throbbing. If he doesn't touch me there soon, I think I might literally explode.

Liam makes eye contact with me, his gaze hungry and a little wild. The force he used to push me down on the bed makes me embarrassingly wet, and also curious about what he likes to do in the bedroom. I've been known to walk on the wild side a bit and his touch makes me think he does too.

His gaze drops to the triangle between my legs and now I know exactly what he's thinking. With my knees bent over the mattress, I spread my legs apart to give him a better look. He groans, throwing his head back like he's praying. Then before I can blink, he has his shirt tossed over his head. It lands somewhere behind him and then he's prowling toward me. His beautiful, chiseled chest is on full display, and I can't wait to get my hands on him. But much to my dismay, he stops just as his kneecaps touch mine.

"Take off your shirt, *Ms. Wilder*."

Fuck he's good at this. I knew he would be.

"Not my pants?" I ask, my voice teasing. He's a breast man, I knew it the moment we reunited in Atlantic City and he couldn't keep his eyes off them.

A sexy smirk plants on his face. He takes one of his strong fingers and tilts my chin up so we're staring directly into each other's eyes. "Take off your shirt first, Birdie."

My stomach clenches. "Say please..."

He takes his finger and brushes it down my cheek gently, then taps my swollen lips. "Please," he croons.

Even hotter now, I bring my hands to the hem of my T-shirt. Just for a moment, I have a fleeting thought of self-doubt. Liam's seen my rolls before. Not only during my horrible bathtub incident, but also inside the sauna. I'm happy with my body and I've worked hard to love it. But lately, it's been difficult to stay on the self-love train. And having Liam before me, my childhood crush, my unrequited love...

I'm not sure if I can be as confident now as I usually am. Even if we've cleared up why he said what he said ten years ago, it didn't erase the years of damage it caused. It didn't erase the last few weeks either.

"Birdie," Liam says calmly. He tilts my chin up to meet his eyes once more. His chocolate eyes look a little sad, but they also hold such adoration I want to cry. No one has ever looked at me like that except for him. I missed that look.

He brushes a loose strand of hair behind my ear, then tugs on the lobe. "You're beautiful. Never doubt how incredibly sexy you are. I want you. And I *really* want you naked and spread out before me like fucking yesterday. Got it?"

My mouth goes dry at his words. I believe every syllable that just came out of his mouth. He said them with such conviction; there's no room for any more doubt in my mind.

I pull off my shirt and swiftly throw it to the floor. I don't have a bra on, which, I'm not going to lie, I'd done on purpose. When I changed—I blame the bourbon for my decision—I knew it would drive him crazy. Part of me was hopeful that something like this would happen tonight, but I didn't actually think it would.

Liam looms over me, then steps between my legs. His eyes are focused on mine before he gently pushes me the rest of the way down onto the soft sheets. I'm spread out, my shorts still on, with my top half totally exposed. His gaze roves over me, landing finally on my breasts.

His mouth opens slightly. "You have no idea what you do to me, Birdie Wilder."

I look down at his crotch, then smile. "I have a little idea... or should I say... a *big* idea."

He lets out a breathy laugh then kisses me hard, plundering my mouth as he puts his hands on my breasts and gives them a nice squeeze. I moan, wanting to clench my legs together, but his legs stop me from doing so. His rough hands feel so good on my bare skin. The friction from his hands on my nipples is almost too much to handle.

Is it possible for women to come from just breast stimulation and kisses? I feel like it's a thing because I may combust just from this alone.

Once he's done thoroughly kissing me, he brings his mouth to my neck, then to the valley between my breasts. He keeps his right hand on my right breast, playing with my already taut nipple, and then puts his mouth on my left breast. He lets out a throaty moan as his tongue swirls around the tight bud; then he bites it gently, causing me to gasp. Wet warmth floods between my legs and my entire body lights on fire.

"You have amazing boobs. I really, really, like them," he manages to say before switching to the other breast to give it equal attention.

"Thank you," I breathe out, and then Liam really laughs.

"God, you're so fucking cute."

I let my head fall back as he continues to pay great attention to my breasts. He's not lying, he really does like them. After a few minutes, or maybe it's a lot longer, he starts to kiss down my stomach. His five o'clock shadow tickles the soft skin there and I shiver.

As he gets lower, he bends down to his knees, his face level with my pussy. He inhales and another gruff sound leaves his lips. For the love of all that is holy, how is everything this man does so sexy?

I lift up my head, but Liam runs his hands over my thighs in a calming motion. "Relax, Birdie girl, let me take care of you tonight. Just let yourself enjoy us."

Birdie girl. *Us.* Is there an "us" now? Or maybe there's always been an us. My heart tightens in my chest, but I don't have time to dwell because Liam is tugging at my pajama shorts. They come off easily, and I'm pretty sure there's a wet stain on them.

A pained noise comes out of Liam, so I lift my head up to look at him. He's staring between my legs at the sheer white thong I have on, his eyes glazed over like some rabid dog.

"Did you wear these for me?" His voice is dangerously low. I bite my lip and nod. Liam swallows then runs one of his long fingers over the seam of my panty clad lips. "Perfect," he murmurs. "Lay your head back down Birdie," he commands. So I do.

He takes his time running his hands back up and down my thighs, he even rubs my calves. By the time he returns to the elastic waistband of my thong, I'm delirious with sensory overload and ready to beg if he doesn't touch me soon.

Finally, he hooks his fingers in the sides and pulls them down. The cool air of the room hits my wet center and I moan.

"Liam," my voice sounds rather pathetic. "Please..."

He presses his thumbs into the creases near my hip flexors. "Please what, Birdie baby?"

Birdie baby? Geez this man. His words alone will do me in. "I need you to touch me. Please, Liam."

"I am touching you," he teases.

"Liam," I whine.

He chuckles. "Well since you said please."

I don't have time to chide him because he leans forward, hands opening me like a budding flower. After what feels like hours, his tongue is on me. Euphoria may be the best word to describe this moment... *fuck*. I'm going to have to write a song about it so that I can remember this feeling forever.

He swirls his tongue around my clit then gently sucks. "You taste like honey."

I've never had a man comment on my taste before and it's empowering to say the least. I grasp the bed sheets as his movements increase. He's worked me up so good I'm not going to last much longer. But Liam isn't finished with me yet.

He takes his mouth off me, then starts to kiss and bite my thighs. Just as I'm about to tell him I need his mouth again, he runs his fingers down my center and seeks entrance into my pussy.

One long finger... then two... he starts moving slowly, building the pressure inside me. I can't help the raunchy sounds that come out of my mouth. I reach one of my hands up and manage to grab Liam by the hair. He lets out a chuckle as I direct his mouth back to my clit.

"So bossy," he says around me, the vibrations of his voice almost undoing.

"Liam," my voice is breathy. "Faster... please"

"Whatever Ms. Wilder wants, Ms. Wilder gets." He adds a third finger and I push my hips off the bed, taking care to hold his face in place.

"Yes Liam! Fuck. Right there." He moves faster and sucks harder and with one final tug on my clit and a few fancy moves of his wrist, I come undone, falling hard and fast.

Twenty-One

Liam

BIRDIE LAYS PANTING ON the bed.

I can't help but stare at her. Every part of her glorious body is on display to me at this angle—I fucking love it. If I died between her legs, I'd be a happy man.

I kiss the inside of her knee then bite and suck her inner thighs as she rides the aftershocks of her orgasm. If she wasn't famous, and I wasn't her bodyguard, I would most definitely have snapped a picture. But a mental one would have to do.

After I'm sure I've wrung out every last bit of pleasure from her, I remove my fingers and lick them clean. I've never enjoyed the taste of a woman so much in my life. She tastes like honey candy and spring. I want to taste it again and again.

Birdie is still panting as she stares up at the ceiling. I brush my hands up her heated skin, taking time to enjoy the way her skin molds to my hands. It feels soft against my calloused skin. When I reach her breasts and squeeze, she gasps.

I grin. "Still sensitive?"

"You're—" I give them one more squeeze and her breath catches.

I grin wider and kiss her neck. When I meet her green- and gold-flecked gaze she looks ready for sleep. My dick is still hard against my jeans, practically begging me to sink into her tight wet heat. But that's not going to happen tonight. She needs to rest, and I want tonight to be all about her. I will survive, at least for now.

I nip at her lips and kiss her softly. "You okay?"

"I don't think I've ever come that hard in my life."

I raise a brow. "That can't be true."

She bites her lower lip all cute. "Trust me, it is."

"Well then, Ms. Wilder, you're in for quite a treat. Because I could do that all night if you let me."

She squeaks. "All night?"

I rub my nose delicately against hers and kiss her again, this time opening her mouth to mine. I let her taste herself on my lips and bring my hand to her messy hair. The bun is practically non-existent now. Loose strands are spilling out of the hair tie, so I grip the back of her head. The scent of fresh lemon hits me, and I realize that must be her shampoo. I smile against her lips before pulling back so we can catch our breath.

"What is it?" She taps the curve of my lips.

"Your hair smells like lemons."

"And that makes you smile?"

I bury my nose in her hair and breathe deep. "I've always wondered what it smells like."

"Really?"

"Even when we were younger," I admit. Because even if I didn't know I liked Birdie back then, it didn't mean my teenage hormones never got the best of me when we hung out. Especially when she'd sing.

A warm smile graces her lips, and she kisses me sweetly. I can feel her happiness in it, and it makes me want to pleasure her all over again. I have decided that a smiling Birdie is the Birdie I always want to see from now on.

As we kiss, Birdie's hands begin to wander down my chest. She gently drags her nails across my skin, and I shiver at the feeling. I dream of the day when they will dig into my back and chest as I thrust into her. *Shit.* I want to fuck Birdie every single way possible, just not tonight. She needs to rest.

Right as her hand grazes my dick, I gently grab her wrist and break our kiss. If she touches me right now, I won't be able to stop myself. She opens her eyes and gives me a questioning look. I can see the hurt in them too.

"Not tonight," I say quietly.

She squeezes her eyes shut; and just like that, she shuts herself off. I feel her body start to go rigid as she takes her hand from my wrist then pushes it against my chest. I'm stronger though, so I don't budge.

"I need to get up," she mutters.

I shake my head. "Absolutely not."

"Liam," she whines, pushing her hand into my chest again. "Please let me get up."

This time I do, but just as she's about to stand, I pull her naked body into my lap. She lets out a shout of surprise, smacking my chest. "Liam! What the hell!"

"Birdie..." I pull her chin to look at me. She moves around in my lap, her ass rubbing against my still hard cock. I'm in big trouble with this woman.

"Would you just stop for a second? I know what you're thinking and you're incredibly wrong." Finally, she stops squirming.

I pull her in for a kiss and at first, she doesn't kiss back. I wrap my arms around her and use one hand to grasp the back of her neck. It doesn't take long for her to stop resisting and soon we're making out like horny teenagers.

I flip her around so her back is flat on the bed and place my legs on either side of her hips. She lets out a small sound of shock. I know what she's thinking now too, that she's too heavy for me to toss around. Another BS lie she's told herself. I hate that I contributed to those shitty thoughts in her head. I'd have to find a way to make it up to her.

She looks up at me through hooded eyes, her dark lashes fluttering. I brace my forearms so I'm hovering over her.

"I want to have sex with you," I tell her as I press my hardness into her. "No, scratch that. I REALLY want to have sex with you, but not tonight. You've been through a lot, and you need to rest. I want tonight to just be about you."

She takes a deep breath. "That's sweet but..."

I kiss her to shut her up. When I release her lips I almost growl. "No, Birdie. I don't want the first time we have sex to be after some trauma. Let me have this moment with you. Let me hold you and we can talk like we used to."

"What if that's not what I want?" Her hand quickly finds its way to my groin, and she squeezes.

I groan and let my forehead drop against hers. "You're so stubborn."

"I want what I want," she smirks.

"I'll be here, Birdie. I'm not going anywhere. I promise." I kiss her deep before putting my lips to her ear. "And when we do have sex, I'll fuck you so hard you won't walk for days."

Her gaze turns hot. "And that can't be now?" she plays with my dick again.

"You drive a hard bargain."

She moans as she pushes her hips into mine. "Give in to me, Liam."

I groan. "Please baby, I want it to be special."

"What if I want to take care of you, too."

"You are," I kiss her softly. When I look into her eyes, I try to convey how much I mean it. "God, you are."

I kiss her one more time and see she's finally starting to give in. When I make the kiss a little deeper, she suddenly pulls back and yawns. Her cheeks turn rosy with embarrassment. I can't help but give her a shit eating grin.

I kiss her nose. "We should sleep."

When I try to stand, she grabs my hand so I have to turn back. Fear flashes across her beautiful features and my heart feels like it's been stabbed. The events of the night come rushing back. Being here with her, it's been easy to forget how close she was to danger just hours before.

I squeeze her hand and make short work of the distance between us. I cup her face and brush my thumbs over the apples of her flushed cheeks. "I'm not leaving. I'm just going to clean up."

"You'll stay?" Her voice is quiet.

I press my lips to her forehead. "For as long as you want me."

I wake up to a warm soft body, pressed into me, and my dick hard as a rock.

Sun streams through the window and I wince from its light. I should've never drunk that cheap vodka. Birdie shifts in my arms and a stupid grin clings to my face. When I run my finger over the flesh of her bicep, she lets out a cute sound then snuggles closer to me.

Last night after we'd cleaned ourselves up and got into bed, I hadn't hesitated to pull Birdie in my arms. My actions surprised me. I've never been one for cuddling, but now I know that Birdie makes me say and do things I don't expect. I rubbed her back and reassured her that she was safe, and she'd fallen asleep within minutes.

Bringing my attention back to the present, I brush a piece of hair off her round cheek, then check my watch. It's already approaching nine in the morning. Which means I'm skipping the gym. It also means that Birdie has to get up to start her Atlanta press tour. Just as the thought crosses my mind, I hear a knock on the door. Birdie mumbles something but I decide to let her sleep for a few more minutes.

I gently get out of bed and quickly find my clothes. I stop to check myself in the mirror to make sure I don't look like a guy who almost had sex with his boss last night. I run my fingers through my tousled morning hair and resign myself to the fact I look... well, tousled.

When the knocking gets louder, I quickly leave the bedroom and look through the peephole. A groan escapes my mouth. It's Shea. I flip on the light and hope she doesn't have a sixth sense. I'm not sure if Birdie would want her assistant to know that we did anything last night. I sure as hell wouldn't pick Shea as the first to know.

I take a deep breath then open the door to the awaiting purple haired thorn in my side. When she sees me, her smile falters.

"Liam. I didn't expect you to be here."

"Good morning to you too, Shea."

She looks me up and down, clearly noting that I'm wearing yesterday's clothes. "Is Birdie awake?"

"Not yet."

"Did you sleep in here?"

I tap my fingers on the door. "I'm Ms. Wilder's bodyguard."

Shea almost rolls her eyes, causing all the alarm bells in my body to go off. There's something not right with this girl. I start to ask questions in my head like, where did she go to school? How did she get hired? Did she have a history of jealousy?

"Right. Well, can I come in?" She asks.

The voice in my head stops. "What do you need?" I puff out my chest, feeling the need to protect Birdie. I really don't trust this girl anymore.

"Are you her assistant now?" She scoffs.

Despite her annoyance, I don't budge. "What do you need, Shea?"

"Hair and makeup will be here in thirty minutes. She has an interview at the local rock station downtown in two hours, then soundcheck after."

"I'll make sure she's ready for them."

Shea checks me out again, then meets my eyes. Her green ones are cold, and I stop myself from looking away. "Did you sleep on the couch or in her bed?"

"Woah," I hold up my hands and take a step back. "That's way out of line, Shea."

She clicks her tongue against the roof of her mouth. "If you're looking for beds to keep warm, mine is open."

I try hard to keep myself from laughing. She's actually serious. "I'm good, thanks."

"Right. Well, if Birdie's bed goes cold, you know where to find me."

Anger flares inside me. It takes everything in me not to tell this girl off. But she's Birdie's assistant, and I'm not going to do that. At least not yet. But I am going to make sure this girl doesn't even have a parking ticket on her record that I may have missed the first time around.

Instead of saying what I really want to say, I push down my anger. "Goodbye, Shea."

Twenty-Two

Liam

I CLOSE THE DOOR on Shea's smirking face then lock it.

I'm happy Birdie is still asleep. I wouldn't have wanted her to hear that insane exchange. She has enough to worry about.

Shaking off the conversation, I make my way to the service phone. When the concierge picks up, I order coffee and pancakes for us before I head back to the bedroom. To my surprise, Birdie is sitting up in bed texting on her phone. Her head snaps up when she hears me enter.

"Liam!" Her voice is squeaky. Like a little kid caught red handed.

I walk over to her side of the bed. "Hey you."

I pull her to me before she can say anything and mold my lips to hers. She lets out a small moan before returning the kiss. I make sure to taste her and let her feel my tongue against hers as my hand winds in her silken hair. I want Birdie to remember me for the rest of the day. Especially when she's in Shea's presence.

When I finally release her, she's flushed and dazed. "Good morning," she giggles; and it's the cutest thing I've ever heard. "I thought you left."

I brush my thumb over her swollen lower lip. "Shea came to the door. I didn't want to wake you."

"Oh. What did she need?"

"She said you have hair and makeup coming in thirty, then a meeting at some radio station in two hours and soundcheck after."

"Crap. I forgot that's today." She goes to get up off the bed, so I help her. She's adorable with her hair a mess and cheeks flushed—both my doing. I fucking love it.

She putters around the room gathering her white thong and shorts off the floor. My dick gets hard when I see her holding them, memories of last night coming to the forefront of my mind. She must be thinking of it too because her neck begins to splotch. When I catch a glimpse of her face, I realize it's tense.

Great—she's freaking out. My brain starts to develop theories as to why. First off, she thought I left this morning, and now I bet she's wondering where we stand. This is why I usually don't do relationships. Too complicated. And this relationship is more complicated than most. But that doesn't stop me from feeling the way I feel right now.

I stride over to her and stop her movements. She stares at me, hazel eyes wide. "Stop worrying. I'm here with you, Birdie girl. I told you I'd stay."

Her features relax and a smile lifts the corner of her lips. "I wasn't sure how you would feel this morning. We drank last night..."

I brush my knuckles on her cheek. "Trust me. I didn't drink nearly enough to not remember or regret anything that happened last night."

She swallows, her mouth having gone dry. "Me neither."

"Good."

There's a knock on the door and Birdie startles. I lean forward and kiss her forehead. "It's just room service. I ordered coffee and pancakes."

A real smile covers her lips now, that cute little dimple appearing on her left cheek. "Pancakes?"

"What, you think I stopped liking pancakes?"

"You never know."

I grab her hand and pull her toward the main room. "Come on. No time to waste!"

She laughs at me. "You're chipper this morning." She's right, I am chipper. I can't help it, when I'm around Birdie, my body buzzes. Is this how it felt when I was a teenager, too?

I pull her to me to make sure she feels the hardness of my dick on her plush stomach. She lets out a gasp. "I like being here with you," I tell her. Shit. I've really gone sentimental. Maybe Birdie gives off some type of vulnerability serum.

I kiss her cheek. "Sit. I'll get the pancakes."

"Okay. Thank you."

Reluctantly, I walk away from her warmth, my body literally calling me to go back. It's another new sensation, and even though it should, it doesn't scare me. Especially since the last time I felt any sort of tug was with my partner Maria.

Abruptly I'm hit with the realization that last night, though we only slept for a short time, I didn't have nightmares. I'm feeling refreshed for the first time in weeks, minus the slight headache. I have no doubt that finally coming clean about Dad to Birdie was part of the reason. Maybe next I'll tell her about my accident, about what happened to Maria. But there's time to figure that out later.

I quickly retrieve the room service cart and scan the hallway while I'm at it. Once I'm satisfied, I close the door and turn to meet Birdie's devouring gaze. Immediately my hunger is forgotten and instead I'm hungry for something else. But we don't have time, her people will be here soon, and I have work I need to get done. Starting with figuring out Shea's deal and checking in with the Atlanta Police. So, I tell my little brain to chill and wink at Birdie.

"Pancakes?" I ask, pushing the cart in front of her.

Her face lights up. "Thanks for ordering. I would have skipped breakfast and then at some point realized I haven't eaten anything since yesterday at soundcheck."

Something in me turns. Does anyone on Birdie's team make sure she's taking care of herself? I'll have to speak with Eric about that. I want to make sure she's eating and not only drinking coffee and bourbon. Now that Birdie and I made up and... other things, something deep inside has activated. I want to protect her, and not just from her stalker, but from everything.

Well, I've got it bad. I can practically hear Ben's teasing and Wren's awwing.

With a smirk, I sit down next to Birdie and make sure our legs are touching. I kiss her cheek before I get to work on pouring her a cup of hot coffee. "Still drink it black?" I turn slightly to find her staring at me, a sweet look on her face. "What?" I start feeling shy with her looking at me like that. Like she can see my soul.

"I feel like I'm dreaming. You're exactly how I imagined when I was sixteen." She turns splotchy again, embarrassed she just admitted that to me.

I hand her the hot brew. "I'm glad we cleared the air. It feels good to not have it hanging around us."

"Agreed. Though I think I owe you an apology."

"For what?

She sighs as she puts her coffee down. "For that day at school."

I take her warmed hands in mine. "You don't owe me an apology for that. We were both upset. I hurt you—"

"I know, but it doesn't excuse my behavior. I said some pretty harsh things."

"We both did," I say, the events of that horrible day coming back to me...

A Green Day song plays on the radio.

It's the first day of junior year. I should be looking forward to it. I'm popular, have great friends, I'm on the football team...

Well, I was on the football team.

Dad's drinking got worse over the summer, and Mom started working more to avoid him. Not to mention Birdie and I are still on the outs. After we chatted online that night, she's been avoiding me like the plague. She even made sure she had all opposite shifts at The Daily Scoop. I'd see her sometimes during shift changes, but work was not an appropriate place to speak about whatever the hell happened that night.

I pull up to the school, and as luck, or bad luck, would have it, Birdie just pulled in as well. She's driving her mom's car, which means her mom is in town—that's rare. I put my car in park and look up to find her trying to get out of her car as fast as possible. She's obviously seen me and wants to high tail it into the school. In the process of hurrying, she drops some books and supplies all over the ground. I hop out of my car, using this opportunity to try and talk to her.

"Birdie," I say as I kneel in front of her. "I'm glad I caught you."

She glances up at me, her green- and gold-flecked eyes hesitant. It looks like she's shaking. No wonder she dropped all her stuff. Do I really make her that nervous?

"I don't have time to talk, Liam." Her voice is so angry it makes me pull back a bit.

My jaw clenches. "We're both early. Where do you have to be?"

She stands and I give her the few things I picked up. When our hands brush, she pulls away like my touch burns her. Now I'm starting to get angry.

Sure, I didn't like her back, but she made me promise we would still be friends. She's the one not allowing me to do so. Not me.

"Liam..." *she sighs.* "Just leave it, okay? I don't want to do this right now."

I run my hands through my hair, "Then when? You've been avoiding me all summer. You won't even answer my calls or the door when I come over."

She stands straighter and rolls her shoulders back. "I thought you were busy with Jen."

"So that's what this is about? You're jealous."

"You're such an asshole, you know that? I'm over you, Liam. Just leave me alone and go kick a football or something!"

I let out a sad laugh. "I quit football."

"What? Why?"

"Why do you care? We're not friends anymore. You made that clear."

Her face goes cold. "I have no idea why we were ever friends, Liam. You're not who I thought."

"I have no idea why I liked you at all. You're such a shitty person."

Right as I say it, I regret it. I'm just so angry and confused.

"Well, now we know the truth. Goodbye Liam. When you see me around, don't talk to me."

"Not a problem. You're forgettable anyway."

Lie. All lies. Nothing about the girl in front of me is forgettable. Fuck. This did not go how I wanted it to go at all. But this is better. I want to protect Birdie from my life, so this is for the best. Maybe we really were never meant to be friends, we did come from different worlds in some ways, even if we shared a lot of similarities.

Birdie's eyes turn hateful and glassy. "I'll have no problem forgetting you, Liam. You just made that easy, at least. Have a nice life, asshole." *Then, she turns on her heel and walks away. As she does, I can't help but think we just made a huge mistake. But Birdie Wilder is right about one thing...*

I am an asshole. I never said I wasn't.

Birdie squeezes my hands, bringing me back to the present.

"I hope you know I was lying that day, Birdie. I didn't mean any of it. I was just hurt and confused."

She smiles sadly. "I know, and I'm sorry I pulled away like that. I was so young and crushing so hard. I didn't know how to deal with being around you when I knew how you felt."

"I get that now. But Birdie, you weren't a shitty person. You were a teenage girl with her heart broken and—" I tilt her chin up, "You were... no, you still are... completely unforgettable."

She blushes, "And you're not an asshole."

I laugh, "That remains to be seen."

She gestures toward the pancakes and coffee. "You're thoughtful and sweet. You've been taking care of me this whole time, even when we didn't like each other."

I grin, brushing my thumb over her hand. "You deserve to be taken care of."

Her cheeks turn red, but she doesn't acknowledge my comment more than that.

"Liam..." she says tentatively. "Why did you quit football?"

My palms turn sweaty. Those memories still hurt. I don't think I ever really mourned the loss of my favorite sport. I sometimes wonder if I could have gotten a scholarship or been somebody different.

"Dad's drinking got worse. Mom started working more. Someone had to take care of him. I took more shifts at The Daily Scoop to help with some expenses."

Birdie's face morphs into sadness, not pity. Which makes me like her even more. I never want pity from anyone, even in my worst moments.

"I feel bad about last night now that I think about it. I forced you to drink that cheap vodka."

I shake my head. "I've got my shit handled Birdie. I'm not like him."

She exhales a breath. "Now I get why you were so concerned about me that night in Atlantic City. Every time I took a shot you looked upset."

I brush a lock of hair behind her ear. "You'd tell me if you had issues, wouldn't you?"

She smiles warmly. "You don't have to worry. I enjoy drinking sometimes to relieve a little stress now and then or to relax and have fun—not to get through my days."

I nod. "I just needed to ask."

Understanding is written on her face. "Thank you for being open with me about everything."

I want to say, "not everything," but again, it's not the right time. Instead, I focus on her dusty pink lips and warm expression. After that, I can't help myself. I kiss her. Hard. When I grasp the back of her neck, my other hand still holding hers, she moans into my mouth. That sound—I want to hear it every day. I want to bottle it up or have it as my ringtone.

Just as she reaches her free hand up to twine in my hair, there's a loud knock at the door. Birdie jumps so violently it pushes me back a little.

"Hey, hey," I whisper. "You're fine. You're safe."

Her neck goes splotchy, and she turns her eyes to the ground. "Guess I'm still jumpy after yesterday."

I tilt her chin up. I don't want her to hide from me. "That's understandable. You don't have to be embarrassed. It's a very scary thing you're dealing with."

She groans. "Don't remind me." The person at the door knocks again. "I guess the real world is calling."

I stand to answer the door, but Birdie stands with me. "Make sure to eat your breakfast."

"Yes, Sir," she winks.

I slap her sexy ass as she walks away. She lets out a cute yelp that makes my dick twitch. I'll have to do more of that later.

When she opens the door, her hair and makeup people are there with all their gear. Birdie must know them because they act like old friends. Gia assured me that anyone who works with Birdie is being thoroughly vetted and searched by hotel security upon arrival, but it's nice to know that Birdie has a rapport with these people.

"I'll leave you ladies to it," I say when there's a lull in the conversation. Birdie's gaze meets mine and I can see she doesn't want me to leave. I don't want to either, but I have to. I need a shower, badly, and I've got limited time to do what I need to do before soundcheck.

"I'll come get you before the interview, Ms. Wilder."

Birdie smirks at that. "Thank you, Mr. Miller. You're just so good at your job."

I hold back a laugh as the makeup and hair women both look at us funny. With one last look at Birdie, I make my exit.

Twenty-Three

Birdie

THE RADIO HOST, GABE, is droning on about his favorite 60s bands to his listeners. He's an okay guy, and he's interviewed me several times, but he always checks out my tits and asks me to the club after my shows in Atlanta.

I said yes once—and unfortunately, we had sex. Which means that every time I come here, he thinks he has a chance.

My eyes search for Liam. He's watching from a nearby sound booth. When he came to get me at my door earlier wearing his typical white button down, skinny tie, and navy slacks, I almost jumped his bones. If Shea hadn't been there, I would have.

My eyes follow the lines of his gelled hair. I've never seen it styled this way, and it makes me wonder what he looks like in the shower with water running in between his hard muscles and over the angled planes of his face. I only saw him shirtless for the first time last night, but I'm dying to find out what below the belt looks and feels like.

Reflexively I squeeze my thighs together, glad that my lower half is covered by the table in front of me. I wouldn't want Gabe to think I'm turned on by him. He's not a bad looking guy, with his salt and pepper hair and well-trimmed beard, but in the sack he lacked. Not to mention I don't want him flirting more than he already is. Especially in front of Liam.

Liam's chocolate brown eyes catch me staring at him and a discrete grin sneaks onto his lips. Despite what went on between us last night, and this morning, he's still all business. The moment we walked out of my hotel suite earlier, he changed his demeanor completely. He was also kind of rude to Shea, which surprised me. Usually everyone likes Shea.

"Well Birdie, shall we take a few calls from the listeners to wrap up?" Gabe's question returns me to the present.

I flick my gaze back to Gabe, his blue eyes flirty. I put on a fake smile. "Sounds good! Let em' rip."

"Right on! First call is from Damien. Damien, what would you like to ask the one and only Birdie Wilder?"

There's silence on the other end.

"No need to be shy," I encourage the caller. This wouldn't be the first time someone got scared when they called to talk to me.

"Anyone there?" Gabe asks.

My eyes catch Liam's. He's watching with concern as he puts on a pair of headphones so he can hear better.

"Damien?"

"Birdie Wilder."

I jump at the sound of his now familiar voice. Immediately my gut churns. It's the man from last night. I just know it is. I heard that voice echo in my head for hours before Liam helped me think of *other things*.

"What do you want," is all I say. It's not even a question. I glance back to Liam; his expression is asking what he already knows.

There's silence. Then the man answers, "You."

I don't even take a breath. "You can't have me."

"Well." Gabe interjects, cutting off the call. "That's all the callers we're going to take for the evening. Birdie, it's been a pleasure. And remember, tonight's show is all sold out, but you can still win a pair of tickets after the break. While you wait, enjoy Birdie Wilder's newest single, *Time Again*." Gabe hits play and then the on-air signal turns off. I throw down the headphones and abruptly stand.

The little box we're in feels suffocating, and I need air. Everyone is staring at me. I know what they're thinking, *poor weak girl*. I'm not weak, and this stalker is really starting to piss me off. Last night was bad enough, but how the hell did he manage to get on air. Who is this guy? He's got to be hella smart or have connections in the industry.

I hear Gabe calling my name, but I don't respond. Instead, I make a swift exit. When I hear footsteps following me down the hall and my name being called, I don't stop.

I push the emergency exit open, glad an alarm doesn't go off. And then I start running.

I'm not a runner but fuck this feels good. The Atlanta air is hot, and it burns my lungs, making me feel free. Thankfully the station is out in the suburbs, and we're in some type of corporate strip, so I don't have to worry about paparazzi. I know it's stupid that I bolted, but I was going to cry in front of all those people. Or maybe even scream. I'd rather run away and have them make fun of me later.

I start to feel my breath come up short, so I turn around a corner of a building and move into an alley that houses trash. It kind of smells, but there aren't any people around, and I'm blocked from view. I take a deep breath, the burning of my lungs fueling me. I hear footsteps and before long they stop in front of me. I don't have to look up to know who it is. It's his job, and he's my... Well, I don't know what he is.

"Jesus, Birdie. What the hell?!" Liam puts his hands on his knees to catch his breath.

I wipe sweat from my forehead then lock eyes with him. "I couldn't stay there. I—" my voice breaks.

Liam walks over to me and grabs my chin like he did so many times last night. He searches my face, then cracks a small smile. "You can run very fast, Birdie. You gave me a run for my money."

I snicker. "You think I'm out of shape, Miller?"

He shakes his head. "I've seen you on that stage. I know you have great lung capacity. I just didn't expect you to have such a stellar sprint."

I shrug. "Long legs."

He barks out a laugh then leans his damp forehead against mine. "You can't run off like that. What if that creep was waiting for you outside?"

I swallow. "I thought of that, but my panic won out. Sorry." Liam stares at me for a moment. I'm not sure what he's thinking, but then he does the last thing I expect. He kisses me.

As I'm quickly learning, Liam's kisses are like a drug. The way I feel when his lips touch mine is very close to the high I get from singing on stage in front of thousands of people every night. He makes my heart race and my palms sweat.

When he finally pulls away, he brings his kisses to my neck, groping my breast and then down to my hips and ass. I press my hips into his and let out a breathy moan. "Liam..."

"You make me insane, Birdie." His voice is hot and breathy.

"Did chasing me turn you on?" He chuckles against my skin before he touches his lips to the shell of my ear. His warm breath makes me shiver.

"I'll definitely be punishing you for running out like that later." He kisses my ear and tugs on my earlobe.

Later. I want to groan. Not having sex last night was hard enough, I don't know how much longer I can wait.

He eases away from me then scrunches up his nose "We're right by the trash."

"We are."

We both laugh together before Liam grabs my hand. His tone turns serious. "Are you okay? You really worried me back there."

I squeeze his hand. "I haven't had a panic attack like this since my first sold out show. But I'll be okay."

It looks like he wants to know more, but he doesn't ask. "Are you sure?"

"Positive."

He tugs me to him and kisses me one more time. "Let's get back before Eric sends out a search party."

I grin. "Probably a good idea."

Liam drops his hand from mine, and I immediately miss his touch. But he stays close to me, scanning the area to see if anyone's around. When he's satisfied it's safe, he leads me back to the station.

I turn my eyes up toward him as we walk, the sun hitting his face at just the right angle. He's so stupidly handsome. If he weren't in bodyguard mode and people weren't nearby, I would probably give in to my desire to pinch his sculpted butt, that looks sinfully good in slacks. But I didn't want Eric to know Liam and I had a thing happening, whatever this thing is. At least not yet. I have to know what's exactly going on between us first.

When we approach the studio doors, Eric is waiting to usher us inside. Shea and Gia are there as well, they had just been in another room listening. Unfortunately for me, Gabe is waiting there too.

When he sees me, he abruptly grabs me out from under Liam's arm and hugs me. I stiffen against him.

"Birdie! I'm so sorry that happened. I have no idea how! We had at least a hundred or more people who called in. The fact he got on... it's, I don't know."

I pull back from Gabe and Liam steps right up beside me. I don't have to look at him to know he didn't like the fact that Gabe just grabbed me without my consent. I hear him crack his knuckles beside me and almost smile from the dramedy of it. Gabe glances at Liam, and he immediately leans back in fear.

"Can I speak with you and your switch operators for second, *Gabe*," Liam interjects, his tone condescending.

Gabe's face turns sour. "Uh yeah, sure."

"Are you good here, Ms. Wilder?" Liam checks in with me. I fight my lips turning up at his, *Ms. Wilder*.

"Yeah, I'm good."

"We got her covered," Eric chimes in before putting his palm on my shoulder. I can tell by his jittery hand that this event has him shaken up again.

Once Liam and Gabe are out of sight, Eric leads us to a private lounge area for talent. Gia, Eric, and Shea all sit around me, much like they did last night. Their eyes turn to me and wait for me to say something about what just happened back there.

"I just needed a moment," I finally say.

"You ran like a bat out of hell, Birdie. You've never done that before," Gia worries.

"I'll make a therapy appointment if that will make you guys happy. But I'm really fine."

"I think therapy is a good idea," Eric nods. "I don't like this, Birdie. I don't like any of it."

"And you think I do?" I raise my voice. "Let's just go to soundcheck."

"We can cancel the show tonight, Birdie."

I stand up. "No! We will absolutely not cancel the show tonight. It's sold out."

Eric stands with me and puts up his hands in a calming motion. "Okay, okay! Calm down. You aren't going to go spiriting out of here again, are you?"

I huff. "No, I won't. But I can't make any promises against hitting you."

He shakes his head. "You're crazy, Birdie. Dedicated, smart, wonderful, talented, insane."

"I never claimed to be sane," I wink.

Shea looks up from her phone. "We should get going. Sound check is in thirty."

I take a few deep breaths. "Let's hit the road."

Twenty-Four

Liam

GABE FROM THE RADIO station is here. He's watching Birdie on stage like she's a piece of meat. He was doing that all afternoon, too. Then, when he grabbed her, I almost kneed him in the balls.

I do have to admit he was helpful in getting me a recording of the stalker. It irked me to no end this guy was able to get on air and the fact he called himself Damien. Really original... not. No way that's his real name.

I grind my teeth. Today's display confirmed what I had already been starting to think—someone on tour is involved. There's no other way *Damien* would be able to get close to Birdie and know her schedule in this way. That led me back to Shea.

Her comments this morning, her taking a liking to me... But most of all, the fact that she has access to Birdie's schedule and all her personal and private information. No, I didn't like that at all.

Unfortunately, my morning search had come up squeaky clean, yet again. Shea Crane, age 22, from Los Angeles, California. Went to Pepperdine University and studied communications. She has nothing on her record, not even a parking or speeding ticket. Her family is average and has nothing to note either. All I'm going off is a hunch and intuition from my years of being a cop. Nothing more.

"She's amazing!" Gabe yells over Birdie's voice rocking out. I turn my head to him, my mouth in a hard line.

"She is."

"You know," he smirks, "We were together once!"

My muscles tense. Birdie and this guy? No fucking way. My girl had to have more taste than that. *My girl.* Is she though? *Shit.*

I get a bitter taste in my mouth. I may not know what Birdie and I are to each other yet, but I do know that I don't want to know about her and Gabe. The dude is a social climber. I can smell his desperation a mile away.

Instead of giving in to Gabe's bait, or whatever the hell he's trying to do by telling me that information, I turn my focus back to Birdie. She's singing an Aerosmith cover, and someone just threw their bra on stage. Such a bizarre thing to watch.

Birdie picks it up and acts like she's going to put it on, but it's meant for someone with small boobs. She shakes her head and mouths, *it doesn't fit*, before throwing it back into the audience. I smile. I know why she refuses to cancel the tour, she's at home on the stage. A whole other side of her comes out—it's brilliant to watch.

When we were "fighting" I'd skip her show because I couldn't stand to watch her while we were at odds. But tonight, everything is different.

When I woke up this morning with her in my arms, it's as if I saw clearly for the first time. Then today, watching from the control room, helpless, seeing the way she panicked when the stalker called in, every instinct in me flared. Before I wanted to protect her, now there's no other option. The thought of even a hair on her head being harmed makes my blood boil. I'd only just found her again, if anything happened—

No. I can't let myself think like that.

Flashes of Maria and the day of the accident march through my mind. The loud sound of Jane doing a drum solo is the only thing that pulls me out of it. I flinch. Usually my PTSD is just memories, but the sound of the banging drums is starting to bother me. I look at my watch, the show is almost over. I can grin and bear it.

After a minute the song finishes, and Birdie addresses the audience. She has them in the palm of her hand. It's amazing how she can get that many people to listen to her at the drop of a hat. Then, for just a second, her eyes dart to mine and she winks. She has me hook, line, and sinker. *Double fuck.*

"Atlanta!" she yells. "Do you want to hear a little story?"

"YES!" they collectively yell back and cheer wildly.

"Okay! Okay! Everyone calm down," she laughs. "Well, you all know my little song "Desire Reigns," right?" The audience goes nuts. "As most of you know, that song is about an unrequited love. And recently I had the chance to reunite with him." A collective round of awws and cheers erupt through the stadium. My pulse skyrockets and my palms sweat, but I can't take my eyes off her.

She continues, "Though I'm not sure where it all will lead, my message to you is this, you never know where your life will lead. Open your heart. Open your mind. Be willing to listen and forgive. If you close yourself off forever, you may miss out on something wonderful."

Birdie glances at me again just before her band strikes the first chord of the song. She winks again and my pulse spikes for a totally different reason. A feeling of adoration wraps around me as I listen to her sing.

"This is going to be all over the news," Shea says to my left. When I look at her, there's a smug smile on her lips. Just like the one from earlier this morning. "You're the unrequited love, aren't you?"

"I'll let Birdie tell her story. It's not my place." I move my attention away from Shea, my eyes back on the blonde in question. She's swaying back and forth—I can't help but smile at the image. Today she's wearing a knee length snakeskin skirt that's deliciously form fitting with a short pink T-shirt she's knotted at the side. Of course, she's barefoot, as usual.

"Be careful. If you break her heart, it will end the tour," Shea clips.

I can feel her eyes burning into me. She wants me to admit I'd never break Birdie's heart. Thus confirming what she already knows. "Birdie would never cancel the tour," is all I say.

She lets out a tight breath then turns on her heel to leave. As she walks away, I swear I hear her say, "We'll see about that."

Birdie is talking with a reporter from some music magazine. I'm standing close to her, the amount of people in this room is making me nervous. We should have canceled the meet-and-greets, but Birdie would hear none of it.

"On stage tonight you mentioned you recently reunited with the person you wrote *Desire Reigns* about. Care to divulge who he is?" The reporter asks.

I try to keep my face neutral, but my shoulders pull back a bit. Birdie doesn't even bat an eye at the question. I'm sure she's been asked worse than that before. She takes every question in stride like a pro.

"He's an old friend. That's all you need to know," she smiles.

"As always Birdie, you keep your life close to your chest."

She laughs sweetly. "It's my private life. Emphasis on private."

"Well, thank you for your time, Birdie. See you next time you're in Atlanta."

"Thanks, Trixie."

Trixie walks away and Gia tells Birdie she's done with interviews and meet-and-greets tonight. She then addresses me, "You can take her back to wherever she needs to go. Just let the extra security we hired know when you're transporting."

"Copy that," I nod.

"See you tomorrow, B. Today was... well, I'm beat." Gia sighs.

Birdie hugs her tight. "Sleep well. Thanks for everything, Gia."

Once Gia's gone, I turn to Birdie, my face still neutral. "Where to, Ms. Wilder?"

She raises one of her eyebrows at me. "Hotel?"

The crotch of my pants gets a little tighter at the way she says "hotel."

"Of course, Ms. Wilder."

"Thank you, Mr. Miller," she grins.

"Birdie!" I see her go tense at the sound of Gabe's voice. This guy is really starting to be my least favorite person. She puts on the fakest smile I've ever seen her wear and greets the radio host.

"Hey Gabe, thanks for coming to the show," she says, her tone purely friendly.

"I was telling your bodyguard here that you were simply amazing. I've never seen you hit it so hard!"

She puts her hand in a prayer form. "Thanks, I appreciate it."

Gabe glances at me then puffs out his chest. Dude is just shy of Birdie's height and half my size. I could breathe on him wrong and he'd fall over. He shies away from my gaze and focuses on Birdie. This man must have a death wish.

Gabe clears his throat. "I've got VIP tickets to Cobra tonight. I was thinking you would like to come with me. Let loose after today." He winks at her. Fucking winks. I almost step in but I know that Birdie's fully capable of telling him to sluff off.

"Sorry Gabe, with everything that's happening it wouldn't be appropriate."

"Isn't that why you have a bodyguard?"

She rubs the back of her neck awkwardly. "Sorry Gabe, maybe another time."

Disappointment covers his features. "Alright then. I'll see you around." Then, without warning, the bastard leans in to kiss her. Just in the nick of time, Birdie turns her face so he hits her cheek.

My blood boils. If I was a better man, I wouldn't have done anything. But I'm not, so I lean forward and grab him by the back of his neck, pushing him to the side. It's a light shove, but enough that he gets the message.

"Woah, dude! What the hell was that for?" Gabe cries, his hand going to rub the back of his neck. He acts like I sucker punched him.

Pushing my shoulders back, I take a step toward him. "You need to learn to treat women with respect. She didn't give consent for you to kiss her, and if I remember correctly, she politely declined your invitation tonight. Your behavior is uncalled for. I thought you needed a little reminder of that."

I feel Birdie's hand on my arm then she gives it a squeeze. "It's fine, Liam."

I shake my head vehemently. "It's not fine."

"Liam," she pleads. Her eyes dart around, and it's then I realize she's embarrassed because there are still some crew mulling around and a few of her band members.

I move my fists to my side but keep my eyes on him as I stand down. Gabe looks like he's about to shit himself, for that I'm proud. He glances at Birdie again, "I'm sorry, Birdie. I didn't mean—"

"Goodnight, Gabe." She cuts him off, then turns to me. "I'm ready to go Mr. Miller."

She sounds pissed; but even if she is, I'm not going to apologize for defending her from a creep. I place my hand on Birdie's lower back and start to lead her away toward the back door. I quickly take my walkie out and alert the security team we're on our way. Birdie is tight against my hand, and she hasn't said a word to me in the few minutes we've been walking. I'm unsure of what to say, so I decide to let her lead the conversation when she's ready.

Once we're at the back of the stadium, we meet a bunch of fans waiting there. Thankfully, we've got extra security detail keeping them at bay. She puts on a smile and waves at them, apologizing for not being able to stop and sign autographs.

Before long we're in the car with our driver and making our way back to the hotel. I've never been more grateful that we have a night in Atlanta instead of getting straight on the tour bus. Birdie and I have to talk about not only what just happened with Gabe, but everything. I'm chomping at the bit to get her alone. We may have kissed near some trash earlier, but it wasn't enough. I'm not sure that anything would be enough when it comes to Birdie.

As the car moves onto the street, I stare at her and hope she'll look at me—but she doesn't. "Birdie—"

She closes her eyes then she holds up her hand. "Just let me think."

For a millisecond I think about obeying, but I don't. "While you're thinking, just know that this is who I am. I'm going to be protective and probably do things that piss you off, but I care about you. I don't take kindly to people who think they can do whatever the fuck they want with no consequences. Especially men who used to fuck you."

That does it. Her eyes snap to mine and she narrows them. "I can't believe you just said that."

I can't either, but I'm not going to let her know that. She's pissing me off with her reaction. "I said it, and I'm not taking it back."

"Why are you even jealous?"

Heat flairs in my chest. "I can't believe you just said that. Are you attempting to make me angry?

"I'm not having this conversation with you."

"What? The past relationship conversation?"

"Exactly. Gabe is a mistake from the past. Did he go over the line tonight? Yes. But it's not that big of a deal."

I feel my face getting red. "It is a big deal. And you're my—" Shit. I'm not even sure what she is. My tongue gets lodged in the back of my throat.

Her cheeks turn pink, and her breath becomes shorter. After a few moments of silence, she licks her lips. "Your what, Liam?"

My mouth goes dry. Do I say what I really want her to be? What I *think* I want her to be? If I'm being honest with myself, I've known what I want even before we became physical last night. But I think it's too soon—I don't want to scare her away.

"Birdie...I—"

"You what?" she clips.

Nervously, I run my hands through my hair. Her tone makes me think she's not ready. "Can I be straight with you?"

"No, lie to me," she rolls her eyes.

I smirk at that. That would be her answer right now, especially when I'm trying to be serious. I sigh. "I don't know what to call you yet." And in some ways, that's true. I think I do, but my rational side says it's crazy to want so much so quickly. "Do you know what to call us?"

For a moment she blinks at me, a little shocked that I threw the question back at her. Then she sinks back into her seat, slightly defeated. "I suppose I don't, no."

I unbuckle my seatbelt so I can move next to her. Once I'm situated, I take her hands and hold them in mine. "Look at me Birdie." To my surprise she does. "I sure as shit don't know what to call us. But I think that's okay. We'll figure it out together, alright? We just started this thing between us."

Her coal-colored eyelids flutter open, her beautiful hazel depths burn into me. "Alright," she agrees. "Together."

I lean forward and kiss her gently, then pull back after a few seconds. When our foreheads rest together, I cup her cheek and run my thumb along her cheek bone. Her eyes close and she leans into my warm touch with a sigh.

"Just promise me something," she asks, her eyes opening.

"What is it?"

"Don't go around beating up radio hosts that I have a past with, okay? For one, I don't want to end up in the news, and two...well..."

I chuckle at that. "Let me guess, there's more than one radio host?"

She lets out a groan. "When you say it like that, I sound—"

I cut her off with a kiss. "Your past isn't my business, and honestly, I'm proud of you. You're enjoying your life and owning your pleasure. There's nothing wrong with that. And I potentially overreacted just a little, but Gabe was out of line, and you know it. You're just too stubborn to admit it."

A puff of air hits my cheek from the breath she'd been holding in. "Okay fine. You may be right there."

I release a smug grin, "I know I am."

Birdie swats my arm gently. I grab the hand before she can take it away from my chest and pull her in close again. She lets out a surprised sound just as our mouths meet, but she quickly melts into my kiss. I put everything I have into it, all the feelings from the last twenty-four hours and all the jealousy toward Gabe. When I'm finally through with her, our lips are swollen and we're both gasping for air.

Birdie holds her hand over her chest, then opens her eyes to gaze into mine. "Stay with me tonight," she says. It's not a question and I know what she's asking.

"Are you sure?"

She trails a hand down my stomach, then places her palm on my growing erection. "I've never been surer about anything in my life."

"Shouldn't we go on a date first?" I laugh, only half serious. Even though we have never been on a real date, Birdie and my relationship went beyond dating. In a way, we'd been on a lot of dates, just not a romantic date. Unless the spa counts, which I'm positive it doesn't.

Birdie squeezes my cock and I suck in a breath. Shit. This woman means business.

"Screw the date, Liam. I only want you."

Damn. I must have created Birdie in a dream because she's one hundred percent a dream woman. Not only is she beautiful, but she's crass, bold, and takes what she wants. Exactly what I want in my life. Exactly what I need.

I've spent the last two years since my accident hiding away, trying to get better and rehabbing my shoulder and fucked-up mind. Once I'd been someone who took what I wanted, but in the last few years, I'd become scared. Hell, the only reason I took this gig with Birdie is because Ben and Wren practically forced me to. Then last night Birdie had wanted to have sex, but I'd denied her.

But with her looking at me the way she is now and her hand on my dick—I think it's about time I let myself give in and take what I want. And I want her.

I want to feel her come around my cock and milk me for everything I have. I want to feel her lips around me and watch as she swallows every drop. God, there are so many dirty things that I could dream up for Birdie and me to try, and I can't wait to do every single one of them. And by the way Birdie is rubbing her thighs together, I have a feeling she's thinking the same thing.

As we pull up to the hotel, it takes everything in me not to grab her and drag her into the nearest dark corner. And if Birdie was normal, and she didn't have a creep after her, I would do just that. But it's not safe.

I take her hand and remove it from my hard-on, then press a kiss to her palm, sucking lightly. A little promise of what's to come. "I'm going to check the perimeter; security will be standing right outside while I do. You'll be safe here." She nods as she licks her lips. This woman... *everything* she does is sexy.

I pull away, but right before I open the door, Birdie pinches my ass. I turn my head back toward her, "Really?"

"Just a little payback for your show back there."

I chuckle. "Oh Birdie, you're going to pay for that later."

"I'm looking forward to it," she grins.

Twenty-Five

Birdie

I HAVE NO IDEA what the hell happened, but I went from being one hundred percent livid to one thousand percent turned on in under five minutes.

When Liam grabbed Gabe by the neck after he tried to kiss me, I was both embarrassed and yet secretly turned on. I internally roll my eyes at myself. I need to get it together and keep my emotions in check.

Now the word, *together*, repeats in my mind as I run my hand down Liam's chest. Surprisingly we made it to my hotel room with nobody bothering us. Which I'm *very* glad about. I'm so turned on right now that I may combust if I don't have him inside of me soon. But as he groans from my touch, I can see in his chocolate eyes that there's no turning back now. Liam is going to have sex with me tonight.

He puts a hand on my lower back, pulling me closer. It's heavy and warm. I feel his strong fingers dig into the skin there slightly more than usual. His gaze moves up and down my body, and my eyes zero in on the crotch of his pants. I can see the outline of his erection and heat pools low in my belly.

"Have I told you how much I like this outfit?" he breathes against my cheek, fingers delicately touching the waistband of my worn fake snakeskin skirt and pink T-shirt that I've knotted at the side like a crop top.

"No, you haven't."

He kisses my nose, then the corner of my mouth. "It's fucking hot."

"I'm glad you approve of my wardrobe choices."

Warm breath hits my neck as he goes to suck just below my ear. "I always do. Though I'd love to see your birthday suit again, that's what I'm really interested in. Especially this part." He reaches one hand down to trace the juncture between my legs then presses the heel of his hand into the sensitive skin there. My head drops to his shoulder, and I bite my lip.

"Liam," his name falls gently from my lips.

"Yes, Birdie girl?" He kisses my lips now, just small little kisses, his hands cupping the back of my head. When he begins to massage the base of my scalp, a soft moan leaves my lips.

"You're good with your hands." I press my head back into the pressure and put my own hands on his waist so I can bring our bodies closer together.

"I'm good with a lot of things," he says, his voice low.

I turn my eyes to his, searching them for answers neither of us have right now. "I'm sure you are."

Liam removes one hand from my scalp and drags it down my breasts, then to the soft flesh of my stomach. I shiver in anticipation, but just as he reaches the band of my skirt, I grab his hand.

A flash of concern moves over his features. "Everything good?"

I swallow thickly, "Everything's great. It's just... I played a show tonight. If I don't at least freshen up, you're going to regret it."

Liam licks his lips. "And if I like it dirty?"

I laugh. "Wow. Didn't know you preferred sweaty rocker chicks."

He presses his groin into mine, letting me feel the length of his cock against me. "Just ones named Birdie Wilder."

"Well, I'm going to at least freshen up. Or..."

"Or what?" he cocks an eyebrow.

"I never said I had to shower alone."

He taps my nose. "I could use a shower."

I lean down and sniff his armpit. It doesn't smell bad, but I pretend it does. "I'll say."

A barking laugh leaves his mouth. "Did you really just smell my armpit?"

"You saw me do it."

He closes the distance between our mouths and kisses me silly. The kind of kiss that romance novelists write about. The kind of kiss that little girls dream of while they watch Disney movies. I want to be kissed like this every day for the rest of my life. My stomach twists a little at the thought.

I haven't thought too much about our future—at least not since my teenage fantasies. We just started seeing each other in this way last night, and I've never been one to want commitment. I was like Mom in that way, free love and all. But could I put that aside for Liam? I don't know. Would I even be any good at being a girlfriend? I'd never really had to be one before. At least not for more than a few months.

Liam pulls back, resting his forehead against mine. "What are you thinking about?"

"It's nothing," I assure him.

"Birdie—"

"Really Liam, I'm fine. Just kiss me like that again and we'll go back to real life tomorrow. Okay?" My voice is solid, thankfully no pleading or emotion colors it. I know what I want, and tonight, since Liam is offering, I'm going to take it.

"If you're sure..."

"I'm sure."

He brushes his knuckles along my chin then down the crown of my head before he tucks a strand of hair behind my ear. There is a reverence in the way he stares at me, as if he's memorizing every inch and line of my face. My gut clenches and my body temperature skyrockets.

Liam's lips tip up, and he half-grins; brown eyes burning with desire. "Let's hit the showers, Birdie girl."

Color blooms on my neck as he takes my hand and leads me to the large bathroom. The shower itself is a masterpiece in its own right. Liam opens the glass door and turns on the massive rainforest shower head and sets the pressure to his liking. His other hand is still holding on to mine, as if he doesn't want to break the connection. After a few moments, once he's deemed it a perfect temperature, he closes the door and turns his attention back on to me.

I swallow when his eyes meet mine. They're set in a determined stare and sparkle with something wild. He lets his gaze roam down my body before he sets his sights on my heaving chest. Licking his lips, he takes a step forward, brushing his palms down my sides before landing on the hem of my shirt. "May I?" he asks.

An emotion I'm not used to springs up inside me. His care for me, his desire to make sure I feel safe... Sometimes I really feel how much not having a completely present mom and absent dad screwed me up. I'm not like Wren or Ben, and neither is Liam. Our parents didn't tuck us in every night or take us to our doctor appointments or come to our concerts and sports games. We both missed out on so many tender moments.

"Birdie," his voice cuts through again. "Are you—"

I take control and kiss Liam with everything I have. In that kiss I pour the emotion of the last three weeks, the pain and fear, but also the excitement and happiness. I love what I do and now that we've cleared the air, it's like my sweet summer boy is back. Like we're sixteen again and we can make up for lost time.

Once I finish the kiss, his fingers find my shirt again, but he stops before he pulls it off. I smile against his lips. "You can do whatever you want to me, Liam. I want this."

He's breathing harshly, and his lips are swollen from my kiss. In his eyes I can see he felt what I felt in that kiss. With one more short peck, he tugs my shirt and starts to pull it upwards. I lift my arms and he quickly yanks it off. Before I can blink, he's already unzipping my skirt and sliding it down my hips. I step out of that too, and when he rises, I'm left standing in my bra and underwear.

Today I'd chosen a cute little pink set I had buried in the bottom of my travel bag for moments like this. By the look on Liam's face, he's sure as hell excited that I chose this lacy number.

"Fuck, Birdie. Looking like that, I sure as hell wouldn't be able to deny you even if I wanted to."

I smirk. "It's a good thing you don't want too then."

He soaks me in for a moment longer, and just as I'm about to turn as red as an apple, he starts to remove his clothes. First comes his tie, then his button-down shirt, and when his fingers go to his belt, I stop him with my hands over his.

"May I?" I echo his last question.

"Whatever you want," he says, removing his hands from under mine. I give him a teasing smirk as I start to undo the buckle. His eyes flash down to the tops of my breasts as they shift from my movements.

"I like the color pink on you."

"Really?"

He brings one of his hands to my cheek, "You're beautiful."

I flush harder but push down his kind words. I've been called beautiful many times, but never by someone I've cared for like I care for Liam. Instead of using words to say my thanks, I finish opening his belt, then push down his slacks. Once he's stepped out of them, I'm left with the beautiful sight of his hard cock beneath his tight navy briefs.

God he's huge.

I've been imagining what it looks like in the flesh for several weeks now, and as I gaze at the outline hiding beneath the thin fabric, I have a feeling it's a wonderful sight to see. Just as the rest of him is. When I meet his eyes, they're dark pools of brown.

"Take them off for me Birdie," he says huskily, his voice a gentle command.

I glide my hands to his hips, running my fingers over the tight waistband. He shivers under my touch, which is a feat since the heat from the shower is beginning to steam up the room. I smile at him; glad I make him feel the same way he does me.

When I push the fabric down over his narrow hips, the V leading to his groin is revealed and my breath hitches, inspiring me to reveal his toned ass and length a little quicker. When I'm finally met with every glorious inch of him, a sound of awe leaves my lips. My eyes focus on the crown of his erection—it's slightly wet and looks deliciously smooth. I gently run my thumb over it, and Liam lets out a hiss. I grin to myself and pull back just slightly so I can take in his entire body.

Liam naked is... *holy gods*. I don't think there are words to describe the way he looks. His cock is proud, thick, long, and his body is toned and muscular in all the right places. He's obviously worked hard to look like this, and I want to explore every inch of the masterpiece that is him.

"Birdie," his voice is so low that it sends shivers up my spine.

My eyes stop their perusal. "Yes?"

"You next."

Liam's right hand comes up to my shoulder and he pulls down one of my bra straps, stroking my skin lightly as he goes. He does the same with the other, then reaches behind me to unsnap the clasp expertly. In a split second my breasts fall free, causing him to suck in a breath.

Before I can say anything, he's tugging at the lacy pink underwear and leaning over to help me step out of them.

The steam from the shower is fogging up the glass around us. It's almost as if we're wrapped in a warm cocoon. Liam takes my hand then gives my knuckles a kiss before opening the shower door. He leads me inside and gently guides me under the heated spray. It almost feels too hot against my skin, but it also feels good on my sore muscles.

Once Liam is inside the shower, he secures the door then joins me under the spray. He captures my lips in a fast kiss, pressing our slick bodies together. I let out a soft sound as his hot erection prods into my stomach.

"Liam," I breathe out, reaching for him. "I don't want to wait any longer."

He pulls away from me for a moment as one of his hands squeezes my breast and the other grips the wet skin of my hip. "Let me take care of you first."

"You did that last night."

He chuckles. "That's not what I meant; though I do plan on tasting you again."

My skin feels like it's on fire. "Oh?"

He turns around, giving me a wonderful view of his muscular ass, then pumps some shampoo in his hands. He positions us away from the water, turning me away so my back is to him. When he begins to massage the shampoo through my long hair, a loud and embarrassing moan leaves my lips.

"Feel good?" he asks against my ear, his blunt nails scratching down my scalp.

"Yes. Amazing."

He spends longer than he needs to washing my hair before he tells me to rinse. While I'm doing that, he lathers body wash in a washcloth and starts to rub it down my arms, then my chest. He pays special attention to my breasts before he moves down my legs.

Before I can protest, he kneels in front of me, right there on the hard shower tile. I suck in a breath as he runs his tongue along the seam of opening.

"God you're so wet."

The vibrations from his words have me wanting to squeeze my thighs together and I have to rest my hands on his slippery shoulders so I don't fall over.

He uses his thumbs to spread me open and brings his bowed lips to suck on my clit. I let out a choked noise as his hands gently scratch my thighs and he does something wonderful with his tongue.

I feel myself getting closer to sweet release and use my hands to grip Liam's wet hair. He must've had a lot of practice because this man is doing A++ work down there.

When he takes the hand from my thigh and gently spreads my legs wider, I know what's coming next. He plunges two fingers inside, stroking just the right spot. I don't think anyone I've ever been with has been able to find my g-spot that quickly. Damn he's good.

My knees begin to weaken as my orgasm nears. Liam notices, so he pushes me against the wall, letting me hold on to him while he supports me from the front. His fingers start to move faster once I'm secure, and he goes back to sucking on my clit with just the right amount of pressure.

"Shit. Liam. Fuck—I'm going to come."

He looks up at me, his forehead wet with sweat and water, his eyes proud and happy. "Then come for me, Birdie baby."

He flicks his wrist just right and that does it.

I come around his fingers, praying that the sounds of the shower drown out my loud cry of pleasure. Liam continues to hold me up as the shockwaves from my orgasm roll through me.

After what seems like hours of floating through the clouds, Liam presses open mouthed kisses up my thighs. It brings me back to earth. When he stands and meets my lips in a kiss, I want to cry in pleasure. My body feels like jelly, but all I can think about is having every inch of his beautiful length inside me as soon as possible.

"Soon," Liam whispers against my mouth, as if he read my mind.

I drag my fingers down his chest, the pads of my fingers catching rivulets of water as I go. When I reach his hard cock, I gently wrap my hand around him. Liam closes his eyes and groans.

"You're so hard for me..." I whisper.

His eyes flutter open and he grasps my chin between his thumb and pointer finger. "I like it when you talk dirty to me."

With a demure smile, I start to pump him up and down. His head falls forward and his breath leaves him.

"I want to put my mouth on you," I tell him then, pumping a little faster. He feels silky and heavy in my hand; I want to know what he tastes like. What it feels like to have him bending to my will as I suck and lick him to oblivion.

After a few more strokes, Liam puts his hands on mine. My stomach drops and my eyes narrow. "Don't try to tell me to stop. I don't want to stop."

Liam shakes his head. "No, it's not like that. I hate to sound clique, but I really want to fuck you. But if you keep doing that, I'm not even going to last one second with your mouth or pussy around me..." I swallow hard. "And Birdie," he breathes hotly against the shell of my ear, "Tonight I want to fuck you till your voice is hoarse and you need another shower."

My toes curl against the tile floor. His words aren't a threat, they're a promise.

I gaze up at him through my damp hair. "Then what are we still doing in here?"

Twenty-Six

Liam

I push Birdie back on the hotel bed. The look of her spread out, her pink skin flushed and damp, her wet blonde hair spread around her... it's an amazing sight to see.

The huge bed and plush white sheets make her look delicate. I smile at the fact that her blonde hair looks dark, almost brown when it's damp. It reminds me of teenage Birdie—of the girl that I adored so many years ago.

Only a few days ago, I would've never thought something like this was possible between us. Now I'm beginning to think anything is possible.

Spending time with her, watching her come undone in the shower, tasting her come on my lips... feeling her soft hand wrap around my dick... I'm starting to think being with Birdie is my new favorite thing in the world.

Her hooded eyes meet mine. I let my gaze travel down her plush body, her pink pussy glistening with arousal and her dark nipples pert and pretty, just begging for me to suck on them. *Fuck*. My thoughts are erratic around this woman, and most of them are dirty.

Birdie smiles at me through her dark lashes, her neck turning slightly blotchy from my attention.

"What are you waiting for?" she asks then, her voice sweet.

"I want to memorize this moment."

"Memorize later," she demands, and my dick twitches.

I salute her playfully and she bites her lower lip. As I approach her splayed out body, I notice how she appraises my form in the same way

I do with her. It makes me happy that she likes what she sees. I can't wait to sink myself deep into her wetness and feel our bodies move together.

I gently lay down so we're skin to skin. Her nipples are so hard against my chest that they make the hair on my arms stand on end. I take my hands and tangle them in her wet hair before kissing her hard. As our tongues duel, Birdie hitches one of her thighs on my hip, her warm heat pressing into my groin. Using my free hand, I grip her round ass, remembering my teasing threats of punishment earlier.

So, just for some fun, I bring my hand up and gently slap her ass. Birdie gasps in shock against my mouth, her pretty eyes flooded with lust. I didn't miss the way she rubbed herself on me after I did that. Good to know.

"You just spanked me," she scoffs.

I nudge her nose with mine. "I told you earlier you'd pay for your little comments."

A little puff of air hits my cheek before I feel a gentle pinch on the inside of my arm. "Ouch!"

"An eye for an eye," she teases.

I gently push her off me then roll over so I can trap her arms over her head. When I lower my lips over hers, I kiss her till we're both gasping for air. She rocks her pussy into me and moans as my dick hits her swollen clit at just the right angle.

"Liam," she begs. "I don't want to tease any longer."

I sip at her lips, tasting her like a fine wine. When she presses herself into me with a little more pressure, I finally force myself to get off the bed to grab a condom. The short time I'm gone, I can feel her burning gaze on my backside. When I turn back around, Birdie watches with rapt attention as I open the packet then slide the condom down my length.

I crawl back onto the bed so I'm hovering over her sweet body, then line myself up with her entrance. I hope I don't blow my load like it's my first time. I want to spend as long as I can inside this woman. I want our first time together to be incomparable. Better than Gabe, better than any other groupie or asshole she's slept with. I want to be the best she's ever had. I want her to never forget me.

"Liam," her voice caresses me. "Stop thinking so hard. I can hear you."

My gaze meets hers. She's smiling so wide I can see the dimple I love so much. "I just want this to be good for you," I admit.

An airy sigh escapes her lips. "It already is. Now hop to it, Mr. Miller, or I'll be forced to get my vibrator."

I bark out a laugh. "I'll remember that for another time." Before she can retort, or I can think anymore, I sink myself into her tight heat.

Fuck... If it were possible to see stars or fireworks behind my eyes, I swear it would have happened.

Birdie lets out a throaty moan as I stretch her, my mouth opening but no audible words or sounds come out. She's so tight, so wet, so hot—she feels like a warm hug on a cold night and my dick is practically weeping in delight.

"Shit, Birdie," my breath is shallow as my head falls to her rounded shoulder. "You feel so good, baby."

She brings her hands up my shoulders and digs her nails in before scratching them gently down my back. I shiver and sink completely into her, letting her perfect pussy pull me in deeper.

"You're so big," she breathes out, adjusting her hips to accommodate my size.

"Too much?" I ask, not wanting to hurt her.

"No, no," she almost laughs. "You feel perfect. I like it."

I kiss her lips gently as I start to move my hips back and forth in a torturously slow movement. It's taking everything in me not to just fuck her hard and fast, but I manage to stay diligent in my easy movements. I watch as Birdie's eyes close, her face blissful as she adjusts to my girth.

When she urges me to move faster with her hips, I pick up my rhythm. Her head presses back against the bed as she moves her hands from my back to my buttocks. In a quick movement, she pulls me even deeper into her.

If there is a heaven, I'm positive Birdie's pussy is it. I could live, eat, and die here as a happy man. Shit. I'm really screwed. How did I go from only one-night stands to a romantic fool in less than twenty-four hours? Fuck if I care. As long as I could have this woman lying beneath me.

"Fuck me harder, Liam," she pleads. "Shit, you feel so good."

I suck on her neck lightly before pressing my lips to her ear. "You feel good too, baby."

I thrust my hips faster and at just the right angle that the sounds of our skin meeting and the bed creaking echo in the room. Once I set a good pace, I support myself with one hand and bring my other to Birdie's clit. She jackknifes forward and lets out a beautiful sound. I thought I loved Birdie's singing, but this is even better. This song is just for me.

For fun, I turn my hips to a slightly different angle and thrust upward in long strokes. Birdie's mouth falls open and more sounds come out as I move my fingers with solid pressure against her clit in a circular motion.

As Birdie clenches her pussy around my dick, I let out a few curse words. "I'm going to come," I say against her lips, sucking the bottom one into my mouth and biting down gently.

"Me too," she cries, arching her back. "Go harder, please."

Not wanting the lady to be unhappy, I gain speed and thrust hard and fast in time with my motions on her clit. She wraps her legs around my back sucking me deeper in. Then, without warning, she squeezes her pussy around me hard and I lose myself in her. With a few more shallow thrusts and a squeeze of her breast we both shatter, her orgasm fluttering around my sensitive cock.

I clench my jaw before letting out a breath as my release floods the condom. I drop my head to her shoulder and suck there lightly as she lets out a happy sounding laugh. After my breath catches, I manage to roll to one side of her. She curls into me and rests her damp head on my shoulder.

The room is filled with the sounds of our ragged breathing and a blissful smile rests on my face. The endorphins of our coupling start to calm but I find I'm still happy. Normally after sex I'd clean up and head out. But with Birdie I want to stay by her side until my dick is ready for round two. Which won't be long considering I'm already half hard at the thought.

Birdie brings her hand to my chest and gently glides it down the sweaty skin. Now that I really worked up a good sweat, maybe I can convince her for another round up against the shower wall, but this time with her mouth around my cock. That's a fantasy I would love to see through.

Birdie's eyes find my hard-on and she lets out a playful groan. "Already?"

I smooth a tangled piece of hair behind her ear. "My dick likes you."

She arches an eyebrow. "Just your dick?"

I capture her lips in mine, telling her through my mouth and tongue how much every part of me likes her. When I pull back, I caress her heated cheeks. "You know the answer to that question."

She smirks while looking down at the full condom still on my dick and the mess that is sure to ensue if I don't get up soon.

"Shower?" She licks her lips. "I thought I could clean you up this time."

I rub my thumb over her swollen lips. "You read my mind."

She sits up, holding out her hand. "Come on, Mr. Miller. Let me take real good care of you now."

Twenty-Seven

Liam

I WAKE UP WARM, sleepy, and with a slight ache in my shoulder. I turn to find Birdie asleep next to me, her hair a bird's nest, and breasts on full display. We hadn't closed the blinds fully last night, so light is streaming in through the window. I glance at the clock and find it's just after eight in the morning.

Reaching my hand up, I trace my finger down the bridge of Birdie's nose. I like the way she scrunches her face up and wiggles her perfect nose at my touch. My shoulder twinges again and I can feel exhaustion in my bones, but that doesn't stop me from being the happiest motherfucker on the planet. We'd finally gone to sleep at four in the morning, both over-sexed and sweaty. We'd need a third shower this morning, but this time we'd have to take them alone, so we actually stay clean.

Birdie's eyes flutter open just as my dick reacts to my thoughts. I'm pretty sure that for the rest of this tour I'm going to have a constant hard-on.

"Good morning, Birdie girl."

She smiles softly before stretching her arms above her head. Her chest pushes forward while she does it. My mouth waters at the sight of her hardened nipples.

"You make me feel like a teenager again," I groan, pressing my morning wood against her side.

Her smile widens at the feel of me. "I could say the same."

I kiss her nose. "What time do you have to be up?" I run my palm down her side, tickling her sensitive skin.

She rubs the sleep from her eyes. "I think I have another interview at noon, but I've got my morning free."

I put my hand on her ass and gently dig my fingers into the soft flesh. "You're so sexy in the morning."

Laughter bubbles out of her and she gently pushes her hands on my chest. "Liar."

I pull her back to me, catching some of her long hair in my fingers. "I've been wanting to ask you why you stopped dying your hair."

"Odd question to ask so early in the morning," she quips, letting her fingers brush lightly over my hard length.

My muscles tighten. As much as I'd like to screw her brains out again, I'm trying to behave myself. Birdie makes it hard—in more ways than one.

I unleash one of my charming grins. "It's an honest question—and I remember you saying you felt like your hair was meant to be dark when we were kids. I want to know what made you go back to your natural color."

"Why Mr. Miller, I didn't realize you paid so much attention to my hair," she teases.

I tug on said hair lightly, pulling her close to my lips. "I pay attention to everything about you, Ms. Wilder. Now answer the question."

Her fingers play with a few of my chest hairs. "Women are constantly being told what to do. Especially in this industry. Some people even have contracts that say they can't modify their hair in any way without consulting their labels or studios first. I guess you could call it an act of defiance," she shrugs. "And I don't know, I wanted a change. Felt right to go back to my roots for once."

"Was your label angry?"

"Hell yeah they were. Said I'd lose fans and everything. That I no longer looked like the rocker they signed. That I looked like a chubby Barbie."

Even though Birdie doesn't seem bothered by it, my blood boils for her. What a bunch of assholes. She must see my anger because she presses her thumb against my furrowed brow.

"It's fine. I'm over it now. I went on to win two Grammys and a VMA. And guess what picture of me is on that Album cover?"

I smirk. "Blonde haired Birdie?"

"Oh yeah. I even wore bubblegum pink."

I laugh. "That's my girl." When the words are out of my mouth, I wait for Birdie to pull back, but instead she just looks a little surprised.

Her response comes out soft. "Do you mean that?"

I grab her chin so that her eyes meet mine. I want her to see that I'm sincere. "I do. I know what I said in the car last night, and if it's too soon to call you that, then I completely respect your choice. But after last night, and this morning," I half-smile, "It just feels right."

The corners of my mouth turn up and her cheeks pink. The events of last night and this morning have brought clarity to our situation, and I know what I want now. Her. I don't need to spend months thinking about it or trying to convince myself this isn't me. I may have a lot of fucking baggage but being with her is like breathing. I don't want to lose her again.

She brushes her plum nails over my stubble. "I know it sounds crazy..." she takes my hand and places it on her heart. I feel it thump wildly in her chest. "My heart does this whenever you're around. And after what we've shared, I don't think I can share you with anyone else."

My grin widens so she can see my teeth. "That's good to hear."

"I'm not usually the relationship type—"

I cut her off. "I understand, Birdie. Trust me, I do."

Still smiling, she presses her thumb into the small dip on my chin. "Does that mean you like me?"

I sit up and pull Birdie with me. In seconds I have her face in my hands, cradling her with as much care as I can. I press our foreheads together so our noses touch. "I can't take back what I said all those years ago. But I'm going to spend the rest of time telling you that I like you, Birdie. I really fucking like you."

She closes her eyes and takes a shallow breath. When she opens them, they're slightly glassy. I can't help the tension I feel in my chest. I kiss her eyelids, then her lips. "I'm sorry for the pain I caused you, I was an idiot—"

Birdie stops me with a kiss. When she pulls back, she's smiling. "Liam, I understand. You don't have to say anything else. I like you a lot, too."

"Well good, because I sure as hell have a lot of plans for you," I let my eyes wander to her naked breasts. "And those too."

Birdie smacks me playfully. "I'm sure you do."

I take Birdie's hand in mine then press it against my chest. My heart is pumping hard too, and I want her to know what she does to not only my little brain, but my whole body.

Her mouth opens slightly as she looks from my eyes to my lips. A devilish grin appears right before her free hand begins to wander down my chest then over the V near my hips. Goosebumps breakout over my skin and I grip the back of her head. "Are you sore?" I ask her.

"It's kind of you to ask, but even if I was, I'd still say yes."

I chuckle. "You're insatiable."

"So are you and you know it."

"Now kiss me."

And I do.

Twenty-Eight

Birdie

WE'RE ON THE TOUR bus to Nashville after spending a few days in Atlanta, then two nights in Alabama, then two in Mississippi. Our show is tonight, and tomorrow we have our first full free day since New York City, which is long overdue.

After this we'll head to Little Rock before Louisiana where Ben and Wren will meet us. I'm exhausted and in need of a shower after a long week on the road.

I'm also in need of Liam. Even though he's on the tour bus with us now, I've hardly seen him since our time in Atlanta. We got another creepy note from the stalker sent to the hotel in Jackson. So between Liam doing his job and me doing mine, time is hard to come by. I mean, I do see him, but only when he guards me or at night when we're both so tired we fall asleep almost immediately. Though I admit being held by him is very nice.

"Check," Liam says.

I glance over at him and Kevin, still engrossed in a game of chess. I'm working on a new song with the rest of the band. Kevin chimes in once and a while, but mostly he's focused on beating Liam.

"What if we repeated the chorus here but you did a key change? We could add some sweet harmonies for you," TJ, one of my backup singers suggests. My other backup singers Jenny and Lorraine readily agree.

I look over the song we've written on sheet music and grin. "That's a great idea actually. We could have the entire band swell underneath."

The women clap at the idea. "Oh, this is going to be good. I bet if we work on it in the next few rehearsals, we could play it in Louisiana."

Though I'm not super keen on the idea—only because that means more time is taken away from Liam and I—I nod in agreement since they're all so excited. "I'll have Eric run it by the label."

"Sweet," the rest of the band agrees, even Kevin, who I guess is still half-listening.

"Hey everyone." Shea walks out from the back of the bus, her voice thick with sleep from a nap. The entire crew greets her, minus Liam. I watch as he clenches his jaw, not even turning to acknowledge her. Instead, he's focused on a chess piece like it's going to come alive and jump off the board. I still haven't had a chance to ask him what's going on between them, but it seems like it may have gotten worse.

I turn my gaze toward her as she sits in the empty space next to Jane. "Have a nice nap?"

She shrugs. "Once I turned off my brain, but I've been coordinating all these interviews for the Teen Choice Awards at the end of the tour. Everyone wants a piece of you."

"That's because Birdie is the greatest!" Jane adds, winking at me.

"She is," Shea agrees, but notice her voice sounds a little off when she says it. Am I missing something here? Did Liam and Shea have a thing? When I look back at Liam, I find he's watching me.

My stomach turns. I'm probably being stupid, but now I really want to talk with him alone, find out what's going on with Shea. I've never had any issues with her before, she's always been a perfect assistant. I also hate that I feel jealous.

Just as I'm about to tumble into my thoughts, my phone alerts me that I have a new text. When I look down, surprise colors my face.

"Everything okay?" Liam asks in a concerned tone.

I smile. "All good. It's my mom actually. She wants me to call."

Shea sidles up to me, "Your mom never texts you."

My face burns at her words. Except for Kevin, my band doesn't really know my family history. Just that Mom's a hippie living in Arizona with her boyfriend. I did mention to Shea once that she wasn't around a lot when I was a kid, but it was an off-handed comment one night when we'd had too much wine. After I left Michigan, I left my past behind... well, minus Wren, Ben and Liam. But Liam came with me in song only, until recently.

I slide my phone into my pocket. I'll have to call her later when I'm alone. It's strange that she's texting me during the week, but not strange enough that it makes me concerned. Mom and I have an easy-going relationship. We see each other mostly when the tour stops in Arizona. She'll come to my show, and we'll hang out. But otherwise, she prefers to stay close to home these days. Which I still find hilarious given how much she was gone when I was young.

I turn my eyes to Liam. He's still watching me with a curious look on his face. For a moment I think about what would've happened if Mom hadn't left me alone all those years. Then I wouldn't have gotten so close to Liam. Who knows, maybe it's fate. Or maybe we just both had semi-shitty parents. Either way, I'm glad it brought us together. I wouldn't change any of it for the world.

"What did she want?" Shea asks. It's a strange question for her to ask, and it puts me on edge.

I shrug. "She probably wants to know about the show in Phoenix coming up."

"Want me to call her and take care of the tickets, etc.?"

"Since when have you handled that?" I clip, my tone cold.

Shea's eyes widen before she holds up her hands. "Geez, B. Did you get up on the wrong side of the bed this morning? I'm your assistant, I'm trying to make your life easier."

The tour bus goes quiet, and I try to stave off the embarrassment from being called out. I breathe in through my nose and out through my mouth.

Liam stands and everyone's eyes go to him. "Can I talk to you privately, Ms. Wilder?"

I push my shoulders back and nod. "Um, sure. I'll be right back," I tell my band. Shea glares at Liam, then turns her annoyed gaze back on me. Something is definitely happening that I'm not aware of. I feel my palms turn clammy.

Grateful to leave, I stand and make my way to the back of the tour bus. Beyond the bunks and the bathroom is a small space we often use to call our families, do business, or whatever we need. Once Liam and I are inside, I slide the door closed and lock it.

Before I can blink, Liam's lips are locked on mine. I let out a quiet sound of surprise, then kiss him back with gusto. I melt into him, almost letting my anxiety fall away.

After a few moments he pulls back and brushes a lock of hair off my face. "I've been wanting to do that since this morning."

"Damn tour," I say, wrapping my arms around his neck. Liam strokes my hip through my black T-shirt, and I almost throw caution to the wind. It would be fun to have sex right here, but then I remember the reason for my anxiety. And the reason we came back here in the first place; to talk.

When Liam goes in for another kiss, I bring my hand up to stop him. "We have a day off tomorrow and we can do lots more kissing then. But you said you wanted to talk. So, let's talk."

He licks, yes licks, my hand, then grabs hold of my wrist. "Oh, we'll be doing way more than kissing."

I laugh and shake my head at his antics. After one more peck, he pulls me to the small loveseat, placing us side by side. His face is serious now, but he massages my thigh to calm me, or maybe to calm himself.

"What did you want to talk about?"

He looks down. "I've been meaning to speak with you about Shea."

I pull our bodies apart slightly, that familiar bite of jealousy returning. "Funny, because I've been wanting to talk to you about her, too."

Liam looks taken back by my reaction. "What are you thinking right now, Birdie?"

"You don't want to know what I'm thinking."

His concerned brown eyes search mine, then realization colors his features. "Do you think there's something going on between us?"

My throat becomes thick with emotion. "She keeps looking at you like she wants to jump your bones... or like she wants to kill you. Then you've been glaring daggers at her. Was there something?"

A sad sort of laugh comes out of his mouth. "No. Never. Though she wanted there to be."

Anger flashes through me, but I try to keep my emotions in check. "And you're only saying something now?"

Liam's hand squeezes my thigh again. "She's backed off since we started this between us. I'm pretty sure she knows we have something going on. She's been suspicious ever since she came to the door the morning after I slept over the first time. Then she said some things, trying to get information out of me. Look, Birdie, I know this may be hard to hear but I think Shea might be behind this stalker thing."

My head reels. "Woah, back up. I thought maybe she kissed you or something, but you think Shea, my assistant Shea, is in cahoots with the crazy stalker? Horny for you yes, but that? No. She'd never betray me like that." I shake my head vehemently.

Liam takes his hand from my thigh and runs in through his hair. "It's often the people closest to you that screw you over, Birdie. You of all people understand that. Just like I do."

I inhale deeply. "There's really nothing going on with you two?"

He shakes his head. "Of course not. I would never cheat. Never."

That ugly jealousy quells a little in my stomach at his words. Though Liam has hurt me in the past, I know he's not lying now. I can see it in his eyes. He's not a sixteen-year-old boy anymore, he's a grown man who's here doing a job. A man who I'm sharing something important with. Plus, if he did do something with Shea prior to whatever happened with me, I couldn't fault him for it. Though I still wouldn't have liked it.

"You really think Shea could have something to do with the stalker?"

He nods. "There's something off. I have enough experience in my line of work to know when someone is hiding something."

My stomach twists. "I'll admit her reaction back there was off, but I did bite her head off."

Liam shakes his leg a bit. "You said she's never made arrangements with your mom before?"

"No, never. I've always been private regarding my mom. The whole band knows it."

Liam runs a hand through his hair and hums in acknowledgement.

"What are you thinking?" I ask him.

He sighs. "I checked her background twice and it came up clean. That doesn't mean she's not up to something though. Has she ever shown any jealousy toward you or the band? Or have you ever had any issues with her?"

I shake my head. "Never. She's been the perfect assistant since day one. Everyone loves her."

Liam leans back on the couch. "I think I'm missing something."

"Maybe she's just angry you're not giving her attention?"

He shakes his head. "I think there's more."

"What do we do then?"

"I'm going to see if I can find out anything more about her life before this. She may not have a record, but maybe I can find something. In the meantime, just be careful what you say around her."

"She's my assistant, she knows a shit ton about my life." My stomach sours at the thought. I don't understand what motive Shea could have for hurting me that way. She's paid well, gets time off, bonuses... She's never made it seem like she's unhappy with her work or with me.

"That's why I think she could have a hand in this."

I grab hold of my stomach. "I feel sick."

Liam gently rubs my back. "You're fine Birdie. No matter what, I'm not going to let anything happen to you. I've got your back."

I lean into him, placing my head on his chest. I let the feel of his muscles and the sound of his heartbeat calm me. He kisses the top of my head and I melt further into him.

"Is this what it feels like to be in a healthy relationship?" I blurt out. Liam's laughter shakes my body and I move with him.

"I've never really had one, so... maybe?"

"What a pair we make." I shift in his arms and look up into his chocolate eyes. "You've really never had a relationship before?" I feel him stiffen and his grip on me tightens. A myriad of emotions cross his face, as if he's not sure he should say more.

"I had a partner when I was a cop. Her name was Maria."

Was. Does that mean she's dead? By the look on Liam's face, I think I'm right in my assumption. My heart tugs for him, for the pain I see in him.

"You were together?"

He shrugs. "Not really. But she's the closest I'd had to a relationship. We worked together, ate meals together, but we weren't... together. It was complicated."

A pregnant pause fills the room. "You've never talked about your time as a cop before," I say eventually.

"That's because I hated it. I became a cop out of some weird loyalty to my dad, not because I actually wanted to be a cop."

"You like private security more?"

He grins at that. "It led me to you, so yes, I like it much more."

My heart flutters. In a flash I get up on my knees and straddle him. His face goes from sadness to arousal in a second flat.

I rub my nose against his. "You make me hot when you say things like that." His hands wander down my back, quickly finding my ass. His erection begins to grow under me and arousal pools low in my belly.

He pushes his hips into mine. "You make me hot all the time."

I hear Kevin laugh from the front of the bus and we both stiffen. "We should get back to the band before they send a search party."

He taps my nose. "Ruin all the fun, why don't you."

I lean forward and kiss his lips softly. "I've missed you."

"I'm right here."

"You know what I mean."

"I do. I'm just teasing." He moves some of my hair behind my shoulder then brushes his lips down the column of my neck. When I feel his teeth capture my earlobe between his teeth, I hiss at the sensation.

"Liam—" his name comes out a breathy moan.

"I miss your pussy around my cock, and your taste on my tongue."

I grind myself into him, my body on fire. I love when he talks to me this way. It makes me feel wanton... like a sex goddess or something.

He tugs on my ear again then pecks my lips. When we both hear Kevin laugh even louder this time, I grunt. Hot sex will have to wait.

"You should get back," he says.

I give him a questioning look. "You're not coming?"

He presses his hard dick into me. "I have to let him settle down first."

"*Him*?"

Liam just shrugs. "Leave me and my dick alone. He's not happy he has to wait till tonight."

I giggle. Really giggle. Then get off his lap. I lean down to kiss him one more time. "Let me know if you find anything else out about Shea, and I'll make sure I pay more attention to what she's doing from now on, too."

His features return to business mode, his perfect face going hard. "Good."

As I turn to leave, he grabs my hand once more. "And Birdie?"

"Yes?"

"Be careful."

Twenty-Nine

Liam

THE SHOW IS JUST finishing up in Nashville. I've been on Birdie like a hawk. I don't want a hair out of place on her head unless I'm the one to do it. I grin like a dog at the thought.

As the crowd sings along with her I watch as she loses herself in the music. *Fucking beautiful.* The Nashville show is sold-out, and the crowds have had a lot of alcohol. Though the venue has a ton of extra security for the night, I still can't help but be worried.

Between the event on the tour bus, the call in at the radio station and the letter that followed, I'm not taking any chances. Shea's little outburst toward Birdie on the bus didn't help take the edge off either.

"Hey Liam." *Speak of the devil.*

"Shea." My voice is cordial, but I can't help the edge it has.

"You enjoying the show?"

"Always do."

She clears her throat. "I hear you've been asking questions about me."

My fists clench. When I turn my eyes on her, I try to stay composed and neutral. "I'm asking questions about everyone."

"Jane said you asked the entire band about me."

She's right. I did. "I'm not going to apologize for it. I'm doing it for everyone."

"And yet you started with me first. Why?"

"No reason. I had to start somewhere." I lie.

Shea takes a step forward, her eyes narrow. "I would never hurt Birdie."

"Who says you would?"

"By you asking around about me, it implies that you think I would hurt her. That's what the stalker keeps saying anyway."

"You're the one implying it. I'm simply doing my job, Shea. I'm sorry if it offends you. But if you care about Birdie as you say, you shouldn't care that I'm checking everyone out. Again, I'm doing my job."

"Are you doing your job by sleeping with her too?" she says under her breath.

Anger bubbles up. If she were a man, I would have punched her lights out, or at least gotten in her face. But we're backstage, Birdie is on stage singing her heart out, and I'm a fucking professional. So instead, I remain calm.

My gaze hardens. "It's comments like that that make me think you would want to hurt Birdie."

Shea's demeanor shifts at my words, and she takes a step back. She's said shitty comments before, but now that I've called her out on the implications, her tune changes. "I shouldn't have said that."

"You're right about that."

"Look, I'm just angry. You denied my advances and then I found out you're having me checked out. I love Birdie. I would never hurt her."

I search her face to see if maybe there's some kind of truth there—but I don't believe a word she says. It's usually the guilty ones that try hard to prove their innocence.

"There's really no excuse for your words or actions. If you have an issue with me or anything for that matter, you should take it up with Birdie—she's your boss. I'm just doing my job, that's it."

"Does Birdie know you're asking questions about me?"

"She's aware I'm doing my job."

"You never answer questions straight. It's frustrating."

"Like I said, I'm doing my job. Now if you'll excuse me, I have to do that job."

For a moment I think she's going to say more, but then she huffs and stomps away in a flash. It takes only a second for Eric to fill the spot she'd just left. He claps me on the shoulder as I go back to watching Birdie rock out with Kevin on stage.

"You good, man?" he asks.

"All good."

"I'm sorry about Shea. I heard what she said. She's young and I don't think she gets how serious this all is."

"It's fine." Even though it's not fine.

Eric stays quiet for a few more moments before he speaks again. "It's true what Shea said, about you and Birdie?"

"I didn't realize I signed up for the third degree today," I clip.

"I'm just watching out for Birdie, she's like a sister to me."

My agitation grows. "I don't like that you think I'm not watching out for her." I want to cuss him out right now. These people are a bunch of gossips. I mean, I knew Birdie and I couldn't keep our relationship on the down low for long, but I also didn't expect it to happen so quickly.

"I didn't mean it that way, Liam. You're doing great work. I just want to know if you two are."

"Are what?"

Eric looks up to the ceiling like he's saying a silent prayer. "Are you and Birdie together?"

Just then Birdie appears, like some sort of sweaty goddess sent to save me. Without preamble, she grabs me and kisses me hard on the lips. Her face is damp, and she smells like salty earth, but I kiss her back after my brain catches up to what's happening. In the background I hear the whooping and hollering of the band. They sound like a bunch of lunatics, but I smile against her lips nonetheless.

When she pulls back from me, she looks at Eric, eyes shining happily. "Does that answer your question, dear Eric?"

"I heard that loud and clear."

Birdie locks her wild eyes on mine, then releases my shirt. "I'll see you after the show, Mr. Miller." With one more quick kiss, she skips back on stage to do the encore. Kevin slaps me on the back as he walks by, flipping his long sweaty hair off his forehead.

"If you hurt her, I'll kill you!" Jane yells over the sound of the crowd before she disappears on stage.

Eric chuckles. "Well, that answers that."

If I blushed, I'd be blushing right now. But with everything going on, I'm glad we're out in the open now. I wonder what made her decide to do that. I'm not complaining though. I would kiss her in front of the entire world if I could, let them all know that Birdie Wilder is mine and mine alone.

I look over my shoulder to see if Shea was around to see that, but I find she's not there. My shoulders tighten and my skin prickles. Something is not right with her; I just know it. Now if only I could find out what.

Birdie is sound asleep while I work on my laptop in a chair next to the bed. It's harder than I thought working here while she sleeps. She keeps making cute noises, and the pair of yellow high-waisted underwear she wears makes me want to peel them back and explore what's underneath.

My dick twitches to life and I have to stop from waking her up. She's just too fucking sexy.

But I know she needs sleep, so I let her be. After the show finished earlier, the band insisted on asking us every question under the sun. They were all happy we were together, and we probably all had one too many drinks while we laughed and talked.

Shea never returned to join us, but I'd been so happy sitting next to Birdie and kissing her in front of the band and crew that I didn't care, for the moment at least. But after we returned to the hotel room, Birdie and I showered together, which may have evolved to me on my knees in front of her, tasting her once more. But then as soon as we hit the sheets, she fell asleep, exhausted from the day.

I knew in the morning she'd be sad we didn't have sex, but tomorrow we have a day off. I'll make it up to her then. It's not like I could stay away from her anyway. Her body, her touch, smell, and taste, I'm addicted. That's why I keep staring at her when I should be doing work.

When the page I want finally loads, I peel my gaze away from her and start to scan it. The internet has yielded very little information on Shea, so I've resorted to stalking her on social media. Which I hate. Especially because she's still so young. Going through her pictures feels wrong on so many levels, but I'm determined to find any information I can.

After another ten minutes, I rub my eyes and look at the clock. It's approaching four in the morning, and I should get some sleep. But when I switch to her friends page, I stop. The word Parker, then Michigan, catches my eye. Shea has a connection in Parker?

I click on the link immediately and I'm met with the face of an older man. When his picture completely loads, I feel as if a knife has been stabbed through my gut. But when I look at Birdie, then back to the screen, I know I owe it to her to investigate this further.

I write down the man's name. Nick Squires. I think I have an idea of what's going on here, and if I'm right...

Birdie yawns and reaches for me in bed. When she doesn't find me next to her, her pretty eyes flutter open. They're hooded with sleep, but still stunning in the subtle light from my computer.

"Liam?" Her voice is husky. "What are you doing?"

"Go back to sleep, Birdie baby."

She smiles at the use of the pet name. "Come back to bed and I will."

I stare once more at the open page on my computer. There isn't much more I can do tonight anyway. Tomorrow the real work can begin. I just hope I'm not right. For once, I really do hope that.

I close the laptop and crawl back into bed. Birdie quickly snuggles into my side, her soft breasts pressing against my chest. Immediately my little brain stands at attention. Birdie must have a sixth sense for it now, because in no time her hand is sweeping its way from my chest then down, down, until eventually she's creeping her dexterous fingers under the waistband of my briefs. The moment her soft fingers touch me, my hips lift off the bed, wanting more.

"He wants attention," she purrs. I can hear the smile in her voice.

"He felt left out after the shower. But I told him we had to let you sleep."

She lets out a tired chuckle. "Then please, let me help him feel better."

"You don't have to; you should be resting."

Birdie's head pops up, her blonde locks messy from sleep. She still looks beautiful though. "You're going to turn down an early morning blowjob from a hot rock star?"

I let out a breath. "Well, when you put it that way." I put my hands behind my head and lay back in a relaxed pose.

Birdie looks demure. "Hold on tight." She shucks my underwear off in a swift motion.

Shit. My girl means business.

Thirty

Birdie

"I ORDERED US BREAKFAST." Liam sips on some black tea he made while looking at his phone. I smile to myself. I never knew Liam drank tea, but it's fun learning little new things about him.

"Thank you." I walk over to him, well, more like prowl. He looks like a snack standing in a pair of gray sweatpants slung low on his hips. I've been exploring the V leading to the goods every chance I get, but I can't get enough of it. I want to touch it.

"If you come any closer, we won't eat breakfast," he smirks, his brown eyes full of mischief.

"Pfft, breakfast." I wave my hand like it's nothing. "We can always eat later."

He takes a playful step back. "We didn't eat anything last night, and we've got a big day ahead of us."

I quirk an eyebrow up. "We do?"

"Did you think we'd spend our day off having sex all day?"

I tap my chin as if I'm thinking about it. "I mean, what's wrong with that?"

Just as I'm about to make a move, there's a knock on the door. "Damn breakfast," I mutter under my breath, which makes Liam laugh.

He strides to the door in a flash, looking through the peephole before opening the door to grab the tray the bellboy left. A second later he rolls the breakfast cart into the room. The whole time my eyes follow the way he walks, the way his thighs and forearms flex and his ass moves. It's sexy as hell. Everything about him is sexy as hell.

"Sit," he commands.

"So bossy."

A devious look passes over his face as I follow his demand. "Oh Birdie, you haven't seen me bossy."

I swallow at the promise. "Well, I'm looking forward to it."

He leans forward, pressing me into the back of the couch. His breath is hot on my lips as he closes in on me. "Trust me when I say, you shouldn't."

My mouth goes dry, and I lick my lips. God, he's good at this game we play. As I lean in to kiss him that devilish look returns.

He pulls back. "Breakfast time, Birdie girl. You need your strength."

Left hot and bothered, he starts to open the domed lids like he didn't just make my panties wet.

When I see all the food he got - pancakes, bacon, eggs, toast - I snort. "Holy crap! There's enough food for the entire band here."

"I wasn't sure what you'd want so I asked them to send whatever is the best on their menu. Coffee?" he asks, holding up the carafe.

My stomach flutters at the thoughtfulness of this man. He can be a big tease, but he sure is sweet.

I push my cup toward him. "Please."

Once we're both settled with food and coffee, Liam chooses the seat across from me so that I "can't touch him," then we dig in. It's just after ten since we both slept in after the early morning activities we had, not that I'm complaining, but I'm starved.

"So, what are the big plans for today? I thought I had to stay inside at all times," I joke, though that's really how it had been since the stalker approached me on the tour bus.

Liam gives me a serious look, his jaw clenched. "I don't want you to feel like you're caged."

My face softens and I take a sip of bitter coffee. He's heard me talk about it before, and it's true, I don't want to feel like that. "Ever since we started things, my cage is a lot brighter," I smile warmly. "But I understand why things are so tight."

Liam's gaze darts from his fist now clenched around his coffee mug to my eyes. "Well, we're going out today."

"Just us?" I'm hopeful that he says yes, though part of me wonders if he's ready to go public. If the paparazzi caught us, the trash magazines would be brutal and relentless. Especially since he's my bodyguard. I don't think he realizes how much his life will change when the world finds out.

Liam notices my hesitation. "We don't have to go alone if you're not comfortable."

I shake my head. "No, that's not it... I—" the words fall away, and my vulnerability bubbles to the surface.

Liam's hand lands on my knee and he squeezes. "What's wrong?"

I smile warmly at him. This beautiful man before me that I've loved for so long, even when I denied it—he cares for me more than he probably should. I can feel it in every action and every word.

My chest tightens. "Can I be honest with you, Liam?"

He sits straighter at my words, "Of course, Birdie girl. You know that."

I place my hand over his on my knee. "I'm worried about going public." Something like hurt flashes over his features and I quickly put an end to it.

"No, not like that, Liam. It's one thing for my band to know about us, but to go public, that puts you in the spotlight. And not just any spotlight, but the Hollywood one. Your life is no longer going to be your own. They're going to air your dirty laundry and drag you through the mud. And what if the stalker..." I trail off as gory images of the dirtbag hurting Liam fill my mind. I would never forgive myself if anything happened to him because of me.

Liam gazes at me, his brown eyes thoughtful. I don't know what he's thinking, but it can't be good. I should have known that this would scare him away. Either people want to be with me to get somewhere or they hate that I can't give them a private life. There's never an in-between.

My eyes start to burn with tears. "Right, well..." I try to stand, but Liam's grip on my knee stops me.

"Where do you think you're going?"

"I—"

He moves to the space next to me on the couch and takes my hands in his. "Look at me Birdie."

"Liam—"

"Please look at me, B."

When I finally do, the corners of his mouth are upturned slightly, and his gaze is warm. "I appreciate your concern over me," he grips my hands harder, "And I think you're right that we should keep it from the public."

My heart sinks. He doesn't want to be seen with me; I knew it.

"No, Birdie," Liam says strongly, taking my chin between his fingers. "You have it all wrong, I meant for now. Only because of your safety. I'm not worried about mine; I never have been."

"You should be, Liam."

"I'm your bodyguard."

"And I'm your—"

"Girlfriend," he finishes for me.

My heart pounds in my chest. "Really?"

"It feels like such a silly word for what we have. People will say it's too soon, but I've never cared about what people think, so yes. You're my girlfriend; my girl, my Birdie girl," he winks. "It's not like I could ever let another guy touch you. I might kill them. Example number one, Gabe."

"That's a little dramatic."

He grunts like a caveman. "I'm being serious. I'm not worried about my safety. But there are some things I'd like to clear up with you about my past, and if they dig around about my dad and rehab, I need to give my parents some warning. I also want you to myself for a bit before the entire world knows. Is that okay?"

"Of course it's okay. I just thought—"

He brushes some hair behind my ear, then runs his knuckle over my cheek. "I want this with you Birdie," he leans his forehead against mine. "You do something to me, something I didn't even know was possible—I'm not making sense. All my thoughts are cliche, sweet and gross; all the things I hate. But it's all true."

I let out a breathy laugh. "I understand. And I agree, boyfriend." The word feels foreign on my tongue, but when I use it to refer to Liam, it doesn't seem so bad. A wide smile breaks out on his face, and I can't help but smile with him.

"And for the record, when I meant we'd be going out by ourselves, I meant with some other security detail as well. I had Gia arrange a few things for us, stuff that won't draw any attention. You have nothing to worry about."

My cheeks flush with embarrassment. "Oh..." is all I manage to say.

He chuckles. "Now let's eat. We have a solid day ahead of us, and I need to get a few things done before we go."

I take a piece of bacon and tear off a large bite. "What things?" I notice his jaw tick, but he swallows his bite of toast, waving me off.

"Just doing some background check stuff. Nothing I want to worry you about."

It's obvious he doesn't want to talk about the stalker, and to be frank, I don't want too either. "Okay."

He turns his head toward me and gives me another beautiful Liam smile. "Better eat up, *Girlfriend*."

My stomach tingles. But instead of kissing him, I reach for another piece of bacon. He just laughs at my choice.

Midafternoon, Liam and I are close to our first destination. He's been mostly quiet during the drive, like he has a lot on his mind.

"You're really not going to tell me what we're doing?" I ask, breaking the silence.

"We're here. You can't wait another minute?" he chuckles.

"I'm not really a fan of surprises."

"Isn't that something people who like surprises usually say?" he quips.

I shake my head at him. "I don't."

He leans over from his seat and gives me a short kiss. "You'll like this one." We hear a tap on the door once we come to a stop. Liam gets out after he gives me one more kiss.

There are two security guys outside standing guard while Liam turns to help me down. He's in full bodyguard mode and I make sure I don't gaze at him all googly eyed in case there are photographers around. Once I'm out of the car, I take in the building before us and the surrounding area. We're somewhere outside of Nashville, and I know why when I see where we are.

"You brought me to a distillery?" I ask once we're out of earshot of the extra security men.

"Of course, I did."

I smirk. "Trying to get me hammered?"

"No, but I do think you'll enjoy this place's bourbon," he says happily while opening the door so I can walk through.

"How is this private?"

"Liam. Fucking. Miller," a loud voice booms. My eyes focus forward on a large man who has a shaved head and looks like the incredible hulk. He's... massive. Tattoos run down his arms, and he has a wide smile on his face.

"Hammer! Nice to see you man," Liam greets him with a big hug and pat on the back.

Hammer? I admit that nickname, if it is a nickname, is appropriate.

"And who is this little lady here?" he drawls, his southern accent thick.

Liam lets out an amused sound. "You know who this is, Hammer."

Hammer hits Liam on the shoulder roughly, "I'm just trying to get you to say it again. Never thought I'd hear the word girlfriend uttered out of your mouth." Hammer turns his blue eyes on me, "No offense."

"None taken," I say, holding out my hand. "I'm Birdie."

He half-smiles at me. "Nice to meet you, Birdie. I'm Hammer. Welcome to my humble abode."

I look around the space. It's not a huge distillery, but it's a decent size. The space is all wood and has a very modern southern vibe about it. Bourbon memorabilia peppers the walls, as well as a few tasteful pictures of nude bodies, which surprises me. Not something I'd think a guy like Hammer would have up on the walls.

"My wife paints those," he chortles. "I told her this is a distillery, you can't have naked paintings on the walls, but you'd be surprised how many she sells when people come in here and get sloshed."

"She's a smart woman."

"That she is. Now have a seat, Liam mentioned you have a love for bourbon."

My eyes find Liam's. He's looking at me like I've hung the moon, and I have to stop from blushing. I can also tell he's happy to be here. I have no idea where he met this guy, but it's clear they're close. I get why he chose this place now; he trusts Hammer not to tell anyone we came here.

I flick my eyes back to Hammer and nod. "That I do."

"Well then, you've come to the right place."

Liam moves closer to me to press a hand to my back, then leads me toward a table near a window. Outside it's a nice summer day, and green grass blows in the breeze. The sky is blue with fluffy clouds and green trees line the property. In the distance I see some horses out in a pasture, enjoying the delicious grass.

Once we're seated, Hammer hands us both a drink menu and a tasting sheet. "I'm going to get some things started for you, I'll be back out in a few minutes."

Hammer's large form retreats to the back of the bar some distance away, and I turn my attention to Liam. "Now I understand why you brought me here."

Liam nods. "Hammer and I go way back."

"How do you know him?"

"He's my cousin actually."

Shock colors my face, "I didn't know you had a cousin."

"Mom has an older sister. Hammer is her son."

My eyes find Hammer and I watch him for a second. I can see a little resemblance. Liam and Hammer have the same wide shoulders and sharp jaw. They also share the same tall height.

"I can't believe out of all the things you could have; you have a cousin who owns a distillery in Nashville."

"I'm just full of surprises," he says gleefully.

"That you are."

After a few moments, Hammer returns and sets down a tasting flight full of several amber colored liquids. "Here we are."

"These look great," I smile up at him. "I actually haven't done a lot of bourbon tastings."

He holds his hand over his heart like he's wounded. "A bourbon drinker who doesn't do tastings? You're hurting my heart."

"I don't have much free time, but I'm excited to try all of yours."

He nods like he understands. If he didn't know who I was before Liam told him we were coming, I'm sure he does now.

Hammer starts explaining the different kinds of bourbons, and how he makes them. It's clear by the joy on his face that he enjoys what he does. He also makes sure that while we're tasting each one, he explains the notes on every bourbon and why they're special.

After a few tastes, I feel Liam's eyes on me. He's smiling at me with a warm expression, but he's lost in thought. From Liam's own words I can gather that not many women, if any, have met Hammer or even know he has a cousin. My stomach flutters at the importance of this moment, especially since he looks so glad that I'm here with him.

"Any you'd like to have a glass of?" Hammer asks once we've tasted them all.

"Hmm... I think I like the rye most," I announce.

"Good choice!" he beams. "That's my favorite, too. Want anything, Liam?"

Liam shakes his head. "The tasting was perfect. Really good shit, Hammer."

Hammer pats Liam on the back, then walks away. I raise my brow at him, "Nothing for you?"

He shakes his head. "Gotta keep my girlfriend safe. No more for me tonight."

My stomach flutters again. "Thank you for bringing me here. I hope he didn't close the shop on my behalf."

Liam grins, "He would have if I asked him too, but no. He's closed on Mondays and Tuesdays."

"And I'm happy to always help, Liam," Hammer chimes in, placing the bourbon in front of me. "He never asks for it, so it's nice to be able to do this for you both."

"Thanks, Hammer," I say, taking the sip. I love the smokey flavor as it slides down my throat. "I live a strange life. It's nice to feel almost normal for a moment."

"No problem. Enjoy," he winks before turning to walk away, but I stop him.

"Why don't you join us for a drink? It's your day off, after all."

Hammer looks at Liam as if to ask for permission. Liam's face is surprised, but not in a bad way. He looks a little excited that I've asked.

"I don't want to intrude," Hammer says.

"Nonsense. I'm sure Liam doesn't get to see you that much, and I'd love to hear stories about him if you've got 'em."

Hammer lets out a deep belly laugh. "I do have some pretty funny stories. Including the time we went to Cabo and he woke up next to—"

"Not that story, Hammer." Liam looks annoyed now. "Maybe you shouldn't join us."

Hammer chuckles. "Okay, I won't tell that one."

"Now you have to tell it!" I laugh.

Liam winces. "No, he really doesn't. It's not something I'd like to relive."

"Oh Liam, you have become so boring since your accident."

My stomach sinks. Accident? The air suddenly becomes heavy, and my eyes shift to Liam. He's staring at Hammer, his eyes taut.

"What accident?" My voice is quiet when I ask. Hammer's shoulders shift back. He knows he's messed up.

"Sorry, man. I thought—"

"It's fine, Hammer."

"Really I—"

Liam shakes his head. "Mind giving us a moment?"

"Yeah, of course." With one last look of apology, Hammer retreats to the backroom, presumably so he can't hear us. I stare at Liam, who's running his fingers over the rim of an empty tasting glass.

"Liam," I say breathily after a few moments. "What accident?"

"Can we talk outside? I need some air. There are some grounds in the back that are safe for us to move around."

"Yes, of course."

Liam holds out his hand, which I gladly take. I'm not mad he didn't tell me about this accident, just sad that Wren or Ben never said anything. Yet, I always told them to leave me out of anything concerning Liam, so I really had no one to blame but myself.

Once we're outside, we start to walk on a small trail that leads to a gazebo with a small table. The property itself has picnic tables littered everywhere, which I imagine Hammer uses for events.

After we reach the safety of the shade, Liam waits for me to take a seat before taking his place beside me. He looks out at the cornfield then, the knee-high stalks swaying in the breeze. Pain is marred on his face, and I feel bad that our day off has turned into this. I know it's not my fault Hammer said something, but I wish I could ease Liam's suffering.

"We don't have to talk about this now, Liam."

He shakes his head. "I wanted to tell you sooner. I should have told you sooner."

"It's okay," I reiterate.

He clenches his jaw and swallows, his Adam's apple bobbing as he does. "I told you about my partner, Maria." I nod. "She was an amazing woman. We were partners for two years and I had a stupid crush on her." Liam darts his eyes to me as if I'll be jealous he's talking about having feelings for another person.

"It's okay, Liam. You're fine," I reassure him, placing my hand on his thigh.

He clears his throat, as if that can take the emotion away. "Even though we were both attracted to each other, and we flirted, we never acted on it. As we've discussed, I didn't do relationships, and definitely not with my work partner. We had a good flow, but I wouldn't allow myself more. But one day, I decided to hell with it, and asked her out while we were on patrol. I should've known it would lead to something bad, I just didn't know it would be that soon."

He looks down at his hands, then out to the cornfield again. "We got called to a burglary in progress. It should have been standard, she shouldn't have—but we were ambushed and there were more perps than expected. A car drove up; she was shot and killed instantly. I didn't even have time to react. I was distracted by my feelings for her, and I made a rookie mistake. She lost her life because of it, because of me. I tried to save her, but they took advantage and shot me too."

I let out a small gasp, my heart wrenching. I know that Liam is safe and healthy, he's sitting right in front of me. But the image of him being shot; of him suffering in that way... he must have been so terrified.

He lets out a shaky exhale. "Unlike Maria, I got out with my life. But my shoulder was wrecked. It took a long time for me to heal, and it still bothers me if I work it too hard. But I want it to hurt sometimes. The pain makes me remember."

Tears burn my eyes. "Liam, I'm so sorry. I don't know what to say."

His chocolate brown eyes flicker to mine. The midafternoon sun makes his tanned skin glow, and his cheeks are flushed with emotion. The dark green T-shirt he's wearing is tight across his chest, and his jaw is twitching, as if he's trying to stop himself from breaking down.

"You have nothing to be sorry for." His voice comes out quiet and pained.

"Selfishly I wish I was there back then. I'm sorry I wasn't," I say gently.

He shakes his head, taking his hand from my thigh then lacing our fingers together. "As my therapist always tells me, we can't live in the past. I'll admit I'm still learning how to do it, but it's true. Our paths are this way for a reason, and Birdie..." he brings his free hand to rub his thumb over the apple of my cheek, "I'm glad they crossed again. You make me feel alive. For the first time in a long time, I have something, someone, to look forward to every morning."

A tear tracks down my cheek. Liam has such a way with words, and he doesn't even know it. I could write a million songs simply about him, but I could also write a million songs with his words.

"Don't cry, baby." He wipes the tears from my cheeks with both of his thumbs.

I almost laugh at the fact he's comforting me. I should be the one comforting him. "I'm happy you're here, Liam. Not just with me but—" my voice chokes, the thought is too painful to imagine.

Liam presses our foreheads together. "I'm happy I'm here too, Birdie girl. You have no idea." The way he says it makes me want to cry more. But when his lips press to mine, I melt into him. It's a sweet kiss, but there's a lot more said in this kiss than our usual passionate ones.

When he pulls back, he cups my cheek again, kissing all over my face in gentle caresses. "Thank you for listening."

My heart thumps. "Thank you for telling me." I hold his hands in mine, and we both look out at the corn swaying in the breeze.

"It's peaceful here," I say after a while.

"It is. I came out here for a couple months after I was released from the hospital. I was in a bad way and didn't want to impose on Ben all the time. Hammer and his wife Bria offered me a bed and some quiet. I took them up on it."

"Did it help?"

Liam shrugs. "A little. Honestly, I just needed time. I pulled myself out of it eventually when I started seeing a therapist. I hadn't wanted to at first, but the NYPD required it. It was a good thing though. I'm glad I did it."

"And you're sure you're okay now?"

Liam squeezes my hand. "Sometimes I still have nightmares, and my shoulder will ache as I mentioned. But for the most part I'm okay."

"Good. But you'd tell me if you weren't?"

He plays with my fingers, then smiles a little. "I would."

"Good," I sigh.

Instead of saying more, Liam pulls me into his lap with an easy tug. I let out a surprised sound just before his lips cover mine. He tastes like bourbon, home, and something sweet. When his arms encompass my back and I push my nails through his tresses, fingernails massaging and threading through the feathered locks at the base of his neck, he lets out a small moan.

Just as I start to bring one of my hands down his chest, a loud bang interrupts us. I pull back, and Liam immediately spurs into action. He jumps up, still taking care to ease me off his lap. As soon as I'm standing, he shoves me behind him and reaches down to flip up his pant leg. When I see a handgun there my stomach bottoms out. He quickly pulls it from the holster and cocks it with ease.

"Liam..." My voice is quiet. He had a gun on him this entire time. My mind is reeling.

"It's okay," he says in a calm tone.

My mouth is dry, and I feel my heart in my throat. It's not exactly an appropriate time to discuss his hidden gun. Especially when I'm pretty sure that bang we heard was also a gun. My stomach twists and acid burns my throat. *Hammer...* I make a step to move toward the building, but Liam stops me.

"Don't even think about taking another step." Liam's voice is stern.

"We have to see if Hammer is okay!" I whisper harshly.

Liam stays strong, his muscles flexing as he scans the area with his handgun at the ready. "Stay behind me Birdie and do as I say."

Even if I don't want to listen, I know I have to. He's doing his job and I need to not let my emotions get the best of me. So, I stay behind him as he scans the perimeter. He looks out to the cornfield, listening intently. When he seems satisfied that the area is clear, he turns his gaze to me. "I need to go check on Hammer. Stay here, Birdie."

"Let me come with you—"

"No. Not until I make sure it's safe."

"It could have been a hunter or something. I'm sure we're overreacting."

"I'm not taking any risks. Stay out here. The extra guards are in the area—and call the cops. Do not move from here unless you absolutely have to."

I nod vigorously. "Okay."

"I'll be right back."

With one last look, Liam takes off toward the distillery. I can hear my heartbeat in my ears now and my hands are clammy. A million scenarios run in my head. What if something happens to Liam's cousin? What if something happens to Liam? This is my worst nightmare coming true. When Liam disappears inside the building without even a glance back, I reach for my phone to call the cops.

"I wouldn't do that if I were you."

The hair on my neck stands on end and I freeze in place. I know that voice.

"Turn around Birdie."

Thirty-One

Liam

I STEP INTO THE distillery with my mind racing in a million different directions.

I didn't want to leave Birdie alone outside, but I had no choice. If that was a gun that went off, I couldn't risk her getting shot. Maria's death is now fresh in my mind, and I work hard to shove those horrible thoughts away. I will not allow myself to freeze now, not when the woman I'm damn sure I love, is outside. Not when my cousin could be hurt or—*fuck*.

I keep my handgun cocked, ready to take down anyone that plans to harm the people I care about. Birdie's face when she discovered I carried will live with me forever. I should have said something earlier, but I didn't want people to know I carried, especially the stalker. I just liked knowing that if I ever needed it, it was there. I was hoping I would never have to use it. But here we are.

As I come through the back room, I hear a noise and my back goes straight. I keep myself flat against the wall, getting ready to shoot whoever may be around the corner. Right as I'm about to attack, I hear Hammer's booming voice begin to sing. I'd spent enough time in his home to recognize his terrible scratchy voice. I breathe a sigh of relief and lower my handgun. He's fine. I shake out the nervous energy I'm feeling and make my way into the room, clearing my throat.

"Hey man," his eyes look remorseful. "Sorry about that back there I—"

"It's fine," I cut him off, my nerves still shot. "We sorted it out. But care to tell me what that noise was? It sounded like a gunshot."

Hammer smirks, "You worried about me?"

His playfulness grates on me, especially since I thought he could be hurt or worse.

"What the fuck was that noise?"

Hammer's eyes go to the handgun at my side, and he holds up his hands. "Chill, man. Didn't you notice the woods nearby? We have gunshots go off all the time around here. It's not a big deal. Your security dudes checked on me, too. Everything's good."

I rub my hands over my brow. "Sorry Hammer, I'm on edge."

"I noticed. But I'm good here. You should get back out to your girl."

Birdie. *Shit.* She's still outside freaking out. My heart starts up again and I immediately make my way back to her without another word to my cousin. When the sun hits my face, I squint from the harsh change in light. But as soon as I adjust, my heart leaps right back into my chest, because Birdie isn't there.

"Birdie!" I yell, but I'm met with the sounds of birds and wind. I start to run toward the gazebo, my pulse hammering and handgun at the ready. I'm there in a flash, but there's no Birdie. "BIRDIE!" I scream this time. But there's fucking nothing. I hear Hammer yell and then he's right there beside me.

"She's not inside," he says, looking around with me.

"Where the fuck else could she be?"

"I'll check the barn," Hammer calls, already on his way. Panic bubbles up in my stomach, and the familiar feeling of failure washes over me. I can't lose Birdie, not after everything we've shared, not after what I just told her about my past.

"Get your head together, Liam," I tell myself out loud. I can't lose it, not when Birdie is missing. *Fuck.* I look out at the cornfield, and I begin to run. I should have never brought her here. What the fuck was I thinking? Scratch that. I wasn't thinking. I was feeling—just like when the accident happened with Maria.

As soon as I reach the stalks, I notice that some of them are broken. "HAMMER!" I yell, "THE CORNFIELDS!" I'm not sure if he heard me, but I'm not waiting. I follow the trail, it doesn't really look like she struggled, which could mean the stalker forced her to go with him in other ways that didn't involve direct force. It's not long before I come to a road on the other side, but there's nothing there except for the faint smell of exhaust.

"FUCK!" I yell loud enough for the clouds to hear.

"Liam!" Hammer calls as he approaches, the two hired guards following close behind him.

"Did you see anything?" I ask them both.

"No, we were double checking the perimeter after we heard the noise," one of them says. "But we found this in the dirt near the side road."

The guard hands me a dirty note that looks just like the other notes all have. I take it from him and read the script.

Wait for my call. – Damien

I crunch the paper and squeeze my eyes shut.

What the fuck have I done?

Thirty-Two

Birdie

I'M IN A VAN with a blindfold on and my hands bound. The man kept his mask on when he took me, and he had one thing he didn't have the last time he visited me—a gun.

It was probably stupid of me to not fight back, but he threatened Liam and Hammer, and of all people... my mom. His exact words were, *"If you don't come with me, I'll kill Lorri and your lover boy, maybe even his big cousin in there."*

This stalker did his research, and I don't trust him to not follow through on his words. Maybe instead of screwing Liam's brains out, I should have had him teach me self-defense instead. If I make it out of this, I sure as hell am going to learn.

"I won't hurt you, Birdie. You can relax."

My back stiffens at his words, and suddenly I want to cry. This man really wants me to relax? "I don't believe you," I tell him, trying to keep my voice strong.

"My plan was never to hurt you. I told you I wanted you, and I got you."

My stomach turns. I shouldn't ask this question, but I do anyway. "What are you going to do with me?"

"You'll find out soon."

I bite my tongue to keep from crying as we continue to drive in silence awhile longer. Honestly, I don't know how long because my thoughts are clogged with Liam, Hammer, and Mom.

The man says he didn't hurt Hammer, but I don't know if I can believe him. I'd be stupid to. This is all my fault; I shouldn't have let

Liam take me on this day trip. I should've stayed inside like everyone wanted me to. The worst part is, I know Liam's going to blame himself. If I die, it's going to break him—especially after what he told me today.

When the car eventually pulls to a stop, the door is thrown open and I'm shoved outside. For a moment we're in the warm afternoon air, but then I'm assaulted with the smell of smoke and gasoline. It reminds me of a mechanic's shop. I wrinkle my nose and wonder why this guy would risk kidnapping me in broad daylight.

"Took you long enough," a woman says. The voice sounds familiar.

"Took us longer than we thought for them to go outside. Good call on hiring those two actors though to play guard. They set off that gun and it worked like a charm."

My stomach turns. Those guards weren't real, and if they were hired, then—I know that voice.

"Shea?"

I have a sense of her watching me. But instead of saying anything, she says, "I have to get back before they notice I'm gone."

I hear the telltale sign of heels click away and I have to stop myself from crying again. Liam was right. I can't believe she'd do this to me. And working with this creep? I feel like I'm living in a weird-ass movie.

The man abruptly grabs my arm, he doesn't hurt me, but he pulls me around before pushing me down into a chair. After a few seconds he pulls the blindfold off. His mask is gone and for a moment I feel like I'm looking into a mirror. Green- and gold-flecked eyes, high cheekbones, tall stature, long blonde hair. He's got to be in his late forties and he's muscular with tattoos on his arms.

"Hello Birdie. It's nice to see you again."

An awkward laugh bubbles up out of my lips. "Seriously?" What in the Twilight Zone is going on right now? "Who the fuck are you?"

His face turns stony. "Don't act like you really don't know."

I stare at him, and he stares at me. I try to place him. He looks like me but—my mom doesn't have any brothers and my dad... no way. He can't be...

"Are you sure you don't know?" he asks again, his eyebrow raised.

I push down the growing unease in my stomach. I try to be brave, to channel my inner strength. If this man is my dad, then he wouldn't hurt me, right? I stare at him square in the eyes, the ones that look exactly like mine. "Why don't you tell me?"

"Did Lorri never show you pictures of me?"

Right. Well, that answers my question. How could a dad do this to a daughter? The things those letters said... I want to vomit, and I almost do.

"What do you want from me?" I say weakly.

"I want to talk with you."

"You could have called," I snort.

"Lorri wouldn't give me your number. Said you didn't want to see me or talk to me."

My stomach sinks. Mom always told me my dad was a passing fling, that he didn't even know I was born. Said she couldn't find him. At a certain point in my childhood, I stopped caring that I didn't have a dad. I had Mom, and Liam for a while, then Ben and Wren, and of course my music. I stopped thinking about the fact that I didn't have a father figure in my life many years ago.

"You had to know about me. Lorri made it seem like you knew."

I shake my head, bile burning the back of my throat. I have a dad who actually wanted to be in my life. As I look at the man before me though, a man who can do what he's done, and now kidnapping me, I'm one hundred percent sure Mom must have kept him away for a reason. But that still didn't explain Shea and why she's helping him.

"Why are you doing this? I don't understand."

"I'm entitled to money. Your half of me and I deserve a little bit of the pot. The rest of your family isn't like you, kid. We've got bills to pay, and times are hard. I tried to ask Lorri politely, but she said that you didn't want to talk to me. That you weren't a bank. But I disagree."

"So, you decided to stalk and kidnap me? Those letters you wrote you—"

"Those were Shea's ideas. She thought we should scare you. That it would make you more pliable and easier to take advantage of."

My tongue feels like a weight in my mouth. "Your plan makes no sense. The letters... you coming to the bus! None of it makes sense."

"Well, I wasn't planning on kidnapping you. Just asking for money to make the letters go away, but Shea said that wouldn't work. That you wouldn't pay unless we did this."

"You're wrong," I spit. "And why is Shea even helping you?"

The man before me chuckles darkly. "You haven't caught on?"

"Why don't you spell it out for me?" I cry. "I'm not one for games."

"She's your half-sister."

I feel my world begin to close in on me. A half-sister?

"If you're wondering why that didn't show up on your little boyfriend's background check, her mom's sister took her in after she was born, and I wasn't on the birth certificate. But she found me when she was a teenager and we've had a relationship ever since. I told her all about her sister, Birdie—the famous rock star," he smirks.

"How long have you both been planning this?"

"A long time."

I really am in some twisted movie. The dad I never had and the half-sister I never knew about hatch a diabolical plan to scare me shitless and weasel money out of me? It's sick. It's twisted. It's—

"I know what you think of me. But you've been flouncing around for years, acting like you're better than everyone. You have a ton of money while your family is left to suffer."

"I didn't know about you! Or Shea! And do you know how much I pay her? She's taken care of."

"She's your help!" he cuts. "She tells me all she does for you. The long hours she works and the sleepless nights. You owe her more than a shitty job."

"I don't owe you or her anything! Especially you. How could you do this to your own flesh and blood?"

"Look kid, here is what's going to happen. You're going to give your long-lost family money every month. If you do that, you won't hear from us. You don't even have to look at us. Just give us our due and that's it. The letters stop, the public embarrassment stops. All of it. I'll even leave your bodyguard lover alone."

"If you fucking touch him—"

"You'll what? I hold all the cards here."

"And you just expect to walk away from this and there'll be no consequences? How did you and Shea think this would end?"

"After we're through here, you're going to be a good little girl and let this all slide. And you know why? Because I have friends, kid. Friends that do bad things. Those friends will hurt people if I want them too. Trust me, you don't want that in your life. So, you give us money, and we leave it at that. It's simple really."

My mind spirals. I may be scared, but I'm also not stupid enough to let this guy and Shea get away with it. The world doesn't work the way he thinks it does. This is going to be all over the news. Nothing ends well in this scenario. Nothing.

I swallow. "You expect me to walk back into my hotel room and just dismiss this entire thing?"

"Of course not. That's where Shea comes in. We're going to ransom you."

"And how do you plan to do that?"

"Shea of course. She has access to all your accounts."

My heart clenches. Once I get out of this, I make a mental note to check if that bitch isn't stealing from me already. God, this is all such a mess. I can tell this man really thinks he's going to get away with this. My eyes flutter to his gun and then back up to his smiling eyes.

"I'll give you your money. Just let me go," I say.

He shakes his head. "I don't think so. I want to get to know you. You're my daughter after all."

"I'm not your anything."

"See, it's comments like that that make me think you did know about me, yet you chose to ignore your other family. Lorri always thought she was too good for me."

"I didn't know about you. She never even mentioned your name. I still don't know what it is."

"Nick," he says. "You have my eyes and my hair." His offhand comment throws me. It's true, I do, but that doesn't make me his daughter. I'd never want a man capable of this to be related to me.

"Did you know about me when you left?" I ask quietly.

He stands and I can't help but flinch. He says he won't hurt me, but a man who could write such horrible letters to his own daughter and then kidnap her and threaten those she loves... I don't trust him for one second.

But instead of walking toward me, he goes to a small fridge and pulls out a cheap beer. "I was in the military. Me and Lorri met in a bar in Michigan right before I shipped off to the Persian Gulf. I didn't know about you until a friend of mine told me."

"And you didn't try to see me?"

He takes a long drink from his beer. "Not at first. It was hard to get in touch with your mom back then. Eventually I came to Michigan. You were four. You don't remember but I met you. Lorri and I had a big fight and she told me to never come back."

"So, you just gave up?"

"I was young and stupid. I had shit going on."

"And now you want money from me? You hardly even tried to be in my life," my chest heaves. I start to feel daring, even though I really shouldn't, "You just lucked out that I got famous. Now you want a piece of the pie. This has nothing to do with me being your kid."

He huffs a dark laugh. "You don't know anything, kid. I think you know the time for a relationship has long since passed. I'll get what I'm owed, your sister too, then we'll be out of your hair. As long as you keep paying up of course."

"You're sick."

He shakes his head. "I've been called worse."

His phone chimes and Nick grabs it from his pocket. Without saying a word, he exits into what I think is an office, closing the door behind him. I pull my hands and legs against the bindings that hold me, testing their strength. He's tied them pretty tight, tight enough that I'm starting to lose feeling in my fingers a bit. I look to the ceiling and pray that Liam or someone finds me soon.

After a minute or so goes by, Nick returns, his booted feet clunking on the concrete as he approaches me. I notice he keeps his hand on his gun as if to scare me.

When he stops about a foot away, he slides his phone back in his pocket and says, "It's showtime, kid. Get ready for your best performance yet."

Thirty-Three

Liam

I FEEL LIKE MY blood is boiling beneath my skin as I pace the floor of the distillery. Hammer is talking to the police, telling them everything that went down and how he found the note.

Eric and Gia have also arrived. They're off to the side, Gia on the phone speaking wildly to the press making statements while Eric is working to postpone tonight's show. Birdie is going to be so upset she couldn't perform for her fans.

Every time I close my eyes, I see her face right before I leave her standing alone at the gazebo. I'll never forgive myself for doing that. Never. Every second since she went missing, I've had to keep horrible thoughts from my head.

My phone buzzes, giving me a short distraction. When I pull it from my pocket, I feel disappointed that it's not Birdie. But when I see who's calling, I'm not surprised to see it's Lorri Wilder. We'd only just talked this morning.

My gut churns when I think of what I learned from her. I felt guilty the entire ride to Hammer's not telling Birdie what I knew, but I planned to tell her tonight after dinner. That plan obviously failed. I run a hand through my hair. Lorri Wilder confirmed what I knew after seeing that man's face on Shea's profile. The moment I mentioned the name Nick Squires, Lorri went into shock, nearly hanging up on me.

But eventually she told me the truth. Nick is Birdie's dad. She asked if I would keep it a secret for her, but I'd refused. I couldn't depend on Lorri to tell her. Now I see that I should have told Birdie right away. I'll live with that mistake forever. The only solace I take now is that I have a connection of mine looking into Nick Squires. I hope he finds something soon. Something that will lead us to Birdie.

I have a feeling he's the one who kidnapped her. I've already told the police my theory, but they can't find him in any records in Nashville. For once I wish Shea were here so I could get information from her, but she's yet to show her face. Which leads me to think I'm correct in all my assumptions.

When my phone continues to ring, I know I need to answer it. "Hello?"

"LIAM! Jesus, Liam!" Lorri yells through the phone. "Tell me what I saw on the news isn't true!"

"I'm sorry, Lorri. I wish I had better news."

She sobs through the phone and my heart breaks again. I've let Birdie down bigtime, and now I'm fucking standing here waiting for this asshole's phone call.

"Liam, you have to go find her."

My fist clenches around the phone. "Lorri, do you have any information about Nick that you haven't shared with me? Does he have connections in Nashville?"

She takes a shuddering breath. "Do you really think Nick has something to do with this?"

I rub the back of my neck. "I think he does."

"I didn't want to believe it but—"

I cut her off. "Believe what?"

"Nick made a threat a few years ago. He wanted me to get Birdie to pay him some money to start a garage. I told him that Birdie had no interest in him and refused to give him money."

"Nick thinks that Birdie knows he's her father?"

There's a pause before she answers, "Yes."

Fuck. "Wait, Lorri—did you say he wanted money to start a garage?"

"Yeah, he was a mechanic before he enlisted. Why is that important?"

Before I can answer, Eric interrupts. "Liam! They were able to ping Birdie's phone and we have a location. Fucker must have forgotten to get rid of it."

Hope bubbles up in me for the first time in hours. "Lorri, I've got to go. We'll call you as soon as we hear something." I ignore Lorri's protests as I hang up and turn toward Eric. "You know where she is?"

"We have a general idea. Patrol cars are on their way."

"I think I know—" My words are interrupted by the sound of the door opening. Shea walks in, her face streaked with tears. She's holding up her phone.

"The kidnapper is on the line!" she wails. "He wants to talk to Liam."

The room goes still and silent. Everyone's eyes are on me, and I feel the heat of the cops' gaze on me too, like they think I have something to do with this. I don't have time to focus on my failures though, because I know Shea is a lying piece of shit. Her tear-stained face is all a lie. I don't know for sure what her relationship with Nick Squires is, but I do have a feeling it's not good.

With my eyes still locked on Shea, I lean over to Eric and whisper the information about the mechanic's shop in his ear. He's confused, but I can't risk Shea overhearing. Her eyes are already curious as to what I said, though she's trying to keep her little act up. I pat Eric's shoulder but still don't look at him. I just hope he's a better actor than Shea.

I take a cautious step toward her, conscious of the fact my handgun is now tucked into the back of my pants. I don't trust anything about the woman before me and I'm glad I have assurance. I'm surprised when all she does is thrust the phone in my face.

I grab hold of the phone but keep my eyes on her. Her gaze is flat, her little act crumpling. She knows that I know. She can tell in my movements. I have to be careful since I have no idea what Shea is capable of. The last thing I want is for Birdie or anyone in this room to get hurt.

I hold the phone up to my ear. "Hello?"

The voice that comes through the phone is the same one from the radio station. "Mr. Miller. Nice of you to speak with me." His tone is scratchy, like he's smoked one too many cigarettes.

"Give the phone to Birdie," I say calmly. In the background I can see Eric talking to Gia. When she looks at Shea, which doesn't go unnoticed, Shea starts to get nervous. She pushes some of her purple hair behind her ear. *Shit*. I have a bad feeling.

"She's fine," Damien, or should I say Nick, barks.

"Liam, I'm here!" Birdie calls from the background.

"Shut up, kid! Or I'll gag you again."

I almost lose my cool at his words, but relief floods me at the sound of her voice. "What do you want?" My voice is tense.

"Five million in small bills by tomorrow morning."

"Not going to happen," I say automatically. "I'm not sure if you know how money works, but most people don't have millions just lying around. Money like that takes time to get."

"Birdie says her assistant can get it. She knows her accounts."

Shea has the decency to look shocked. There is no doubt in my mind that she's involved now. Their plan is idiotic and very sloppily done. They may have been smart when it came to the stalker bit, but this plan? It was never going to work.

"Is that so?" I say into the phone, my voice condescending. "Even if we can get that type of cash by the morning, how do you propose we get it to you?"

"I'll send instructions via her assistant."

"Of course, you will." There's a pause at the end of line, then he says tightly, "I'll be in touch."

When the phone call is over, the room remains silent. Shea and I are in a showdown. She knows her jig is up. Nobody in the room knows what I know, but I can see it in her eyes. She's scared.

"I know what you've done, Shea," I say calmly. I watch as her shoulders tense.

"I've got nothing to do with this," she retorts.

"You're lying."

"What's going on here?" Gia's voice interrupts us.

I hold my hand up to stop Gia from moving any closer. I can tell Shea is about to do something stupid. Her body language is undeniable. When I see Shea's hand move toward her back, I spring into action. I lunge forward, Shea's phone flying as multiple voices shout out in the room. Shea's fast, I'll give her that, but I'm faster. Just as she's about to pull out a pistol I manage to grab her arm. I twist hard, bracing it against her back. She cries out, the gun dropping to the ground.

"It's over, Shea!" I yell, still trying to subdue her. She's wriggling against me, her legs trying to knee me in the groin. It doesn't take long for the cops to come help me grab her and soon she's maneuvered on the ground. It gives me more delight than it should to take a pair of cuffs from the cop and bind her.

"You fucking asshole!" she screams. "You have no idea! Really, you don't."

I shake my head. "That's where you're wrong. I do know. You should be more careful who you're friends with on social media, Shea. The internet is full of bad people."

Her face turns white, and for a split second, I feel bad for her. Her greed and whatever else has blinded her into ruining her young life. I'm not sure of the whole story but I know we'll find out soon enough.

Once the police have righted her, a silly smirk plasters her face. "Without my cooperation, you'll never find her," she spits.

Though her words are a threat, she just admitted in front of the cops that she had a hand in all of this. I bend down so my mouth is next to her ear. "That's where you're wrong, Shea. I'm already one step ahead."

Thirty-Four

Birdie

HEARING LIAM'S VOICE THROUGH the phone was exactly what I needed to keep my spirits up. Knowing he's fine makes my heart clench with joy. I just hope Hammer is okay, too.

Nick on the other hand doesn't look so hot. He's sweating and chain smoking as if it's his last night on earth. Clearly something's wrong. And when I heard him ask for five million, I wanted to laugh out loud. The fact that Shea really thought they could get that much money on a whim is insane. Then once they got it, what would they do with it? Disappear to Panama?

"Your people better get me that money, kid." His voice is shaky as he takes another drag from his cigarette.

I don't answer him because I don't know what to say. Instead, I squeeze my hands and wiggle my toes to bring some life back into them. Hopefully there won't be any permanent nerve damage. I need my hands to play piano. I hold back a groan as a shooting pain moves through my back from sitting on this hard chair. My ample ass doesn't help pad me as much as I wish it did.

When Nick starts to pace, I can't help myself. "Why are you really doing this?"

His hazel gaze, my gaze, stares into me. His smirk is gone, and a sad look is on his face. "It's unfair. The way you rich live. I served this country, and I can't even get proper health care. I should own my own shop but instead I work here for a shitty hourly wage!" He chuffs, kicking a loose piece of drywall.

My eyes wander his body and I really take him in from head to toe. The way he stands, the way his muscles look weak and his face tired. "You're sick," I say as more of a statement.

"It doesn't matter what I am."

"You could have just come to me—"

"And what? You'd just fork over money? Lorri said you wanted nothing to do with me. Time and time again I asked, and you denied me."

"I didn't know about you!" I say again. "It's the truth! I didn't know."

He lets out an anguished laugh. "It doesn't matter now. What's done is done."

Sadness fills me. He did wrong here, so did Shea, but nobody deserves to suffer. I take a deep breath and lower my head. This whole situation is such a mess. Once I get out of this, I for sure need to have a long talk with Mom. The fact she kept all this from me, I—fuck. I don't know what to feel. All I know is that I'm confused, and I really wish he'd untie me so I could feel my hands again.

I'm about to ask for him to loosen the bindings when I hear a faint noise. At first, I'm unsure what it is, but as it gets closer, I know. It's a helicopter. My gaze darts to Nick as he begins to freak out. He mutters something under his breath, then digs out his phone. I think he tries to call Shea, but there's no answer.

Relief floods through my veins at his obvious disappointment. They're coming for me. Liam is coming for me. Thank God. But before I can get too excited, I see something in Nick's features shift. I've seen it before, too. It's a look some of my obsessed fans get, a look that I've seen too much of. Nick is desperate, and desperate people do stupid things.

In seconds he's hoisting me up roughly. He bends down and opens a pocketknife, cutting the bindings on my ankles. "Walk," he demands.

"Nick—"

"Walk, kid. I won't ask again."

I stumble as the blood rushes back in my legs, but I manage to walk forward. When we reach the front of the garage the doors are closed, but there's a front door that has glass on the front of it. I see the familiar flash of red and blue lights, followed by the sound of car doors shutting. I should have felt safe then, but by Nick's actions and body language, I don't think he's just going to hand me over without a fight. He doesn't have anything to lose.

"Nick," I plead softly. "We can work something out."

"I'm not stupid, kid. I know how this ends."

"I won't press charges if you just let me walk out there. You can leave unharmed."

"You may think I'm an idiot, but I'm not going to believe that."

"NICK SQUIRES, COME OUT WITH YOUR HANDS UP," an amplified voice calls from outside.

"Do as they say, Nick. Please."

He doesn't listen to me. Instead, he pushes me forward toward the door with one hand, the other cocking his shotgun. My stomach knots. Is he planning on killing me? What would that achieve?

"You said you weren't going to hurt me," I plead.

Nick clenches his jaw but refuses to meet my eyes. Once we reach the door, he cracks it open. I hear sounds of movement then the amplified voice again, "COME OUT WITH YOUR HANDS UP. WE DO NOT WANT TO CAUSE YOU HARM."

Nick laughs mechanically as he peeks his head out. "I want my five million and to walk away from this alive. But that's not going to happen!" Nick calls back.

"COME OUT WITH YOUR HANDS UP," the officer yells again.

"Please Nick. Just do as they say. I'll help you get the treatment you need. We're family, after all."

He turns his head to me for a split second. "Family," he shakes his head. "We'll never be family." Before I can say more, Nick pushes the door open then shoves me in front of him. My hands feel like they might fall off, and I let out a cry of pain from the jolt. If anything happens to my hands... They're part of me, my music. God, how did I end up here? How is this man my dad? Tears collect in my eyes as the bright headlights of the cop cars hit me.

"Release the hostage and put your weapon on the ground!" the cop tells Nick, no longer using his megaphone.

When my eyes adjust to the darkness, I immediately find Liam's eyes. His face is tight with emotion, but I can see the relief in his eyes. He's also angry as hell. He stands at the ready, gun aimed right at Nick. I can't help but smile at him. Even though I haven't been gone that long, seeing him feels surreal.

Nick holds me tighter to him, then places the gun to my temple. My heart skips a beat, and my eyes fall closed. Is this how it ends? When I open my eyes again, Liam is staring right at me. I can't help it, but just in case this is the last time I see him, I have to let him know.

I love you; I mouth silently. *I love you.* I see his jaw tick, his features distressed. After a moment he shakes his head, and I know it's not because he doesn't feel it, but because he doesn't want to say it right now.

A tear slips down my cheek as Nick grips me, pressing the gun further into my skull. "Walk away now and no one gets hurt!" Nick yells. But I know he doesn't believe his own words. I can feel him shaking.

"Nick," I manage to say. "Please just put the gun down."

For less than a second he looks at me, but it's just enough time for someone to fire their gun. I let out a strangled noise at the loud bang, my brain not able to put together where it came from. When I feel no pain, my eyes find Liam's. His gun is smoking slightly, his gaze is flat. When he starts to move toward me, I realize that Nick is on the ground.

There's more yelling going on around me right before my knees hit the concrete. Without Nick holding me I can't keep myself upright.

Within a moment, Liam is kneeling in front of me, but the sound ambulance in the distance makes me look toward Nick. It's hard to see, but I catch a glimpse of his face. He's staring at me and for a moment I think he's dead. But after a few long seconds, he blinks. My heart beats fast and I breathe out the tight feeling in my chest. Nick did wrong here, and I'm not sure if he was really going to hurt me, but I didn't want him to die.

Liam's hands move to my face. "Birdie, are you okay?"

His brown eyes are warm as he looks into my eyes.

"I'm not hurt," I manage to say, pulling my wrists against my ties.

"Let me untie you," he says, emotion thick in his voice.

He gently eases me forward and rests my head on his shoulder. I breathe in the scent of him: cedar, musk, and pine. He unties the binds, but I still can't help the hiss that escapes my mouth. When the blood rushes back into my fingers it feels like thousands of pins are being stuck into me. My arms fall dead at my sides and my head throbs.

Liam uses his good arm to pull me into him, letting his chin rest on top of my head.

"You're safe now, baby," he mutters against my hair. "I've got you."

I release a loud sob, and he only holds me tighter.

"You're safe," he whispers again. "You're safe."

Thirty-Five

Liam

IT'S BEEN FORTY-EIGHT HOURS since the incident.

Nick Squires is being treated for a gunshot wound to the left thigh but is expected to make a full recovery. I've since found out he's been suffering from colon cancer. But unlike Birdie, I can't find it in my heart to feel bad for the man who terrorized her and held her at gunpoint. I don't feel bad for Shea either, who's currently sitting in a local precinct after being denied bail along with the two men she hired to play security guard for the day.

Birdie whimpers and I turn my eyes toward her sleeping form. It's just after eight in the morning, and the early sun makes her skin glow and her hair look like spun gold. My heart squeezes in my chest when I think about what could have happened that night. I almost lost her forever.

Watching her own dad hold a gun to her head, I don't think I'll ever be able to erase that image from my mind. Every time I close my eyes I see it, and my sleep has been absolute shit because of it. It appears that my life is meant to be plagued with horrible scenes of those I care about being threatened, or worse.

It doesn't help that every time I catch sight of her bruised wrists, my stomach sours. There's no nerve damage, she'll just be sore for a bit. The doctor said there's no reason to believe her piano playing would be affected. The relief on her face when he told her that—my eyes burn at the memory.

The worst part is, my slip-ups, my prioritization of our relationship over her safety, it's why the other day happened. If I acted faster on the information I discovered on social media, I could have gotten ahead of Nick and Shea. When I mentioned this to Birdie at the hospital, she quickly brushed it off. She told me she understood why I didn't tell her right away. But even with her assurance I still feel guilty as fuck.

Birdie smiles gently and makes another tiny noise—I wonder what she's dreaming about. The first night after we got back from the hospital, I held her all night while she tossed and turned from nightmares. She hardly speaks about what went down. She'll need to talk about it eventually, but I understand why she can't right now. She's already told the police what happened—and then Gia, Eric, and the band. They were shocked that Shea was the culprit and her half-sister. I think they all blamed themselves for not putting the pieces together.

Eric and the label asked if she wanted to cancel the rest of the tour, and for a moment I wondered if Birdie would consider it. I should have known better. She asked to postpone the next few stops, then pick up back in Louisiana where Ben and Wren would meet us. Eric tried to give her more time, but she insisted she would be fine. Even if she wasn't, I knew Birdie would go on anyway and give them one hell of a show. That's just who she is.

I run my hands through my mussed hair. I've been in emotional turmoil since the event. Not just from what happened, but what to do next. From the moment Birdie mouthed that she loved me, I knew she had accepted the fact that her own dad may kill her. That she could leave this world and be okay with it. It pissed me off. Not only that she resigned herself to that fate, but that I'd put her in that position. That I'd failed her, just as I'd failed Maria.

Over the last forty-eight hours I've tried to come to terms with the love I have for Birdie. I wanted to say it back, but at the same time, I couldn't. I do love her. I love her too much, and that's the problem. Losing Maria changed my life—but losing Birdie—she's better off without me screwing up her life more than I already have. No matter what we are to each other, her life is more important. She deserves to be with someone that won't fail her. That won't let their love blind them like it blinded me. I came here to do a job, and I failed at that job.

I pry my eyes away from the beautiful woman I love, to the suitcases before me. I need to leave before I lose my nerve. But I'm not going to leave without saying goodbye. I may be an asshole, but if I left without telling her why, then I'd be a heartless asshole. I can't do that to her.

"Liam..." Birdie's sleepy voice mumbles.

"Go back to sleep," I say quietly.

"I can hear you thinking from here. Come back to bed. It's early." She opens her eyes a crack, but when she takes in the fact I'm not moving, she stiffens. "What is it Liam?" She sits up then, the tight shirt she's wearing stretching as she moves.

My mouth goes dry, and I hate myself for what I'm about to do. I planned on doing this when she woke up after a good night's sleep, but I should have known she'd wake up when I wasn't next to her. I pause for a moment but decide it's better to just say it. There will never be a good time to tell her I'm leaving.

"We need to talk."

She takes in my bags, and I see her jaw tighten. Wide awake now, her hazel eyes are pained. "You're leaving." It's a statement, not a question. She says it as if she knew I would. That makes my heart wrench even more.

"I have to."

Birdie takes a shuddering breath then moves to get off the bed. She's not wearing any pants, and her white shirt is almost see-through. I focus on her eyes, not allowing myself to succumb to how much I want her. Not just her body, but her mind, her heart, her soul. The worst part is, I know she would willingly give it all to me. She'd go all in and convince me to do the same. But I can't. I can't do that to her.

Birdie crosses her arms over her chest, her stance harsh. "You were going to leave without saying anything."

I shake my head as I stand to meet her. "No, of course not."

Her shoulders ease just slightly, but her anger is replaced with confusion. "I don't understand... I knew you were pulling away, but I thought we'd get through it. I thought—damn it, Liam. What the hell are you thinking?" she cries, her voice thick with sadness. "I thought I meant more to you than this."

My hands itch to touch her, but by some miracle I keep them at my sides. I have to stay strong. "You do. You do mean more."

Birdie takes a step forward, her eyes gleaming with unshed tears. "Then why are you leaving?" Anger lingers in her words, and I can't even blame her.

"I failed you. I can't put you in danger again. You deserve better, so much better."

She shakes her head vehemently, her eyes now hard. "Is this why you've been so quiet? Why you won't touch me? You didn't fail me, Liam. You didn't!" She cries. This time she touches me, her hands trembling on my cheeks. "You can talk to me, Liam. Please, I—"

"Birdie, I can't lose you. And by staying I'm putting you in harm's way."

Her fingers grip my cheeks. "You're speaking crap, Liam! You realize how stupid you sound? You saved me. You got me out of harm's way. And now the threat is gone. And if you leave, you're losing me. If you stay, you have me Liam. You fucking have me!"

I place a hand over her trembling one. "This is all my fault. I can't risk doing something that could put you in danger again. I have someone coming to replace me that will make sure you're safe."

A broken sob escapes her throat. "You keep me safe, Liam. You! I don't want someone else."

"I'm sorry," I say, because I really am. I'm sorry for the heartbreak I caused her, for the damage I've done. I'm also sorry for leaving this way, but I need to do it now before I give in. This is for her own good. I know it is.

Tears roll down her cheeks and I know it's time to leave.

"You don't have to do this, Liam. We just found each other—and I love you," she sobs softly.

A lump forms in my throat. "I—" God I want to say it so badly, but I can't, not now. "I'm sorry," I say instead.

Her hands quickly drop, and she takes a large step back. I watch as the woman I love is replaced by someone cold right before my eyes. "Get out, Liam."

"Birdie..." But the words die on my lips.

"Get out, Liam. You've made yourself perfectly clear. Have a nice life."

I want to reach out and comfort her, but I know better. I've made my bed, now I must lie in it. I grab my bags and walk out of the bedroom, my heart thumping in my ears. Birdie doesn't follow, and I can't help but wish she did. Wish she'd beg me more, slap me or tell me how much she couldn't stand to be without me until I broke down. But this is what I want. This is what's best. Right?

As I walk down the hallway of the hotel, I can't help but feel like I just made the worst mistake of my life.

Thirty-Six

Birdie

THE CURTAINS OPEN AND the bright sun hits my face. I cringe while a noise of protest leaves my lips. "You're evil, you know that?"

Wren stands in my line of vision, her hands on her hips. "I'm here to help take your blues away, not support your vampiric activities."

I snort. "I'm just trying to get some sleep."

She rolls her eyes, "Kevin told me that you've been sleeping all day in the dark since Nashville."

I huff. "Not *all* day." Which is true. I've gotten out of bed for rehearsal and small meals of toast and coffee. My stomach still can't handle much else.

"Come on. Get up, shower. You have rehearsal soon and then we're going to the spa for a little pampering."

My eyebrow lifts. "You planned our day?"

"Duh. Without Ben here you have to keep me occupied. Gia said she cleared your schedule, so besides rehearsal, you're all mine, crazy biotch!"

I can't help but smile at Wren's cheerfulness. Despite having told her to cancel her trip to see me, I'm glad she came. But sadness nags at me because she lost out on the chance to spend time with Ben. I can tell that she's also struggling to not speak about Liam. So far, the only time she slipped was to tell me that Ben stayed back in New York to be with him. I'm glad for it too. I just don't want to know anything else.

"Just tell me there's coffee and eventually pizza involved."

She clicks her tongue. "Duh. Now get your depressed ass ready. I don't want to be late."

"Fine," I sigh, pulling the covers off and making my way out of bed. Once my feet touch the cool wooden floor, I put my hands on my knees. The marks on my wrists have almost faded. I'll have to put some makeup on them tonight for the show, but at least they feel good.

The last eight days have been hell. Not only do I have to continue to talk to the police and deal with the aftermath of finding out I have not only a dad, but a half-sister, my heart aches for Liam. Once again, I feel like my sixteen-year-old self—lost, confused, rejected—the only thing I don't feel this time is alone.

My band is constantly around me. They take everything in stride and don't make a big deal out of what happened. So now my daily routine consists of rehearsal, going to my room, watching bad movies, and crying. Sometimes Gia joins me, but she doesn't try to talk to me about what happened or why Liam left. Of course, Mom keeps calling, but I told her I'll talk with her when I'm ready. There's only so much I can take right now and listening to her excuses as to why she kept family from me is not one of them.

Wren places her hand on my shoulder, her green eyes full of concern. "Are you okay, B?"

I blink away the sadness that threatens to spill forward. "Yeah. I'm fine." Even though I'm anything but fine. Eventually I'll talk to my therapist and deal with what happened in Nashville, but right now I just want to hang out with my best friend and get ready for my show. My fans deserve a good show, and I want to prove to the world that Birdie Wilder can't be broken. Not by a stalker, not by family drama, and sure as hell not by a man.

Once I'm off the bed I give Wren a hug. "Thank you for coming here. I'm glad you did." Her body relaxes against mine. The comfort and familiarity of her feels like home. When I pull back, I think it's the first time I've had a real smile on my face in over a week.

She smiles back, her gaze warm. "Anytime, B. Anytime."

Thankfully, rehearsal goes well, and I feel confident tonight's show will be great. Maybe it will even be one of our best. Given the circumstances, that's a damn miracle.

I take a sip of the mimosa in my hand then lean my head back as the whirlpool jets knead my shoulders. Wren and I just got a massage and facial. I'm feeling loose and relaxed for the first time in a while. Despite everything that's gone down, it's nice to know I don't have a stalker out there at the moment. At least I hope not.

"I wish I could do this every day," Wren sighs happily. "Think if I retire early the flower shop will survive without me?

I chuckle. "Probably not."

"You're right. Well, I'll enjoy it while I can. Do you get to do this often?"

I think of the last time I had a spa day in Florida. Liam and I had our moment in the sauna. My smile falters, and Wren notices.

"I'm sorry, I didn't mean to make you sad with that question."

My eyes meet hers. "It's not your fault. The last time I went to the spa Liam and I—I guess that's when we sort of came to a truce."

Wren sets down her mimosa and moves closer to me. "Do you want to talk about him? I know it's a sore subject but..."

"You want the deets," I finish for her with a grin.

"I mean, I am your best girlfriend, and I didn't even know you and Liam were a thing until... Well, you know."

"Do you know anything?" I ask, genuinely curious.

"Not very much. And please don't be mad at Ben for saying something. He was concerned about Liam and needed advice."

I exhale. "Don't worry. I'm not mad. We're all friends here. And even if Liam did break my heart, I'm glad he has someone to talk to. Especially someone like Ben."

"Maybe it will help if you talk about it, Birdie. I know you know this, but I'm worried about you."

I audibly sigh and take a long sip of my drink. Thankfully it's heavier on the champagne side. "I know you are. I just needed some time to process. It all happened so fast."

"What did?"

"Liam and I..." I make a wild gesture, "...everything."

Wren nods like she understands. "I don't know much, but I do know Liam feels like shit."

I snort. "He should."

"Tell me, Birdie. I want to dish with you like old times." She taps the side of her champagne flute almost mischievously. "It will make you feel better."

I huff a laugh. "Only if we can talk about what the heck is going on with you and Ben."

She groans dramatically. "Do I have to?"

"That's the deal. My boy drama for your boy drama."

She contemplates for a moment, then holds out her hand.

"Deal."

We shake on it, and with another drink, I begin the story of me and Liam.

Wren listens with rapt attention every second I speak. When I get to the kidnapping, my stomach is in knots. But she hears everything and even holds my hand. It feels so good to talk to her, someone who knows me. By the time I finish I'm glad we made this deal.

"God, B. What a dick!!!"

I've just finished the story with the morning Liam left.

"If it makes you feel any better, if Liam told Ben any of this, Ben is going to rip him a new asshole. You're like a sister to him and he'd protect you till the very end."

My heart squeezes. "That means a lot to me. But I don't know, even though it hurts, I think I understand why he did it."

Wren raises an eyebrow at me. "That's very mature of you to say."

A laugh bubbles out of me. "Don't get me wrong, I'm still hurt. Really hurt. When I woke up and I saw his suitcases... I think I knew before he walked out that he was struggling. Right before I was kidnapped, he told me all about his accident."

Wren's shoulders straighten. "About that... sorry I didn't tell you. I wanted to; I swear. But Ben thought it would be best if we left you out of it. You were on a European tour and working on an album. And—"

I cut her off. "It's fine Wren. I'm not mad, just—I wish the past was different sometimes, you know?"

She releases a tight breath. "I know. Me too, but it's not. All we can do is move forward and, can I be frank with you, B?"

"You know you can," I tell her seriously. "You're my best friend. I wouldn't expect any less."

"Liam is a dick for what he did, but I think you know he acted out of fear. And I know you couldn't have, but you didn't see him after the accident. He was a totally different person. I've never seen him so withdrawn and scared. For a while Ben thought he had an alcohol problem, but when he asked Liam about it, he immediately cut back on his usage. Then he went to Nashville and finally pulled himself together, but he never really was the same after that.

"The accident changed something in him forever. I can only imagine what seeing you in that situation was like for him; what memories it brought back. Liam wouldn't leave someone he cares about without a reason, and I think for him this is the best one."

I listen to all her words carefully. Part of me completely understands, but the other part that was rejected—it doesn't.

"So, you think he's justified in his decision to leave me? I told him I loved him, Wren! He just walked away without looking back."

She squeezes my hand. "All I know is that he's scared shitless. He's never had a stable relationship, Birdie, not even with his parents. You're the closest thing he's ever had to one. Then you almost died on his watch. He's broken up about it and he doesn't know how to deal with his emotions. He doesn't know how to deal with loving you."

I feel like I've been punched in the gut. She's right. I know she's right. But there's still a part of me that doesn't want to forgive him so easily. He hurt me once ten years ago, and the second time hurts worse, especially since we were together this time around. My heart aches for him, yet I also want to slap him.

"Relationships aren't easy, B. They never are. But if you believe in what you and Liam have, if you really do love him, just give him time. I think what he said and did is stupid and I think Ben is trying to make him realize that too. But it sounds like what you two have is really special. Not a lot of people can say they found the love of their life at fifteen. And all these bumps in the road? You'll figure out how to work around them. There's a reason you came into each other's lives again after so long."

Love of my life. Is that what Liam really is? I sure as hell have never felt this way about a person before.

"You really believe that?"

"I do. And I know it may be hard to hear, and I know you're hurt, but just give yourself some time, see what happens. I think you'll find your paths will cross again someday; when you're both ready."

I grin at her. "Since when did you become so good with words?"

She chuckles. "Flower arrangements aren't the only thing I'm good at."

I laugh with her. "I do have something to say though, about something you said."

"And what's that?"

"Something about finding the love of your life at fifteen—you know that's rare," I tease.

Her cheeks turn red. "Yeah, yeah. I get where you're going with this. Next, you're going to say I should listen to my own advice."

"You definitely can talk the talk, Wren my friend, but can you walk the walk?"

She shoves my shoulder. "Things between me and Ben are complicated."

"And as you said, relationships aren't easy."

Wren sighs. "No, no they're not."

"What's stopping you from being with him?"

"Distance mostly," she sighs. "He can't leave his gym and I can't leave my shop. He said he wants to open a place in Parker, but he doesn't have the finances yet. His rent in NYC is expensive. I try to be supportive, and I want to wait for him but—it's getting hard, B. Really hard. I want to get married and start a family."

The memory of speaking to Ben about becoming an investor re-enters my memory. I make a mental note to have my financial advisors look into it. If I can help my two best friends be together, I will. Especially for Wren.

I squeeze her hand this time. "It will work out, Wren. You and Ben are meant for each other. And not just because your names rhyme." I joke.

"Ha-ha." Her voice drips with sarcasm. "We're quite the pair, aren't we," she gestures between us.

I finish off my drink in one swig. "That we are, my friend. That we are."

Thirty-Seven

Liam

I HIT THE PUNCHING bag in front of me in rapid succession, imagining it's Nick's face.

"Wow. Glad I'm not that guy."

Ben's voice is full of mirth as he comes to stand next to me.

"If you want, I could get you into a fighting ring, make a few bucks."

I flash him a look.

"What?" he says, "I know a guy."

"Sure you do."

"Anyway, Wren's in town. Thought maybe the three of us could go grab a beer."

Her name piques my interest. The last I heard him talk about her was when she went to visit Birdie in Louisiana. Just the thought of Birdie's smile, her soft, curvy body and golden blonde hair makes my blood simultaneously heat and cool. Every day is a fight not to think of her, and I've been losing miserably. Ben knows it too. He's constantly on my case to get over myself, but he doesn't understand. Nobody does.

"What's she doing here?" I ask. Ben scratches the back of his head, and I feel my stomach flip. "Birdie's here, too?"

He nods. "Tour is on break for a bit while the band records a new album. I guess she has some awards thing this week. She invited Wren as her plus one."

Shit. I totally forgot about that. "I see."

"Birdie won't be there if you're wondering. I know your ass is too scared to see her face-to-face."

I grind my teeth. I have to stop myself from going back to the punching bag and pretending it's Ben's face. "If you're going to be an ass, then no, I won't go."

Ben sighs. "I'll be on my best behavior. Wren really wants to see you, man."

"If you promise not to get on my case about Birdie, I'll go. But I already made my decision. Don't make me go through this with you again."

"Okay, okay. I'll make sure Wren doesn't say a word."

"I'm more worried about your blabbering mouth."

Ben picks up a weight and starts to curl it roughly. "Be at Foxfire at nine tonight," he says.

I grunt. Apparently, I've been dismissed.

"I'll keep my blabbering mouth shut," Ben cuts as I walk away.

I don't turn around, instead I go to the cardio area to burn off some steam.

The Foxfire is dimly lit and smells of stale beer.

It's one of those hole-in-the-wall dive bars that only locals know about. Ben and I have been coming here for years. It's a place I find to be more like home than anywhere in New York City. I haven't been here since before the tour and I feel comforted by the muffled voices and the smack of pool cues hitting their targets.

These last few weeks I've struggled to stay away from drowning myself in poor decisions, which meant I kept out of bars. But this time it felt easier to call my therapist instead of falling down a depressive hole. Working out daily helped too and being near Ben. Even when he busted my balls.

One thing I still can't wrap my head around is all the press. Every day I get calls from reporters for a "sound bite." After having a small taste of fame, it makes me admire Birdie more for how she deals with it all. I understand why she mentioned being afraid of a relationship. It's not something I can't deal with, but it's also not pleasant.

As I make my way to the back booths, my eyes tip up to the TVs on the wall. My heart stops beating for a moment when I see Birdie's face. The first thing I notice is she's dyed her hair back to black. It stuns me at first, then I'm struck with memories of the teenage girl I knew. The captions at the bottom of the screen mention the kidnapping and that her reps say, "She's doing well and fully recovered."

I'm glad, but the image of her tells a different story. Her eyes are sad, and her body is stiff. It makes me want to reach through the screen and hold her, kiss her lips, and tell her she's safe. *Shit.* I may not be in her life but she's sure as hell in mine.

The number of times I've wanted to call her and tell her how stupid I am for running away from the best thing in my life, the number of times I almost texted her to make sure she's okay... I suppose I'm more stubborn than her, but I can't bring myself to do anything about it. I've convinced myself that eventually she'll get over the sadness and she'll move on. She'll find someone better than me. Someone less screwed up and more emotionally available when shit gets tough.

"Liam!" Wren's friendly voice calls through the crowd. "Over here!"

My eyes find her in a corner booth smiling. Her red hair is piled on the top of her head and she's wearing a little black dress that sparkles. She's a little overdressed for this place, but she shines like the joyful beacon that she is. I smile wide at her.

"Hey lady!"

She jumps up and gives me a big hug. My gaze finds Ben and he tips his head in greeting.

"Got you a beer," he says, pointing to the empty place next to Wren.

"Thanks." I see that he's still angry about our conversation at the gym. I can't blame him. I haven't been a good friend lately and Ben has been nothing but kind. That's just who he is.

I take my place in the booth across from them and take a small sip, somewhat regretting my decision to join them.

"It's nice to see you, Liam," Wren smiles.

"It's good to see you, too. It's been a long time."

"Well, I'm here now. Only for a couple of days though, then I have to get back."

"How's your trip been?"

"Amazing actually. Birdie sent a private plane for me. It was freaking wild!" she laughs.

My stomach flips. "She did? Wow."

Wren cringes. "Sorry, I was told not to bring her up and there I go."

I wave my hand. "It's fine Wren, really."

After a few heavy pauses, Ben shifts in his seat. "Look man, we brought you here to share something with you."

At his serious tone I sit straighter. Ben looks like he's about to give me news I won't like. Alarm bells go off in my head. "Is Birdie okay?"

That catches a smirk from both Ben and Wren.

"I thought you didn't care about her," he says.

I grip the pint glass in my hand. "You know I care about her I—" I stop myself from going further. Ben looks like a cat who caught the canary, but instead of indulging him, I dig for his information. "What is it, then?"

Ben and Wren make eyes at each other, then they both smile happily.

"I'm leaving with Wren when she goes back to Parker."

That gets my full attention. "You're leaving New York? I don't understand."

"I'm opening a gym there. Birdie's going to be a silent partner and she managed to get a few others on board."

I feel my heart pounding in my chest. "How long have you been working on this?"

He shrugs. "Not long. It all happened so fast. I'm going to look at spaces next week."

"So, you're moving?"

He places his hand over Wren's on top of the table, a goofy lovesick look now plastered on his face. "Eventually. Things will take time, and of course I'll still have a place here. I've got to train a manager and get things straight but at some point, yes. I'll leave New York."

I'm flabbergasted. "Wow, man. That's huge."

"I know it's a lot but, I wanted to tell you and well—" his gaze goes back to Wren. "Show him, honey."

Honey?

Before I can comment, Wren holds out her left hand to reveal a giant diamond ring. I think my mouth falls to the ground because they both chuckle at my reaction.

"What the hell, dude?!" I exclaim, unable to say anything else.

"I've had that ring for years," Ben pauses. "Tonight just felt right and..."

Wren interjects, "We realized a lot recently, and the only thing stopping us from being together is distance. Our rock star friend helped with that."

An ache cracks through my chest. What Birdie did for the two people before me makes me love her even more. For the last ten years I've watched Ben go back and forth on his relationship with Wren. I've seen him get angry, cry, laugh, and everything in between. I knew they'd end up together, but I also knew he'd been struggling hard with it as of late. *Fuck.* I've been a shit friend. I'm glad Birdie has been there for them since I haven't been.

I stand and surprise Wren by hugging her tightly. "Congrats, Wrennie. I'm so happy for you both."

She laughs, but I can hear the emotion behind it. "Don't start with that name again."

I sit back down then reach my hand out to Ben. He takes it in his strong grip. "I can't believe you finally did it. Proud of you, man."

Ben smiles, but he's watching me carefully.

When he pulls his hand back he says, "You're not upset?"

"Of course not. I've been waiting for you both to figure your shit out."

He studies me carefully. "Have you now."

I nod. "I'll hate not having you here, but I knew it would happen someday. Though I always secretly wished you'd move here, Wren."

Ben slings his arm around her shoulders and kisses her temple. My hands suddenly itch to hold Birdie in my arms again. My mouth goes dry, and my hands turn cold. Regret rushes through me and I can't help the sadness that hits me. Damn it, I'm such a mess.

Wren lets out a noise of protest. "I could never live here long term. I like the calm of Parker. This place is too much for me."

I let out a breath. "It can be."

For a moment there's silence, and then Wren puts her hand on mine. I look up into her emerald eyes. "Liam," she says quietly.

"What is it?"

"I know you didn't want us to bring up Birdie, obviously I've already failed at that," she laughs to herself. "But I need to say something." She squeezes my hand. "When I visited her in Louisiana, she was heartbroken."

"Wren—"

"No Liam, please let me talk," her voice is strong. "Birdie is a badass and one of the strongest people I know—but she's hurting. I know that you think staying away from her is for her own good but you and I both know that's complete and utter bullshit."

I hear Ben cough, not expecting Wren to be so straightforward with me. To be honest I'm a little surprised too.

"You're being selfish, Liam," she continues. "What you both went through in Nashville is terrible, but it's not your fault. Those sick people who call themselves her family are the ones at fault. Your and Birdie's happiness shouldn't suffer because of their actions.

"Now, I've watched you two dance around each other for far too long. It's time for you to get your act together and go after her. I wanted to give you more time, but I can't watch you destroy yourself in the process. Not this time."

Silence fills the table, and I'm at a loss for words. A part of me knows she's right but—

Wren moves, placing a square badge on the table in front of me. "I had Eric make you a backstage pass for tonight. Birdie's doing a special late-night show in about twenty-minutes. If you leave now, you can make it."

My eyes bounce between my two friends. Ben is watching me carefully, all the while holding Wren's hand. They belong together, and I can't help but feel a little jealous of them.

Ben clears his throat, breaking me from my thoughts. "You can have what we have, Liam. In fact, you already do. Just stop being an idiot and go get the woman you love. Take the badge and go."

My heart begins to race as I look down at the badge one more time. "What if it's too late?"

Wren leans forward, a genuine smile on her lips. "As I told Birdie. Relationships are hard, but not many people are lucky enough to meet the love of their life at fifteen years old."

Wren turns her lovesick gaze to Ben, who has the same look.

Fuck. I've been such an idiot.

Without a second thought I grab the pass and head for the door. As I leave, I'm pretty sure I hear my two friends clapping like a bunch of idiots.

Thirty-Eight

Birdie

I SIT IN MY dressing room with a glass of Kentucky Bourbon. I let the liquid burn my throat and light a warmth in my stomach that's otherwise not there.

The show tonight was fun. I agreed to do it to support Kevin. He lived in New York City for many years, so when he asked if I'd perform at his favorite music club with him as a little acoustic duo, I couldn't say no. Gia loved the idea too. She said it gave me lots of much needed good attention.

I glance at my phone to see if I have any texts from Wren, even though I know I won't. She was supposed to attend tonight, but then out of the blue she came to my hotel room flashing a giant diamond ring and screaming at the top of her lungs. I smile a stupid grin at the memory.

After she came to visit me in Louisiana, I jumped into action regarding Ben's gym in Parker. I wanted my best friend to have her happy ending, and I'm glad I could help make it happen. Ben is going to do all the work with another investor I have from my network, but I trust him to do right by me. I know it will be a success, just like his gym here in New York.

My phone rings and I see I have an email from my travel agent. After tonight I'm taking a vacation. Tomorrow evening I'll be on a plane to Santorini. The blue Aegean Sea is calling my name. I'll face the world and all my problems when I get home.

A knock on the door startles me from my daydream.

"Come in!" I yell, thinking it's Kevin. I open my email to have a look at what my agenda is, hoping I have nothing I need to do while I'm there.

"Didn't I tell you to always look through the peephole?"

I nearly jump off the couch when I hear his voice. I turn to him, my hands shaking as I look into the chocolate eyes I've missed so much. They're full of mirth, but I can also see he's upset. In hindsight I should've at least asked who was behind the door. I wasn't thinking.

"What are you doing here? I ask, my voice quiet.

Liam's eyes trail down my body. I'm wearing a pair of jeans and a red tank top. Nothing special, but his eyes eat me up just the same.

He licks his lips. "I need to talk to you"

"Oh..." I breathe out, unsure of what to say.

The last person I expected to walk through the door tonight was him.

I kinda want to knee him in the balls, but I also want him to hold me and never let me go. Ever since Wren and I spoke in Louisiana, I've been thinking a lot about him and if he'd ever be ready to have a relationship. If my heart would be able to wait for him... but now, here he is. Maybe it's fate, or maybe I'm an idiot for wanting him in my life again. I just know that seeing him now, despite my heartache, makes me glad he's here.

As my brain swims in turmoil, I let my eyes admire him for a moment. He looks just as beautiful as the last time I saw him. He's wearing a tight white T-shirt and dark wash jeans. His hair is tousled, and his cheeks are red. It's then I notice he's sweating.

"Did you run here?"

He pushes an awkward hand through his dark tresses. "I did."

"Liam..."

"Can we sit?" He points to the couch.

"I don't know if—"

"Please, Birdie girl?" he pleads.

His voice sounds broken. Maybe it's the way he asks, or maybe it's Wren's words, *"Not a lot of people can say they found the love of their life at fifteen,"* but I agree.

Once we've sat down, I feel the heat from his body. His leg is almost touching mine on the small couch and I can smell his musky pine scent.

"What do you want?" I eventually ask.

He sets his hands on his knees and I watch as he digs his fingers into his legs. He's nervous about whatever he wants to say.

"I saw Wren and Ben tonight. I'm sure you've heard the news," he eventually says.

I can't help but smile. The image of Wren's happy face is burned into my mind. "Yes. I'm happy for them."

He pushes air through his lips. "Yeah, me too."

"If you're here because they forced you again—"

"No, Birdie, god no."

"Then why are you here?" I press.

He leans forward slightly before one of his hands reaches out to tentatively lay on mine. When I don't pull away immediately he relaxes a bit.

"I came because I realized something."

His touch sends a familiar shiver up my spine. I try to quell my nervous stomach, but it won't let me, not with him touching me again and sitting so close.

"And what did you realize?" I ask, becoming impatient.

"That I'm an idiot."

A small awkward sound bubbles from my lips. "That's what you came to tell me?"

He runs a hand through his hair. "No, but I—shit, Birdie. I'm not good with words like you. I always think I'm going to say the wrong thing when I'm around you."

He squeezes the top of my hand and when I look into his chocolate brown eyes, I surrender.

"I'm listening, Liam. Just tell me what you came here to say. *Please.*" I whisper the last part.

He inhales then exhales slowly out of his nose. Like he's counting or something.

"Okay."

After a moment he squares his shoulders back and his jaw hardens a bit.

"When I left, I was scared," he stops again, like he's trying to work out his words. "Fuck," he mutters, his eyes burning into mine. "I'm still scared, Birdie."

"Scared of what?"

"Scared that I'll let you down. Scared that something will happen to you. Scared that I'll say the wrong thing, and that I can't be a good boyfriend to you. After Nashville, my mind hasn't been in the right place. All I can see are my failures. How all the things that make me happy are tarnished somehow. I didn't want my fear to hurt you. I didn't want another person I love to be taken from me. That's why I left. That's why I haven't reached out. I just couldn't."

My heart beats loudly in my ears. *He loves me*. He finally said it. My chest constricts and my palms sweat. Everything he just confessed I already knew, but to hear it from his lips calms my inner turmoil. But it also pains me that he thinks he can't have good things in his life. He deserves to be loved. He's a good man, he just needs to realize that for himself.

"Birdie," he says, his voice laden with raw emotion. "I'm so sorry, baby. I'm so fucking sorry. And I completely understand if you don't want me in your life after what I put you through I—"

I put my fingers against his mouth, stopping further words from exiting his bowed lips.

"Liam," I exhale. "Do you really love me?"

For a moment I see the confusion in his eyes, but it's quickly replaced by amusement. "That's all you heard?"

A small but happy laugh escapes me. "I heard it all Liam, and I want you to know that you're worth more to me than the possibility of loss. I refuse to let it rule my life. And if you're willing to work through your fears with me, to not let them stop you from loving me, then—"

Liam lifts a hopeful brow. "Then?"

I squeeze his hand. "Tell me you love me."

The corners of his mouth lift and he brings one of his hands to gently grasp my chin. My heart flutters at the movement and I watch his mouth as it moves.

"I love you, Birdie Wilder. I fucking love you."

Something bursts inside me at his words and tears spring to my eyes. I can't stop them, and I don't want to. I don't have to ask him if he means it or if he wants me. I can see everything in his eyes. I can see his desire, his pain, his fear, his joy, his worry. But most importantly, his love. His eyes begin to water as I bring my hand to the back of his head, running my fingers through the hair at the base of his neck.

"I haven't completely forgiven you," I say quietly. "We have a lot to work on and it won't be easy," I tell him quietly. "But I think you know that."

He brushes the tears from my cheeks with his thumbs. "I know, Birdie. I don't expect you to fall at my feet. I just need you to know that I'm sorry and that I love you. That I'm here with you. That I'll face my fears with you if you'll have me."

"If we try this again. And I mean really try this, you can't run. I don't know if my heart could handle it. Honestly it wouldn't be good for either of us."

Worry fills Liam's eyes, and he pulls me closer to him. "I know I fucked up. I shouldn't have left. I'll regret it for the rest of my life."

I shush him. "No, Liam. No more regrets. I just want to move forward. But I need you to know that this is it. This is our last chance." I tell him sincerely.

He presses his forehead into mine and closes his eyes. "I understand. I won't waste it."

"I won't either," I promise.

Our breaths mingle, and for the first time since the kidnapping I feel warm inside. As if the spark that died inside me rekindled.

"Liam..." his name like a prayer on my lips.

"Yes, Birdie girl?"

"I love you, too."

"Thank fuck," he huffs out right before he closes the distance between us. When our lips meet my knees go weak and my body comes alive.

I know this kiss doesn't fix what's broken, but I feel like we can do it.

If we made it through every shit thing in our lives, then we can make it through this.

I've known this man before me since I was fifteen, and I want to know him for the rest of my life. He's my best friend, my love, my home. He's everything, and I'm willing to take the risk if he's all in.

Liam pulls his lips from mine.

"Oh, and Birdie?" His tone is playful and grin cheeky.

"Mmmhmm," I hum.

"I like you like that."

I throw my head back and let out a silent laugh.

"You better, Liam Miller. You better."

Epilogue

Liam

ONE YEAR LATER

Birdie screams ridiculously as Wren's wedding bouquet lands in her arms. I can't tell if it's a happy scream or a scared one, but it makes me chuckle.

"You next, man." Ben appears beside me, slapping my back. "I'm surprised you don't already have a ring on that woman's finger."

"Birdie and I are happy as we are. We're not ones for labels."

Ben scoffs. "You two are stuck together like glue. Hell, you're practically married anyway."

He's right. I can't remember the last time I was away from Birdie. Her band calls us the Conjoined Couple. Kevin even gifted us with T-shirts last Christmas. Birdie just rolled her eyes when she opened them, but secretly I loved it. We spent ten years away from each other and I'm never letting her go again.

Birdie skips over to Ben with a silly grin on her face. Her dark hair is curled today, and it bounces as her emerald dress flows out behind her. She looks like a siren in it. Wren had it designed for her, so it fits her delicious body like a glove. I can't help but watch her breasts bounce from the deep V as she stops in front of us. My love for Birdie is strong, but my love for her boobs come in a very close second (though Birdie might tell you they're in first).

She leans forward and plants a kiss on my lips.

"Nice bouquet," I comment, causing her cheeks to flush. I love that I can still do that. I also love watching other parts of her turn the same color. God, my little brain is ready and raring to go. Birdie senses it because her nipples harden through the silk of her dress. God she's so hot. And all mine.

Ben fidgets uncomfortably. Ever since he walked in on me and Birdie going to town on our kitchen counter last year, he's never been the same around us. It was his fault for not telling me he was coming back to pack his things. I smirk at the memory. It's still funny to me, and I enjoy watching him squirm when Birdie and I show any type of PDA. Which is basically all the time.

"I better get back to my bride," Ben winks. But I know he's leaving because he's afraid I'll rip Birdie's dress off right here and now. Which is tempting.

Once Ben is gone, Birdie throws her arms around my neck and presses her chest to mine. The bouquet lands on my back, making me shiver as one of the flowers scratches me through the fabric of my shirt.

"Enjoying the party?" she asks.

Instead of answering, I take her lips in a deep kiss, not caring that a lot of people are around. People that will probably take pictures of us with their cell phones and sell them to gossip rags. After twelve months of being Birdie's boyfriend, I've gotten used to it. It sucks, but to have Birdie in my life is more important than my privacy. I'd give it up time and time again if it meant I got to hold her in my arms and kiss her silly whenever I want.

As our tongues duel, I let my hand explore the open back of her dress. Her soft skin has me dreaming up some new positions I'd like to try. Birdie lets out a quiet moan and my dick stands at attention. I have to pull back so we don't make an even bigger scene. I don't care about people taking pictures, but Wren and Ben wouldn't like if we had sex in the middle of the dance floor while their parents and friends watched in horror.

"What do you say we go back to our room?" My breaths are heavy and hot against her cheek. If she says no, I'm at least getting a quicky in the bathroom.

She flutters her eyes at me, the color amplified by her dress and the darkness of her hair framing her round face. Even though I sometimes miss her natural blonde, Birdie can do whatever the hell she wants to her body and still look more than beautiful to me. I take a piece of it between my fingers as I cock a questioning brow at her.

"Is the sky blue?" she answers.

I laugh. "Do we need to say goodbye?" I look over to Ben and Wren who are locked in a sweet embrace on the dance floor. Birdie's eyes follow mine and she smiles.

"I don't think they'll miss us. We've done all our bridal duties for the evening. Plus, Wren gave me permission to leave after I caught this thing." Birdie unravels herself from me and holds the bouquet in her hands.

I look into my girl's eyes. I try to see if there's a subtle hint in them, that maybe she changed her mind about wanting to get married in the near future. We'd talked about it several times, but we always decided that we'd wait and get married when we felt it was a good time. If and when it made sense.

As Ben mentioned, we're practically married anyway, a piece of paper and a ceremony didn't change the love we have for each other. Even if the caveman side of me did want to claim her in front of the entire world, I'm happy with how we are. I don't doubt how she feels for me, and vice versa. She'd have to kill me to keep me away from her, and I know she feels the same.

I wink at her, giving her sexiest smile. "What are we waiting for then?"

I take her free hand and pull her with me toward the elevator. We smile and nod at the people in the crowd. Wren invited both my parents and Birdie's mom, but they all declined. It wasn't a shock to either of us, we're used to our parents being absent. Though I know it still hurts Birdie that her relationship with Lorri isn't better.

Even with Nick and Shea both in jail, that day still haunts the both of us. Some nights I hold Birdie while she cries. The betrayal she feels from her entire family is too much for her at times. I know Lorri feels bad, and she's apologized in every way possible, but in this case, Birdie just needs time; however long that may be.

When Birdie tugs me inside the elevator, all thoughts of that day go out the window. She presses the button to the top floor, and I grin. She got us a suite on the opposite side of Ben and Wren's. She even paid for the entire floor to be cleared out. It's excessive, but sweet. I'm just glad we don't have any stalkers to worry about. And being in Parker took away the fear I have when we visit big cities. She doesn't always need a bodyguard now, but I stick by her side regardless.

Birdie squeezes my hand in anticipation as we ascend. When the elevator doors open, she pulls me out and pins me against the wall with her body weight. Her lips are immediately on mine and my hands grip her round ass, squeezing hard.

"Is this why you rented out the entire top floor?" I say between kisses.

"I'm not going to screw you in the hallway, Miller," she teases, "but I can if you want me too."

My dick hardens at her words. Birdie and I have some adventurous sex, but there are cameras in this hallway, and I don't want the hotel security to get an eyeful of her sexy body. That glorious sight is all mine.

"Get a move on, Ms. Wilder," I croon before smacking her ass.

She scoffs, but I know she likes it. We quickly make our way to the suite door. As soon as it's open, I pounce, making her drop the bouquet on the ground. Even though Birdie and I will have officially been together for one year as of tomorrow, my desire for her hasn't waned. Some people say that sex tapers in a relationship, but I don't think we'll ever have that problem.

I grip her hips and pull her groin hard against mine. She moans at the feeling of me against her.

"Please Liam," she whimpers.

I bring one hand up to play with her right nipple, rolling the hardened peak between my fingers, while I lean my head down to suck the other through the fabric of her dress. Birdie's head falls back, and I use my other hand to support her neck, massaging the back of her head. She loves it when I do that.

After a few seconds of me playing, she pulls out of my grip.

"Someone's impatient tonight," I tease.

She gives me a wanton smile before pushing me toward the couch. When she goes to remove her dress, I stop her. "Leave it on."

"The shoes too?" Her voice is husky as she asks, the sound going straight to my cock.

"Definitely the shoes." She's worn some strappy dark green heels that make her legs look to die for and her ass pert and lovely. Even though I've dreamt of fucking her in shoes alone, I want the dress on too. It did something to me.

"Lean over the couch," I demand.

A sexy sound escapes her lips. "So bossy."

"You know you like it. Now bend over, *Ms. Wilder*."

Birdie bites her lower lip but does as she's told. She bends at the waist so that she's leaning over the curved arm of the couch. With her dress and shoes still on, ass in the air, she looks like a sexy offering. I stalk forward, making short work of my suit.

Birdie's hungry gaze watches me as I strip. In her current position she has to look over her shoulder, which makes her beautiful hair fall forward. My hand itches to tug on it and expose the peachy skin of her neck to me. Impatient now, I kick off my pants, not bothering to take my briefs off. I just tug them down and let my erection spring free. Her eyes continue to burn into me as I grab the end of her dress and pull it up, folding it over her waist.

With her backside in the air, I'm afforded a lovely view of a matching green thong and Birdie's toned calves. Her thighs are shaking, and I can see she's wet and ready for me.

"Liam," she begs again. "Please, I can't wait anymore."

I can't say no to a plea like that. I push her thong down around her ankles and line myself up with her entrance. I reach for the ends of her hair and pull gently as I sink into her warmth. My dick is so painfully hard I hiss as she encompasses every inch of me. Just watching our bodies join together like this is almost my undoing.

"Yes, Liam!" she practically weeps.

This angle, plus the heels she's wearing give her ass a nice boost so I'm hitting all the right spots. I watch as her eyes close in pleasure as I start to move.

"You're perfect," I purr into her ear.

I move my free hand up her back until I'm grasping her shoulder, then begin to thrust forward harder. She's hot, wet, and tight, a dream come true in so many ways.

"I love you," she breathes and my heart clenches.

Nobody ever mentioned to me how much sex changes when you love someone, but it does. Her words make me even hungrier for her, and I feel as if she's unleashed a beast.

The sound of our coupling bounces off the walls as I piston my hips up into her. Her cries make it hard for me to hold off from coming. But by some miracle I do. Her hips grind into the couch, and she pushes back into me.

"Harder Liam," she commands.

I drive in, my hips hitting her ass. I move my body forward and pull her up so I can play with her breasts and feel her against me. She moves so her head is on my shoulder, her thighs supported by the couch, and one hand moves to her clit rubbing in a vigorous circular motion.

"Fuck. You're so hot, baby. I'm going to come."

A cry breaks free as my hips thrust harder.

"I'm coming," she says suddenly and that's my queue to pick up my pace.

With a shift of my hips, and a pinch of her nipple, she comes undone in my arms. Her body starts to go limp and the sound of my name on her lips undoes me. I come too as her orgasm grips me.

When I catch my breath, I whisper my love for her against her ear. She smiles as she comes down from her high, our bodies both shaky and sweaty. Once she can't stand any longer, I bend her over the arm of the couch and rest lightly on top of her to catch my breath.

"Damn woman," I tease. "That was—"

She huffs a laugh. "You outdid yourself this time."

I kiss her shoulder. "I could say the same for you."

After a moment I stand, helping her up in the process. I grab a nearby tissue box to clean us both. It doesn't take long before I'm pulling her into me and brushing hair from her flushed cheek behind her ear. She's taken off her shoes and dress, and I've kicked my underwear off as well. Naked, our skin pressed together in the afterglow of our lovemaking, I kiss the shell of her ear.

"A year tomorrow," I say with reverence.

"I can't believe it's already been a year. And that Wren and Ben are married!"

I squeeze her tightly. "Thanks to you."

She laughs. "They would have figured it out eventually. I just helped to get rid of an obstacle."

And she had. Ben's new gym in Parker is a smash. The place has been so packed that they plan on opening a second location in the next year. Wren's flower shop is also doing well. I couldn't be happier for my two friends, and they owed a lot of their happiness to Birdie, even if she's too humble to admit it.

Birdie runs her fingers through my chest hair before she places her hand on my heart. "One year," she says quietly. "This time last year I thought I'd be on a plane to Santorini alone."

My body heats just thinking of Santorini. After we made up in her dressing room, I invited myself to go with Birdie on her vacation. She'd been hesitant at first, but that trip ended up saving us. It was two weeks of pure bliss, but it was also two weeks of heart-to-heart talks. We cried, laughed, and had way too much sex (if that's even a thing.)

Now we travel the world together. She does her rock star thing, and I took a job as her head of security. I'm even looking into starting my own private firm to help other people in Birdie's industry. But we'll see where the future takes us.

"What are you thinking about?" Her hazel eyes twinkle with curiosity.

I stare into her eyes, the eyes of my best friend. My everything. Birdie kisses my chest and I feel heat spread from the top of my head to the bottom of my toes.

"Birdie girl?"

She smiles at the nickname. "Yeah, babe?"

"Marry me."

Her reaction is amusing. Her eyes go wide, and the skin of her naked body turns blotchy with red spots. I want to kiss each mark and worship her until she's flushed with need again.

"Is this because I caught the bouquet?" she asks seriously.

I let out a breathy chuckle. "No, baby. It's because you're my forever."

"I thought we talked about this," she says, her tone confused.

"We did. And to be honest, I wasn't planning on it until just this moment. I don't even have a ring."

A smile tugs at the corner of her lips. "Was it the sex? Because even I'll admit it was pretty amazing. I'd marry me in a heartbeat."

This time I let out a booming laugh.

"It's not because of the sex, though it was superb as usual," I wink. "It's because I want to marry you. You're my person, Birdie. You're my best friend, the love of my life, my forever. I want to travel the world with you and protect you from obsessed fans and paparazzi. I want to hold you when you cry and cheer you on. I want to be the first one that hears your new songs and the person you see when you open your eyes every morning. I want to be your everything, Birdie, and I want the world to know it too."

Tears shine in her eyes, and before I know what's happening, she's kissing me fiercely. My hands grip her cheeks, and her arms go around my neck. Our kiss is passionate, hard, and everything I need. When she finally pulls back, lips swollen, I'm crying too.

Her green- and gold-flecked eyes gaze into mine, their depths full of love and happiness. "You know that I don't need a piece of paper to tell me that you're mine, Liam Miller."

My stomach sinks. I feel like I'm being punked. She shakes her head at me when she sees my fear. "Let me finish," she says patiently.

"I don't need a piece of paper, but I do need you. I've always needed you. You're my person, too. You're my forever, too. Tonight, watching Ben and Wren say their vows, it made me realize I want to be married to you, Liam. I want the world to know you're mine and that I'm yours. So yes, my sweet *fiancé*, I will marry you. I'll marry you tomorrow if you want."

"Vegas?" I blurt out.

She laughs. "Okay, well, maybe not tomorrow. But you know what I mean!" I pull her to me; our bodies plaster together like we're two pieces of a puzzle that fit together perfectly.

I kiss the crown of her head and look to the ceiling as if I can see the night stars plastered above us, as if we're sixteen again and listening to music while we lean on each other for more than just friendship.

I didn't know it then, but I sure as hell know it now.

Birdie Wilder is mine, and I'm never letting her go.

Acknowledgments

Thank you so much for reading this book. To date, it's probably one of my favorites that I've written. As a tall, plus-sized woman, I always wished to have romance novels, movies and TV with women that looked like me. Though it's gotten better in years, it still is not enough. Then one morning, I realized I was part of the problem.

Out of all the novels and stories I've written or thought about writing, none of the women I wrote ever looked like me. So, I embarked on a journey to write a novel about a plus-size woman who is not only beautiful, but confident and goes after what she wants.

This story has a lot of my heart and soul written into it, and a lot of my own personal body and even mental health struggles. I hope that by reading this novel, you also saw a little bit of Birdie (or Liam) in yourself. That you can find the confidence inside yourself to speak your mind and live your life to the fullest. That you know that you ARE enough, that you ARE beautiful, and that you ARE deserving of love and everything you dream of.

I also want to give a special shout out to my friends, Lanae, Katelyn, Katie, David, Tyler and all of the Ex-Cold Stone Basement Gang aka The Clot for inspiring a lot of this story. Your friendship since we were fifteen has given me so much more than just friendship. I hope all of you enjoyed this book and spotted all the easter eggs along the way.

AND thank you to all the people who helped this book become a reality. To my beta readers, Taylor, Deanie, Sona, Lanae, and Kim, to my editor April, to my formatter, Beta reader, fellow author, co-author, best friend and more, Nicole Reeves, YOU'RE

AMAZING, and to my cover artist, Nia Oliveira—WOW. Each one of you really did make this book possible.

I also want to thank my family and friends who constantly cheer me on and teach me to never give up. And a special thank you and dedication to my grandpa, who I lost this past May. I would have dedicated this entire book to you Grandpa, but I doubt you'd want a romance novel with sex and swearing dedicated to you! But I hope you laugh at this from up in heaven. We miss you every single day.

Lastly, thank you to all the readers. If you've made it to the end and you're reading this, just know how much I appreciate you. Thank you for hearing Birdie and Liam's story.

Till next time,
Kayla Grosse

CPSIA information can be obtained
at www.ICGtesting.com
Printed in the USA
LVHW032108051022
730040LV00002B/193